UNIDENTIFIED FUNNY OBJECTS 2

Edited by
Alex Shvartsman

UFO Publishing
Brooklyn, NY

Published by:
UFO Publishing
1685 E 15th St.
Brooklyn, NY 11229
www.ufopub.com

Copyright © 2013 by UFO Publishing

Stories copyright © 2013 by the authors

Trade paperback ISBN: 978-0-9884328-2-6

All rights reserved. No part of the contents of this book may be reproduced or transmitted in any form or by any means without the written permission of the publisher.

Cover art: Arnie Swekel
Interior art: Barry Munden
Typesetting & interior design: Windhaven Press (www.windhaven.com)
Graphics design: Emerson Matsuuchi
Logo design: Martin Dare

Copy editor: Elektra Hammond
Associate editors: James Aquilone, Cyd Athens, James Beamon, Anatoly Belilovsky, Frank Dutkiewicz, Michael Haynes, Nathaniel Lee, Fran Wilde

Visit us on the web:
www.ufopub.com

Printed in Canada

10 9 8 7 6 5 4 3 2 1

TABLE OF CONTENTS

Alex Shvartsman
   FOREWORD 1
Ken Liu
   THE MSG GOLEM 3
Esther Friesner
   SERVICE CHARGE 25
J.W. Alden
   ITEM NOT AS DESCRIBED 43
Jim C. Hines
   STRANGER VS. THE MALEVOLENT MALIGNANCY 53
Fran Wilde
   HOW TO FEED YOUR PYROKINETIC TODDLER 73
Matt Mikalatos
   A STIFF BARGAIN 77
Josh Vogt
   THE GIRL WITH THE DAGON TATTOO 93
M.C.A. Hogarth
   IMPROVED CUBICLE DOOR 97
Mike Resnick
   ON SAFARI 119
Konstantine Paradias
   HOW YOU RUINED EVERYTHING 141
Jody Lynn Nye
   INSIDER INFORMATION 151
K.G. Jewell
   THE HAUNTED BLENDER 169
Tim Pratt
   THE RETGUN 179
Heather Lindsley
   THE DIPLOMAT'S HOLIDAY 198
Michelle Ann King
   CONGRATULATIONS ON YOUR APOTHEOSIS 205
Desmond Warzel
   ONE THING LEADS TO YOUR MOTHER 219
James Beamon
   CLASS ACTION ORC 231
Wade Albert White
   THE WIGGY TURPIN AFFAIR 247
Robert Silverberg
   HANNIBAL'S ELEPHANTS 267

FOREWORD

ALEX SHVARTSMAN

How do you follow a hit?

In 2012, I set out to create something that wasn't available in the speculative anthology space—a collection of humorous short stories. As a reader, I was frustrated with the dearth of science fiction and fantasy venues for such material. This kind of book was something I'd welcome, and I was betting there were enough fans of the lighter fare who wanted it, too. And thus, *Unidentified Funny Objects* was born.

The book was a success, well-received by both critics and the reading public. But my ambitions extended beyond creating a single hit. I envisioned *UFO* as an annual series of anthologies, providing a consistent outlet for the type of light-hearted, optimistic short story that is seldom seen elsewhere. But how do you provide that consistent experience and yet keep things fresh? *UFO2* is my attempt to answer this question with:

New headliners: Robert Silverberg and Esther Friesner are among the exciting group of well-known authors to lend their talents to the *UFO* series.

Familiar worlds: Jody Lynn Nye, K.G. Jewell, and Matt

Mikalatos revisit the characters and settings they created for the first *UFO* volume. Each story is a stand-alone and can be enjoyed without having read the previous installment, but it's a nice bit of continuity, and an extra reason for new readers to seek out the inaugural anthology.

Different lengths: *UFO* was packed with twenty-nine shorter stories. *UFO2* includes nineteen mostly-longer tales.

Picture it: This book includes original illustrations for nine of the stories, drawn by Barry Munden.

Bring the wacky: *UFO* stories are often about outrageous settings and characters. From madcap time travelers to orc lawyers to alien beasts in Central Park, this book turns the wacky setting up to eleven.

Please enjoy the stories collected here. If I did my job right, this book will not only be a worthy successor to the previous volume, but will also have you marking your calendar for the release date of *UFO3*. And while you wait, be sure to check out several additional free stories posted at www.ufopub.com.

THE MSG GOLEM

BY KEN LIU

On the second day after the spaceship *Princess of the Nebulae* left Earth, God spoke to Rebecca.

"Rebecca Lau, listen to me. I need you."

The ten-year-old girl took off her headphones. The cabin was silent save for the faint rumble of the spaceship's engines. "Dad, did you say something?"

"It's me, God."

"Right." Rebecca climbed onto a chair to examine the speakers in the ceiling. The voice did not seem to be coming out of them.

She climbed down and peered closely at her computer. "If I find out you had anything to do with this, Bobby Lee . . ." she muttered darkly. Bobby had been jealous when he heard that her family was going on this cruise to the vacation colony on New Haifa for winter break. It was entirely possible that he decided to play a trick on her by programming her computer.

"Bobby has nothing to do with this," God said, slightly miffed.

"So which god are you?"

"*The* God. The God of Abraham, Isaac, and Jacob. *Your* God! Jason Engelman explained me to you over lunch last semester."

"Oh, so you're Jason's god. The Jewish one."

"You are a Jew."

"Um." Rebecca sat down on her bed. "I'm Chinese. We live in New York. You must have confused me with my friend Yael Wasserstein. Now I know we're the same age and we both have long dark hair, but—"

"Be quiet! I need you to make a golem and catch all the rats on this ship. I'll explain everything."

BACK IN THE NINTH CENTURY, Jewish merchants from Persia settled in Kaifeng, the capital of China. The community grew so numerous that they built a synagogue in 1163. The Kaifeng Jews became known to their Chinese neighbors, who always paid lots of attention to food, as the "People Who Remove Sinew."

For a thousand years, this community on the fringe of the Diaspora flourished and prospered. But over time, the Kaifeng Jews intermarried and gradually forgot most of their traditions. Many of them even forgot about God.

But God never forgot about them.

"SO I'M DESCENDED from one of these Kaifeng Jews?" Rebecca asked. "How come Mom never told me about this?"

"She doesn't know either. I haven't...er..."

"You haven't needed to look us up," Rebecca said, "until now."

"I've been busy," God said, a little stiffly. "You try to keep an eye on every molecule in the universe for a few days."

Rebecca tried out the idea of being a Jew. Her eyes gradually lit up. "I get Hanukkah? And all the presents?"

"You get to celebrate Hanukkah, yes. The presents are up to your parents, not me."

"Can I keep Christmas? And Chinese New Year?"

"That's up to you," God said. "I'm not—"

"Deal! But You need to make your presentation a bit punchier. That history lecture needed visual aids."

Rebecca strained her ears and swore she heard God muttering. "What I have to work with... the closest thing to..."

"Hey!" Rebecca was hurt. "*You* came to *me*, remember?"

"Yes," God said. "Don't remind me. Can you get some mud?"

"Back up a minute. Why are there rats on this cruise ship? And what's the big deal about rats? Aren't they Your creatures, too?"

"Some family snuck aboard a pair of pet rats on the last cruise," God said. "They escaped and multiplied. And now a hundred and fifty of them live in the walls of the ship. Ordinarily, I neither favor nor disfavor rats. But if these rats get to New Haifa, it'll be a disaster."

"Why?"

"There's nothing in the ecosystem there to keep the rats in check. They'll eat everything in sight, grains, crops, the eggs of songbirds, and baby chicks. Worst of all, there's a virus on New Haifa that normally doesn't affect people. But if the rats get there, the virus will infect them, and I can already see how the virus will mutate into new forms that will be very dangerous to people. It's just one of those unforeseen interactions when you bring species across the galaxy together."

"That sounds like a planning error on Your part."

"Don't start that again," God groaned. "Everyone wants to blame me. You try to create all these worlds all by yourself, on the first try, no mistakes or oversights allowed."

THE *PRINCESS OF THE NEBULAE* had a number of restaurants. Rebecca's family favored the Chinese buffet, which had a good selection. But since Rebecca wasn't sure exactly which foods were kosher (she knew that pork and shellfish were no good, but that was where certainty ended), she took only a plate of rice and bamboo shoots.

God was no help at all.

"I'm used to looking the other way at Chinese restaurants," He declared, and refused to say anything more.

At their table, Rebecca made the announcement to her parents. David Lau and his wife Helen looked at each other and turned back towards their daughter.

"Is this like when you said you wanted to be Italian when you were seven?" Helen asked, cautiously. "Because you wanted to sing opera?"

"I don't remember that. But no, it's not."

"You know," Helen continued, struggling to keep her tone even, "when people say that the overseas Chinese are the 'Jews of the Orient,' it's not meant to be taken literally."

"Mom, I *really* am Jewish. So are you."

"And God wants you to catch rats on this ship because they're about to destroy an ecosystem? That's not some metaphor I'm too old to understand?"

"No metaphors. God wants to protect the beaches and animals of New Haifa. And to prevent a plague."

"Can I speak to God about this? He's taking my daughter and I don't get a say?"

"No," God hissed at Rebecca. "Jewish mothers are bad enough. Chinese-Jewish mothers are worse. You deal with her."

"God only talks to me," Rebecca said. "He chose me to be his helper. You'll have to ask a rabbi how this works."

"Rebecca, you have an overactive imagination. If you invested one-tenth the energy you spend acting crazy on your school work—"

"*Mom*, I'm telling you the truth."

"*Aiya*, David, are you listening to this? Talk to her."

"What am I supposed to say?" David Lau shrugged. "According to her, she's Jewish because of your side of the family. You read all the books on child development and psychology. Don't they have chapters about stuff like this?"

"Don't make fun of me. None of this would have happened if you paid more attention to her instead of always working."

"Hey!"

Rebecca excused herself and quietly slipped out of the dining room.

REBECCA SCOURED THE DECKS and the halls, peeking into the theaters and dining spaces. The ficuses were in hydroponic planters, not soil. The flowers were fake. Metal, wood, and plastic gleamed everywhere. Not a smidgeon of mud in sight.

"Didn't You realize that with all the cleaning robots running around, it's impossible to find mud on a spaceship? You're God. You're supposed to know these things."

"It would help if I had a more competent assistant. You could have questioned my plan ahead of time and saved both of us from wasting time."

"As if! What would You have said if I had expressed doubts about Your plan?"

"I would have told you to not question me," God admitted.

REBECCA TOOK ADVANTAGE of God's temporary silence to go to the library. The cruise ship's collection on religious studies was rather sparse. The *Children's Guide to Judaism* was the best that she could find.

"Have you thought more about how to get mud?" God interrupted.

"Shhhh. I'm reading about how to be Jewish."

"Can you do that later? We need to focus on acquiring mud."

"Mud, mud, mud. I'm sure we'll come up with something. It's more important that I study. Do You want Your helper to make silly mistakes and be laughed at?"

It exasperated her mother to no end that Rebecca was all or nothing about everything. If she had no interest in something—piano, calligraphy, the spelling bee—she refused to spend even one minute thinking about it. But if she *was* interested in something—computers, baking, the history of gunpowder—she would spend every waking moment studying it, neglecting everything else.

She had decided that she was interested in being a good—no, a great—helper of God.

"But we don't have time! It's already Friday, and the ship docks tomorrow. You need to get out there and find mud."

The ship's lights dimmed as God spoke. It was now evening, ship's time.

"Wait," Rebecca said. "Explain to me exactly how we go about making a golem. It's Shabbat. I don't want to break any rules."

"You can't be serious."

"Very serious. A helper of God must be a role model. Eek, I forgot to light the candles. Please forgive me."

"..."

"God, I couldn't understand a word You just said there. It sounded like You were choking, or maybe You gurgled 'like a convert.'"

"Trust me, no rules will be broken. First, you gather the mud—"

"Gathering is one of the *melakhot*," Rebecca said, looking at the list in her book.

"Only if the produce gathered is in its natural place. And we know that there is naturally no mud on this ship, so what we gather won't violate the rule. *I cannot believe I'm even debating this with you.* Anyway, next, you form the golem out of mud, much like how I once shaped Adam—"

"That sounds like kneading, another *melakha*."

"Only if you do the mixing on Shabbat. All right, so we'll focus on getting pre-mixed mud. After you shape the golem, make it smooth—"

"Smoothing is—"

"Fine, FINE! Leave it rough, what do I care? As long as it can walk. Finally, after you've made the golem, you must write *emet*, truth, on—oh."

"Writing is—"

"I know. Forbidden." God sounded so dejected that Rebecca stayed quiet.

After a moment, God brightened. "If the rats get to New Haifa, there'll be a plague. The Shabbat laws can be broken to save lives."

"Doesn't it take a while for the virus to mutate? If we don't catch the rats, can't we evacuate the people in time?"

"Well, yes, that probably *can* be done. But convincing people will be a lot more work."

"More work later is not a reason to break the rules now."

"Wait, there's a more immediate threat. The rats will eat all the stored grains."

"People will starve?"

"Well, no. They have lots of freeze-dried foods that the rats won't touch. But they *will* have to go without whole grain bagels for a while."

"I don't know," Rebecca said, flipping through her book again. "The connection seems too tenuous. I think You're stretching that saving-lives loophole beyond the breaking point."

"You're arguing against me based on some rules you read in a book?"

"I'm studying to be a good Jew. Don't You want this?"

"But I'm telling you to do this! I command you."

"But You can't just make an arbitrary, random exception against all Your settled commandments and rules. It doesn't work that way."

"Why not? I'm God."

"I thought we're way past the stage where You act like a despot now."

The argument went on for an hour. Rebecca's zeal was implacable.

FINALLY, GOD NOTICED the globe on Rebecca's nightstand. He would have slapped His forehead if He had a forehead (and hands).

"Rebecca Lau, listen to me. It's not Shabbat."

"What?"

"Shabbat begins at sundown, not the dimming of the ship's electric lights."

"It must be sundown *somewhere* on Earth now though."

"Good thinking, except that due to relativistic effects, the ship is in a different frame of reference than Earth. By my calculations—let's see, carry the one, add the ten—it's Tuesday or Wednesday on Earth. And it's not Shabbat anywhere."

"You sure about this?"

"You can argue with me, but you can't argue with Einstein."

"So we're allowed to do what we need to do."

"No restrictions. Let's get to it."

Rebecca would have high-fived God at that moment if God was into high-fives (or had hands).

REBECCA BEGGED TO accompany her mother to the ship's spa in the morning.

Helen was touched. She hadn't felt close to her daughter for some time now. She seemed to be always yelling at her daughter, pushing her to do this or that, to be more disciplined, to try harder. It would be nice to relax together in the spa.

At Rebecca's insistence, Helen ordered both of them mud facials.

With her eyes closed, Helen found it easier to talk to her daughter. She wasn't constantly reminded of what a bad mother she was by Rebecca's unfocused ways. All her friends' daughters could play at least two instruments and never got less than a 99 out of a 100 on tests. The feeling that Rebecca's lack of accomplishments was her fault gnawed at her.

But this sudden interest in Judaism could be a blessing in disguise. The Jewish kids at Rebecca's school all did so well. Perhaps they'll be good influences on her. She just hoped it wasn't another one of Rebecca's crazy enthusiasms that she couldn't understand.

"Why don't you try harder at school?" Helen asked.

"I'm just not interested," Rebecca said. She sat up and, keeping an eye on her mother, quietly scraped off the mud on her face, putting it into a plastic bag.

"Most things worth doing aren't interesting until you get good at them. You have to do the hard work first."

Rebecca made non-committal noises. She gathered up the mud from the bowl by her mother.

Helen decided to change the topic. "You should spend more time with your father. One of the goals of this vacation is for him to take a more active role in your discipline. I just don't know what to do with you."

"I don't know what to say to him. I only ever hear from him when he's arguing with you or when you tell him about my grades and he yells at me."

Helen felt a pang of guilt. "*Aiya.* That's not how we wanted it. Your father works so hard because he loves you. You should give him a chance."

But Rebecca was gone already. She had gathered enough mud.

"She's right, you know," God said. "Honor your father and mother. Big deal in my book. Big in Confucius's book too."

"I do honor them," Rebecca said. "I'm just tired of being a disappointment all the time. I'm not a very good Chinese daughter."

"There are many ways of being a good Chinese daughter," God said. "Not just one way. Just like there are many ways of being a good Jew, even if some people think there's only one way. Being a Jew is about being part of a family. Families aren't perfect, but they're always there for you."

"Yeah, wish my parents believed that."

God started to say something but stopped. He sighed to Himself.

Rebecca went on shaping the mud. She was not a great sculptor, but since God gave her dispensation to be "rough" and liberal in her interpretation, she finished quickly.

"What do You think?" Rebecca asked.

"It's very modern," God said, diplomatically.

The mud statue was about a foot tall. It had two very long arms, a stubby head, and eyes and a nose carved with fingernails. Rebecca had pinched tiny earflaps on either side of the head. One of the legs was longer than the other.

"I ran out of mud."

The statue fell over. Rebecca blushed, and fixed the legs so that they were more even in length. Now the statue stayed upright.

"What's next?"

"Now we practice calligraphy."

TWENTY MINUTES LATER, God was as frustrated with Rebecca as He had been with Jonah.

"Of all the Chinese girls, I had to be stuck with the only one who doesn't know any calligraphy. Don't you know how to write legibly?"

Rebecca wiped her sweaty forehead, which was now covered by mud. "Don't yell at me! How was I supposed to know this would come in handy? I hated brush-writing. I've always typed or dictated."

She had tried over and over to etch the Hebrew letters for *emet* into the forehead of the golem with a chopstick. The *Children's Guide* had examples of what the letters looked like. But time and again, she failed—the proportions of the letters were wrong, the lines were squiggly, the letters ran into each other. She had to wipe out the half-formed letters and start again.

"This is the problem with modern education everywhere. Penmanship is just not valued."

"Sounds like a design flaw. Why did You make writing so hard and typing so easy?"

"Again with the blame."

David poked his head into the room.

"Hi," he said, awkwardly. The fact that his daughter's face was covered in mud didn't faze him. He had seen his wife often looking similar. "Your mother suggested that I take you for an ice cream on the promenade deck. If you're free."

"I'm a little busy, Dad."

"What are you working on?" He came in and sat down on the bed.

"Making this golem. But God is mad at me because I can't do calligraphy."

Since most conversations David had had with his daughter consisted of him yelling at her at Helen's direction for some failure on Rebecca's part that he didn't fully understand, this actually made some sense.

"Your grandfather was the same way with me," he said.

"You didn't like brush writing either?"

"Hated it. I preferred to draw pictures during those classes. The teacher told my father, and I got into a lot of trouble. But I eventually learned to like it."

"What happened?"

"Your grandfather was good at making paper lanterns for the Lantern Festival. Back then, in China, every kid ran around with a homemade lantern for the Festival. He told me that I had to write the characters on the lanterns myself. And if my bad calligraphy ruined a lantern, he would have to start over and make me a new one. I felt so bad about making him do extra work that I practiced a lot and got really good. And then I enjoyed making the lanterns with him every year."

Rebecca liked that story.

"Can you help me with the golem?" She asked.

She showed him what the letters had to look like. He held her hand and, together, they made the letters on the forehead of the golem.

The two stepped back to admire their work. It wouldn't win any awards. But it was functional.

"Thank you," Rebecca said. "Dad, can we get ice cream another time? Right now, God has more things for me to do."

When David was little, he had thought he could fly. In comparison, Rebecca's belief that she was working for God seemed far more reasonable.

"Good luck," he said.

AFTER DAVID LEFT, Rebecca asked God, "Why isn't it moving?"

"Give it a minute. It's still getting its bearings."

The golem sat up, rubbed its eyes, and stood unsteadily on its feet.

"It worked!"

"Now the really hard part begins," God said. "Golems are strong but extremely stupid and literal-minded. You have to give this one very precise instructions to get it to catch all the rats."

Rebecca brought the golem to a little-trafficked corner of the ship. She knelt down and loosened the screws securing the grille over a wall vent. Then she opened the grille and pushed the golem inside the ventilation duct.

"I command you to go catch a rat."

The golem stumbled around, looked left and then right, and went down the right side. Gradually, echoes of the golem's footsteps faded.

Rebecca waited.

Five, ten, fifteen minutes passed.

"You never told it to come back," God said. "Remember: very literal-minded."

Rebecca leaned into the vent and shouted, "Come back."

After a moment, she stuck her head back into the vent: "With the rat!"

"Now you're learning," God said.

Within a minute, pattering footsteps approached the vent, along with loud squeaks.

The golem appeared dragging a struggling white rat by its tail. The rat tried to dig its claws into the sides of the duct but could get no purchase against the smooth metal surfaces.

Rebecca clapped. She directed the golem to deposit the rat inside a shoebox, which she carried back to her cabin. She released the rat in the dry bathtub, a temporary holding cell.

"One down, a hundred forty-nine to go," God said.

THE NEXT EXCURSION didn't go so well. The golem came back to the vent dragging another squealing rat. But five more rats followed the golem. As soon as they were sure that Rebecca could see the golem, the rats attacked together.

They jumped onto the golem, bit through its arms to free their companion, and then turned together to face Rebecca and bared their teeth, grinning. She thought one of them even licked its teeth and smacked its lips. Then they ran away, leaving the broken golem behind.

Rebecca crawled in and dragged the writhing pieces of the golem out. Luckily, mud arms were easy to reattach to mud shoulders, and the golem was soon as good as new.

"What's in the mud?" God asked.

Rebecca smelled the newly repaired golem. "Jujube, apples, grapes... and honey, I think."

"*Aiya.* That explains the problem. When I told you to get mud, did you think I meant 'sweet mud?'"

"Now you sound like my mom. 'Go get mud! Go get mud!' You didn't say anything about what had to be *in* the mud."

"Are you a mindless golem? Do I have to specify everything? God's servants show initiative!"

"I did the best I could. Seems to me that the flaw was the lack of detailed instructions."

"Again with the blame."

"Wait a minute," God said. "What're you sprinkling on it?"

"MSG."

"No. No no no no! I told you to use salt."

"But MSG is better. With this much MSG, even a rat would think twice about eating the golem."

"You think rats care about the health effects of MSG? When I told Noah to use gopher wood to construct the Ark, do you think he just substituted cedars? No. When I tell you to do something, you do it exactly the way I tell you. No modifications!"

"'Show initiative!' 'No modifications!' I'm getting conflicting messages here."

"I get that complaint a lot. Join the club."

God waited as Rebecca sprinkled salt over the golem. "More, more. Lots more. Make it inedible to the rats."

"I'm going to get a taste of this at Passover, aren't I? Parsley in salt water?"

"Where do you think I got the idea? All Jews remember the taste of tears. It comes in handy."

NOW SOAKED IN SALT, the golem was having a much easier time fending off the attacking rats. One after another, it captured the rats and brought them back. Soon, the bathtub was filled to capacity. The rats climbed over each other. A few almost jumped out.

"This isn't going to work," God said. "You need a bigger tub."

Rebecca decided that the best way to hold all the rats was to use the entire bathroom.

She opened the fan vent in the ceiling of the bathroom, and ordered the golem to herd the rats towards that opening until they dropped down into the locked bathroom.

"Whatever you do, *don't* go into my bathroom," Rebecca said to her mother and rushed off before she could ask any questions.

"JUST ONE MORE RAT to go," God said, excitedly. "I think we'll be able to do this."

The last rat was strong, fat, about the size of a cat. His black-and-white fur was getting patchy in places. He waddled a bit when he walked, but he could still put on a sprint when he needed to.

Not for nothing was he the smartest rat on the ship. He knew that he was being herded, and he dodged the golem in the maze of HVAC ducts, refusing to go anywhere near Rebecca's room.

Rebecca ran through the ship, following the skittering and pounding footsteps overhead. She ran through the promenade deck, dodging couples standing by windows full of red-shifted star fields; she excused herself as she rushed into and out of a seminar room full of startled cruise passengers listening to an investment lecture; she ran up and down flights of stairs, hoping to help the golem.

Finally, the rat decided that it was better to reveal his existence to the ship's crew than to be captured by the lumbering, terrifying mud monster. He dropped out of one of the overhead vents and landed in the middle of the kitchen.

Rebecca burst into the kitchen from the dining room and lunged after the rat, but he changed direction at the last minute, leapt onto a nearby stack of boxes, and jumped onto the stainless steel counter.

The head chef, sous-chefs, waiters, and busboys stared, mouths agape. A fat rat was running loose in their kitchen; a little girl was yelling and chasing after it; and *plop*, a pile of mud fell out of the vent over their heads, landed on top of the counter, and stood up like a little person.

The head chef fainted.

"Get him!" Rebecca yelled. "I'll cut off his retreat." She rushed to the other end of the counter, hoping that the rat, trying to get away from the pursuing golem, would skid right into her waiting plastic bag.

The rat kept on running towards Rebecca. *But why was the rat grinning?*

In the middle of the counter was a sink, half filled with water and dirty dishes. The rat jumped right into the sink and swam across the soapy water with little effort. It climbed up the other side and turned around.

Oh no, Rebecca thought. *Water and mud.*

"Stop!" She shouted at the golem and waved her arms frantically, smacking the face of a busboy who was trying to get a closer look at the animated mud statue. "Sorry!" Rebecca glanced at the boy to be sure he was okay while still shouting instructions to the golem, "Go around! Get him on the other side!"

The golem tried to stop, but it slipped on the soapy puddle next to the sink and fell into the water. It sank immediately.

"What happens now?" Rebecca asked.

"I've never seen this," God said. "None of this is very orthodox, you understand."

The water in the sink bubbled and churned, and finally, a much wetter, more amorphous golem emerged, climbing up the other side of the sink. It now lumbered forward like a walking starfish. The water had dissolved most of its facial features, but the eyes were still vaguely there, two small pits.

The golem paused, looked around, and went after the busboy standing by Rebecca. It passed right by the rat, chittering next to the sink, and launched itself into the air. Before anyone had a chance to react, it latched onto the startled face of the busboy, and began to punch his nose and bat him about the ears.

"Aw! OUCH!"

Rebecca yelled at the golem to stop, but the golem ignored her.

"It can't hear you," God said helpfully. "The water's dissolved the ears, which you should have made bigger. The last order it heard from you was 'get *him* on the other side.' Since you were looking at the busboy, the creature thought that's who you meant."

Rebecca ran to help the boy. She grabbed onto the slick and soapy golem. But it was like trying to grab onto a jellyfish, her hands slipped and the golem easily slithered out of her grasp. The creature turned around and stuck out a pseudopod of mud, and punched Rebecca in the lips.

Rebecca reeled back, seeing stars. She could taste the MSG, too. Mixed with salt and apples and grapes. And soap. *Blech.*

The boy was now on the ground, rolling around and trying as best as he could to protect his face with his hands and forearms. The golem was strong and relentless. Rebecca could see bruises and swelling on the boy's face.

"It's really hurting the boy," Rebecca said. "How do I make it stop?"

"You have to erase the aleph from the *emet* on its forehead," God said. "Turn *emet* into *met*, or 'death.' That will stop the golem."

"Which one is aleph again?" Rebecca asked in a panic. "Remember I'm new at all this!"

God groaned.

Rebecca turned around and faced the rat, still chittering on the counter.

"Listen," she said. Her heart pounded. She had no idea if this would work. But God's helpers were always creative, weren't they? *They showed initiative.* She was going to be the best Chinese-Jewish helper of God ever.

"I need your help to stop the golem. If you do this good deed, God will help you and the other rats find good homes."

"I will?" God asked.

"I'm God's helper. I can speak for Him."

"You can?" God asked.

"It'll be much better than hiding on this ship and stealing people's table scraps," Rebecca said.

The rat looked at Rebecca quizzically, chittered some more, stroked his whiskers, and then launched himself at the golem.

"Good rat," Rebecca said, and went after the golem too.

The rat dove into the golem. The golem let go of the boy and tried to defend itself. It wrapped its limbs around the rat and *squeezed,* like a python. The rat squeaked and his eyes bulged out.

Distracted by the rat, the golem couldn't pay attention to Rebecca. She leaned in, and with the palm of one hand, wiped away the Hebrew letters on the golem's head. Grabbing a chopstick from the floor, she wrote the Chinese character for 'death' in their place.

"Good thing I can read Chinese," God said. "And I've gotten used to your chicken scratch."

The golem stopped moving. It was just a pile of shapeless mud on the ground now.

REBECCA SAT ACROSS the large oak desk from the captain. In the middle of the desk was a pile of mud, the remains of the golem. The office was large and spacious, but she felt claustrophobic. She was boxed in and had nowhere to go.

Her father sat to her left, her mother to her right, and behind her, blocking the door, stood a line of stony-faced witnesses: the head chef, sous-chefs and their staff who had to scrub the kitchen all afternoon, as well as the busboy whose eyes were swollen almost shut.

"Mr. and Mrs. Lau," the captain said, drumming his fingers on the smooth surface of the desk. "Your daughter has caused a great deal of trouble for Blueshift Cruise by bringing contraband creatures onto the ship. There are reasons that pets like your daughter's rat and this exotic alien creature that wrecked my kitchen are forbidden! But she apparently thinks rules only apply to other people."

Rebecca silently seethed at the injustice of the accusation. There was no point in arguing. Her parents always thought she was in the wrong whenever authority figures like teachers were involved, so of course they would believe the captain. Indeed, they might even interpret her "crazy" rants about rats yesterday as evidence of her guilt. She was as good as convicted.

The captain went on, "Now, we need to discuss the matter of compensation—"

"Indeed, we should," David said. "Starting with how you're going to compensate my daughter for accusing her unjustly."

Rebecca stared at her dad in surprise. He smiled at her and patted her hand.

"I suggest you send someone to take a look in Rebecca's stateroom. You'll find that she did not bring any animals, rat or otherwise, onto your ship."

Oh no. Rebecca started to speak, but her father gestured for her to remain silent.

Rebecca cringed at the thought of the discovery of the rats trapped in her bathroom. She wished the floor would open up and swallow her before her parents were disgraced because of her.

The captain looked at the Laus suspiciously, but he ordered a steward to do as David suggested.

You have a plan for this? She mouthed silently at God.

"Plans are not as good as surprises," God said.

"Now, while your man is gone, I'm going to address your ridiculous claim about the 'exotic alien creature.' That's clearly just a figurine made of mud, no more alive than any of the plastic flowers that fill this ship."

The captain sputtered indignantly, "I've got a whole room of witnesses—"

"Does this thing look alive to you?" David poked at the remains of the golem. "I made this with her. I know what it is."

Helen got up to examine the mud. "This is from our facial at the spa." She sniffed it and made a face. "And it's gone bad. What did your people put in this?"

"But, but—" the captain sputtered.

"The mud is from *your* spa," Helen said. "If anything was causing this to move, then you might want to check your spa for alien infestations before other customers complain."

The captain sat down sullenly and kept his mouth shut. Helen put an arm around Rebecca, who was too stunned by the turn of events. Not only was her mother not mad at her, but she was actually defending Rebecca.

"Parents, they sometimes surprise you, eh?" God said.

Rebecca wished this moment would last forever. She wished the steward sent to her room never returned.

The door to the captain's office banged open. The out-of-breath, sweaty steward rushed in, came to a halt by the captain, and bent down to whisper to him what he had found in Rebecca's stateroom.

Rebecca closed her eyes and waited for her doom.

"What have you done to MY SHIP?" The captain roared at the family sitting across the desk. "Her bathroom is filled to the ceiling with rats!"

David stood up and leaned across the desk to stare the

captain in the face. "That's what I wanted you to see. The rats came from your ship, not Rebecca. You should be thanking her. She was smart enough to trap the rats in her bathroom."

"That's ridiculous."

"If you check your ventilation ducts, you'll find months worth of rat droppings and hair. Rebecca didn't bring the rats on the ship. She's the *victim* of your poor pest control procedures! She told us that she was going to catch the rats on this ship, and you're lucky she succeeded."

The captain dispatched several men to go examine the ventilation ducts and confirm David's statement. But his face was ashen. He remembered the reports about odd droppings.

"Now, just imagine if you actually docked at New Haifa and allowed the rats to escape. At a minimum, Blueshift Cruise would be fined, and the press would have a field day writing about the lack of sanitation on Blueshift Cruise ships. I'd wager that you'd be fired in a second. So, *let's* discuss the matter of compensation."

The captain considered this. After a moment, he smiled. "How would you like to have your cabins upgraded to first class for the return trip? We'll refund your tickets. And we'd like you to stay as our guest on New Haifa. We'll pay for everything."

David and Helen smiled back. "And daily passes to the spa for me and my daughter," Helen said. "The full treatment. With very healthy mud."

"Of course."

"And the rats," Rebecca spoke up. All the adults turned to look at her. She blushed, swallowed, but continued, "What's going to happen to them?"

"I'm going to throw them out the airlock," the captain said, irritated.

Come on, God, You promised, Rebecca thought.

She could have sworn that she heard God sigh.

"That doesn't feel right to me," Helen suddenly said. "It wasn't the rats' fault that they were put where they didn't belong. Besides, they are descended from rats kept as pets. Hey, I just got an idea. I think you should bring them back to Earth and find families to adopt them."

"Or we can always describe our rat-infested cruise to *Travel and Leisure*," David added.

"Fine," the captain said, defeated.

Thank you, Rebecca mouthed to God.

"YOU DONE GOOD," God said. "Enjoy yourself on the beach down there."

"You aren't coming?"

"I could use a vacation," God allowed. "Thinking about the effects of relativistic dilation on the timing of Shabbat gave me quite a headache. But there are too many things in the universe for me to worry about."

"I'm glad I got to know You," Rebecca said. "God, don't be a stranger."

She walked off the disembarking ramp with her family, into the bright sunlight and salty breeze of New Haifa.

Ken Liu

(kenliu.name) is an author and translator of speculative fiction, as well as a lawyer and programmer. His fiction has appeared in *The Magazine of Fantasy & Science Fiction, Asimov's, Analog, Clarkesworld, Lightspeed,* and *Strange Horizons,* among other places. He has won a Nebula, a Hugo, a World Fantasy Award, and a Science Fiction & Fantasy Translation Award, and been nominated for the Sturgeon and the Locus Awards. He lives with his family near Boston, Massachusetts.

SERVICE CHARGE

by Esther M. Friesner

"Yvitelli is such a charming little kingdom," Naphtheena said, studying her nails as she enjoyed the spring morning at a table in the tavern courtyard. "What a shame I'm going to destroy it." The dragon illustrated her plans for the kingdom in question by spearing a *biscotto* with the spike at the end of her long and graceful tail, and crisping the confection to ashes with a single gout of fire from her nostrils.

The waiter took in this spontaneous demonstration of unspontaneous combustion with a jaundiced eye. Another man might have run away screaming, but M'sieu Bertrand hailed from the legendarily languid kingdom of Sesinaypazoonpeep, and thus was not easily roused from his carefully cultivated aura of ennui. He was also aware that dragons were good tippers. It came from their long-standing (and sometimes sprawling) tradition of slumbering on piles of treasure. For a dragon, bestowing largesse beyond the dreams of avarice was equivalent to a peasant giving you a couple of handfuls of straw from his miserable sleeping pallet.

"Perhaps in that case madame might consider making

alternate plans for *le tourisme*?" M'sieu Bertrand inquired nonchalantly.

"Goodness, no, I wouldn't dream of it," Naphtheena replied, fluttering blue, scaly, lashless eyelids. "I've already filed the parchmentwork." She sipped her tisane of spider blood and silently indicated that she wished another order of biscotti.

"And this time, don't take so long," she cautioned him. "I don't know why you needed an hour to bring the first plate and I have even less of an idea why you then had to fetch the biscotti on an individual basis, but—"

"A thousand apologies, Madame." If M'sieu Bertrand had been speaking his native tongue rather than Hucksterian (or the Extremely Common Lingo) he would have employed the First Person Indifferent, a verb form meant to convey insincerity and disdain like nobody's business. "If I brought you the biscotti one by one, it was to prevent accidental crumbling, for to do otherwise were to insult the baker. Good things are worth the wait, is it not so? But perhaps madame does not know how to appreciate such a refined and sophisticated—"

The dragon's eyes narrowed. "Are you *trying* to annoy me?"

The waiter's brows lifted. "Is madame becoming irked? Peeved? Peradventure piqued? Dare I hazard...infuriated?"

Naphtheena took a deep, centering breath. "I am not. It would be quite unwise of me to permit a mere mortal to provoke me into losing my temper under the present circumstances. However, you might be interested to learn that among my kindred, anger is not a prerequisite to eating what irritates us, or even what attempts to do so. If I were to tell you the number of people I have devoured in cold blood—theirs—it would make your flawlessly coiffed head spin. But it would be much better for us both if it made your butt move into the kitchen and back here with my biscotti right about *now*."

Her words had the desired effect. M'sieu Bertrand dashed off with alacrity and returned with biscotti. When he brought the tasty morsels, he found that another party had joined his customer at the small, round table. The creature that perched on the chair opposite the enormous dragon was much smaller, squatter, and covered in dirty taupe plumage from her garish yellow bird feet almost all the way up to her neck. The only portion of her body that was bare, besides her lovely woman's face, was her equally attractive bosom. While Naphtheena eyed her askance, she cocked her head at the waiter in the manner of inquisitive pigeons everywhere.

"A friend of yours?" the waiter asked Naphtheena.

"Certainly not!" The dragon seemed appalled at the very thought. "Shoo her off at once!"

"Ah, Madame, would that I could." M'sieu Bertrand flicked his fingers in an insouciant manner. "But this newcomer is a customer and our outdoor seating is limited." He needlessly indicated the fact that there was only one table in the courtyard. "I am afraid that you will either have to share your place with her or pay your bill and depart at once."

"All right, if I must. Wrap my biscotti to go and—"

The waiter whisked the plate behind his back. "This tavern is not licensed for takeaway service, alas. However, you are still responsible for paying for them."

Naphtheena's brow lowered. "You *are* trying to get my goat, aren't you? If you were anything but a miserable fetch-and-carry, I would suspect you of dark motives against me." She drew in another of those calming breaths and let it out in the waiter's face. Coming from a dragon, such an exhalation bore the tang of sulfur and the charnel house, with a whisper of almond extract from her previous order of biscotti. It was no fragrant zephyr, as she well knew when she shot it at M'sieu Bertrand, who staggered at the sick-making pong. This mollified the dragon somewhat.

"Very well, I'll share the table," she said, and tapped the surface smartly with one claw. "My biscotti, if you don't mind."

M'sieu Bertrand looked a bit green, but nausea was not the chief emotion that his face revealed. For some as-yet-unknown reason, the waiter did not look so much queasy as thwarted.

It took him a moment to recover his aplomb, whereupon he turned his attention to Naphtheena's uninvited guest.

"Would madame care to see *la carte du jour?*" M'sieu Bertrand inquired suavely, all the while employing the famed Sesinay-pazoonpeepian discretion to feast his eyes upon the feathered monster's generous endowments.

"Don't ask her that, you fool!" The azure dragon leaped to her feet in a panic, upsetting the table in her haste. "Don't you know a harpy when you see one? They don't *talk* to communicate, they—"

A stench of operatic grandeur engulfed the premises. The harpy flicked her tail feathers and fluttered to an unpolluted perch atop the thatched roof of the tavern. M'sieu Bertrand regarded the malodorous mound smothering on the abandoned chair, then turned to Naphtheena.

"Was that a *oui* or a *non?*"

She ate him.

It was at that very moment that a man clad in the robe of a wandering wizard chanced upon the small tavern where M'sieu Bertrand had once been employed. He observed the azure dragon with deep disfavor. "Hail, vile beast!" he called out. "Be thou apprised that by devouring yon mortal you stand in violation of the Basilisk Accords, as laid down by the Council of Wizards, Sorcerers, and Demon-masters and ratified in committee by the Ancient Union of Wyverns, Salamanders, and Dracos."

"Apprise this," said Naphtheena placidly, displaying one claw in a rude gesture. As she was a dragon of the four-clawed variety, the gesture in question did not look precisely the same as if it had been utilized by a human being, but the intent behind it got through. "I know that I violated *nothing* and I defy you to cite chapter and verse showing otherwise. I am painfully aware of all laws, statutes, governances, and plain old down-home *rules* that refer to dragons. You stinkin' wizards managed to kill off enough of my relatives with your miserable rules to make the rest of us pay attention."

The wizard got huffy. Folding plump arms across an equally plump chest, he beetled furiously at the dragon. "You make it sound as if the Basilisk Accords were laid down solely for the purpose of dragon-slaying."

"Weren't they?" Naphtheena's lipless mouth turned up at one corner. (You have not been truly mocked by a smile until you have been mocked by a dragon's smile.)

"No, they were *not*." The wizard snorted at the very idea. "They were compiled by the highest of the high mages, in cooperation with the most revered of the monstrous reptilian elders, as a viable alternative to engaging in a war between mortals and all drake-kind, a devastating, all-out, take-no-prisoners slaughter that—"

"—that nobody really wanted and that nobody could ever hope to win, blah, blah, blah," Naphtheena finished the wizard's bombast for him, moving her claws so that it looked like she was manipulating a garrulous sock puppet. "I *know* all that, Pookie. *I'm* a revered elder; I was there. Which is something *you'd* know if you hadn't napped your way through whatever passes for a history class at whichever miserable excuse for a toad-kissing wizards' academy you attended. Or don't they make you bunch of wand-wagging whelps view Moorbeevil's masterpiece, *The Accords Are Ratified*, any more? That gorgeous blue dragon in the foreground? The one lolling on a pile of skulls? That's me."

The wizard's eyes narrowed. "I know the painting. My grandfather was one of the skulls in question."

"Isn't it a treat to have a familial link to history?" Naphtheena said, lightly. "I know *I've* got one. I have lost five uncles, a brace of aunts, one sister-in-law, Grandma Gridelin, and two score of my innocent hatchlings to *your* people for violating those accursed Accords."

The wizard looked down his nose at the dragon—no mean feat given the fact that she was twice his height and there were bulldogs with more protuberant snouts than his stubby sniffer.

"They broke the rules and paid the price, which is as it should be."

"The rules are a big pile of nitpick stew with a side order of clause slaw!" the dragon roared. This time fire spouted from her nostrils, mouth, *and* ears. The overwhelming power of her emotions turned her flanks from the delicate blue of a summer sky to the sinister, empurpled hue of thunderheads. The wizard observed this with a gloating, anticipatory grin.

Naphtheena caught sight of his expression and cut off the fireworks at once. "Oh no you don't," she said, taking a deep breath and reasserting self-control. "You'd *like* me to lose my temper, wouldn't you? You're practically drooling at the thought of me whipping myself into a frenzy of rage with no bureaucratically justifiable target in sight. If I blast you, your spells will simply deflect my flame. If I destroy anyone or anything else, I've violated the Accords. And if I don't calm myself down before it's too late—"

"You explode," said the wizard nastily. "*Pop!*" He wore a smug look that was absolutely begging for a complimentary butt-kicking.

Naphtheena lowered her eyelids. "I am a dragon. Dragons do not go *'Pop!'* Unlike your head when compressed between two of my talons. Much as that impossible prospect delights me, I must be going. You are a highly irritating two-legged fungus and I will give you no further opportunity to goad me into a self-destructive fury."

"Hold!" The wizard raised one hand, meanwhile drawing his wand with the other. He looked like he was preparing to conduct the village orchestra, but Naphtheena knew that the alternating spurts of green, purple, and silver brilliance fountaining from that "baton" marked its wielder for an Eleventh Level Magister Mysticorrrrr—er, um, something or other threatening in Latin.

It was just such wizards who had compelled Naphtheena and her peers to submit to the Basilisk Accords. She didn't want to get into any needless confrontations with this chubby little itch, especially when the deck was not stacked in her favor. She hadn't survived over three thousand years of stupid but tasty mortals by taking dumb chances.

"All right, Pumpkin-pants, I'm holding. But make it snappy. I have a date with the Grand Gateway and all of the legal documents covering my departure have been properly filed with *your* imbecilic Council. That means if anyone detains me without just cause, I have the right to bring them before said Council and, unless he can provide hard evidence justifying his illicit actions, I get to eat him." She cast a connoisseur's eye over the wizard's generous proportions and added, "On second thought, *do* please make me miss my departure. You look delicious."

The wizard lowered his arms slightly. "You can go as soon as you cough up M'sieu Bertrand," he said.

"What for? He won't be of any use to anyone in his present state."

"Unholy lizard, know that my arcane studies included a full immersion course on the physiology of *your* abominable race. And by 'full immersion' I mean that the first thing our professor did was have a dragon eat us, one by one. It was most illuminating. I mean that literally, for when it was my turn to be ingested, I saw a great light blazing before my eyes. It was the flare from the dragon's fire pouch, and by its brilliance I saw that I was in a large, somewhat fusty sac, in damp but undigested condition. I had no sooner observed this than there came a rumbling, a great shifting, and a yo-heave-ho that propelled me out of my prison and back into the world."

Naphtheena glowered at the wizard. "How dare you violate a dragon's personal space in that obnoxious manner?"

"It was a required course."

"I can *not* believe that one of my kin consented to cooperate with larval wizardlings like that. How humiliating!" She lashed her tail so violently that the harpy on the tavern's thatched roof took wing, settling in an oak tree across the road.

"Nonetheless, and by the grace of a somewhat illegal binding spell, he did. You will be pleased to hear that the professor in question was later dismissed and subsequently devoured for this breach of the Accords. In the meanwhile, he taught a surprising number of us that dragons, like cows, have more than one stomach *and* give excellent milk, to the valiant and nimble-fingered. If you have a scheduled departure flight, that must mean you've still got M'sieu Bertrand in the vestibular paunch because dragons never eat within one hour of flying; it gives you cramps. Cough him up pronto. I know you can."

Naphtheena sneered. "I *can* also share my treasure hoard with you. That doesn't mean I will."

The wizard sighed. "Do I *really* need to say 'or else'? And for you to respond, 'or else what'? And for me to remind you that, per the Accords, the rescue of unfairly endangered mortals supersedes all other considerations, including the enforced delay of a dragon from meeting any and all other commitments? Or, moreover, that such delay will result in your forfeiting the right to complete whatever hideous mission you have on your agenda, which in turn will put you into a snit, which will naturally raise your gorge pressure, which very well might cause you to—?" He stuck a forefinger into one cheek and flicked it out with a percussive *pop!*

"Oh, shut *up*, you worm-wick!" The azure dragon's pique frightened the harpy, who dropped her equivalent of a pithy rebuke. The feathered monster was a garrulous sort, which in her case translated as letting loose much "commentary." Even though her perch was well across the road from the tavern, the wizard's robe was still splashed from waist to hem with her "remarks."

This redolent spectacle restored Naphtheena's good humor. She laughed so hard at the mucked-up mage that she hawked up the considerably rumpled and moist M'sieu Bertrand as a bonus.

"There!" she declared, wiping away tears of mirth. "You've got what you wanted, you miserable dab of magical mucus. The

Accords are fulfilled on my side, so unless you've got another quibble up your knickers, I'll be on my way. I've got an appointment with a doomed kingdom. Ta!" And she soared off without paying her bill or leaving a tip.

M'sieu Bertrand did not seem to be at all concerned by this, which was strange, for a waiter. Rather than pouring forth a stream of denunciation against his deadbeat customer, he instead turned to the harpy in the oak and said, "You might as well get down now, Ma'm'selle Trissa; it didn't work." The harpy spread her wings and floated to the ground so gently that one might almost suspect the wings were just for show. With an artless shrug, she proved this to be true, for the gesture caused those drab pinions to drop to the ground and vanish, along with the rest of her disguise. A tall, freckle-faced blonde in a gown of midnight blue now stood in the harpy's place. She looked disgruntled.

"I suppose *I'm* going to be blamed for the mission failure," she said petulantly, giving both M'sieu Bertrand and the wizard some very hard looks indeed.

"Well, you were a bit . . . *emphatic* in your use of props," said the wizard, indicating the stains on his robes. "You and Bertrand were supposed to do aggravation groundwork on the beast, besetting her with a thousand tiny provocations so that when I finally made my grand entrance as the snotty wizard, it wouldn't take much to push her over the edge of mindless, heedless fury and then—" He made that *pop!* sound with his cheek again.

"I was *setting the mood* by *acting in character*," Trissa shot back. "It's not enough merely to put on the semblance of a harpy; you must *be* the harpy, *live* the harpy, *embrace* the—"

"Pooh," said M'sieu Bertrand, which garnered him a glower from the lady until he specified: "Pooh-pooh, you cavil, Ma'm'selle. We were hired to satisfy our patron, not the critics. I am certain that Prince Gomitino agrees." He nodded to the plump young man in the spattered robe.

"At this point I'm willing to agree to anything that gets me out of these smelly clothes," he said.

Trissa rolled her eyes and with one flip of her right hand transformed the dropping-afflicted garments into a tasteful silk ensemble in shades of green and gold. "Happy now, Your Highness?" she asked in a tone that conveyed the sentiment: *if you're not, tough.*

"I'd be happier if our plan had succeeded," the erstwhile ersatz wizard replied. "And so would both of you. I won't pay for failure."

This declaration did not sit well with the enchantress. "My spells made you look like a wizard, complete with a zappy wand that convinced a dragon that you were too dangerous to attack, even if it didn't have the *real* power to neuter a firefly. I also gave you the temporary brain-boost that let you talk the thaumaturgical talk just as if you were one of my esteemed and arcane order. Such spells don't come cheap, and yet you would dare to shortchange *me?*" She conjured up a lovely backdrop of tame lightning to make herself look more menacing.

"It's no threat but a fact. As we speak, that blasted dragon is en route to the Grand Gateway, the clearinghouse for all winged creatures governed by the Basilisk Accords. Once she passes through, her destination is Yvitelli, *my* kingdom, and once she reaches it, she'll burn it to the ground, slaughter thousands, and take over the royal treasury. You know, treasury? As in: the place where I keep my gold? As in: the gold I was going to pay you if you'd succeeded in annoying the beast to the point of *ka-PLOWIE?*"

"You mean—?" Trissa began.

"No *ka-PLOWIE*, no gold, Ma'm'selle," M'sieu Bertrand provided with equanimity.

"Well, *you're* taking this well, I must say," Prince Gomitino remarked, pettishly.

"Ah, what would you?" the cavalier Sesinaypazoonpeepian replied, spreading his hands. "My part in this little play

Service Charge

was minor, to be rewarded with a comparable pittance when placed beside the enchantress' fee. I have not lost much by the plot's failure, and the one moment of malaise I suffered was undone promptly—which is to say, I was *in*gested but not *di*gested. I have had worse Mondays. Now if Your Highness will but provide reimbursement for the damage done to this table, as well as covering the cost of one spider blood tisane and two orders of biscotti, plus a suitable token of appreciation for the person who conveyed said items to said table, we can call it a—"

"No *ka-PLOWIE*, no gold," said Prince Gomitino. "No gold, no tip."

M'sieu Bertrand pursed his lips. "I don't think so."

"Are you sure this will work?" Trissa whispered, as she peered around the corner of the barracks. Within those daub and wattle walls slumbered the off-shift of the Wand Patrol, wizards whose job it was to enforce the Basilisk Accords at this, the key nexus governing the inter-kingdom flight of dragons, the Grand Gateway.

"We shall see soon enough, Ma'm'selle," the waiter replied

through clenched teeth. "You have followed my instructions to the letter?"

"Yes, such as they were. You didn't exactly give me a *specific* item to conjure."

"Specificity is not our friend, in this case. You are certain you have the magical power to turn my instructions into reality?"

"Your ridiculously *vague* instructions, yes." It was the enchantress' turn to grind her molars. "And the power to turn you into a toad if this doesn't work."

"Oho, but I assure you, it will, for it follows the same inexorable logic that Prince Gomitino himself posited in his simple but elegant *ka-PLOWIE* chain of reasoning."

At the mention of his name, Prince Gomitino pushed his way around the waiter to stare at the Grand Gateway. As usual, the space before that carved obsidian archway was thronged with all manner of wyverns, fire-drakes, and good old down-home dragons, each one patiently waiting its turn to be allowed access. As part of the Accords, the wyrms vowed never to shift their spheres of devastation without obtaining the correct permits, which had to be vetted at the Grand Gateway. In exchange, all wizardkind swore never to provide any heroes, knights, barbarian freebooters, or freelance third-sons-of-poor-but-honest peasant families with enchanted weapons that might give them an unfair whoops-there-goes-your-severed-head advantage over the dragons.

The prince was not pleased by the view.

"*What's* going to work?" he demanded. "All I see is the Gateway. Where's this foolproof solution you promised me to stop that blue dragon from destroying Yvitelli? Look, there she is, just one away from her turn through that abominable arch!"

"Ah, then it is time." The waiter closed his eyes in contemplation and steepled his fingers.

Some distance away, Naphtheena watched the drake ahead of her give his name and destination. The wizard on duty behind the Grand Gateway podium checked a scroll, nodded, and waved him through. Then it was her turn.

"I am Naphtheena the Maleficent," she said calmly, for it was true matter of life and death for dragons to remain as calm as possible at all times, since the Accords. "I am also called Mother of the Thousand Sorrows, Wreaker of Havoc, Devourer of Nations, Despoiler of—"

Somewhere—and yet from no discernable direction—a trumpet blast sounded.

"Lunch!" cried the wizard on Gateway duty, leaving Naphtheena to draw a number of those centering breaths while he skedaddled and his replacement arrived.

The replacement did not arrive alone. He came attended by a squad of identically clad wizards, all heavily laden with some of the strangest items the blue dragon had ever seen. While he spread out a fresh pile of scrolls on the podium, his colleagues arranged weirdly humming wands, piles of shallow bowls, and a smaller archway made of metal which they erected between Naphtheena and the Grand Gateway.

"And you are?" said the wizard.

"I am Naphtheena the—"

"I'm going to need to see some identification."

"I told you, I am Naphtheena the Maleficent, also called Mother of the Thousand—"

"Sorry, but you have to show me some proof that you are who you say you are. Would you have a picture of yourself with your name on—?"

A few wisps of steam began to rise from Naphtheena's snout. "Cast a spell to fetch an image of Moorbeevil's *The Accords Are Ratified*. I'm the blue dragon on the skulls, all right?"

"Well, that's highly irregular, but it is our first day. While I'm summoning that image, please get ready for your screening."

"My what?"

"Oh, it's very simple, really. First you're going to have to nip the points off your hind claws—"

"Off my what?" The white wisps became gray puffs shot through with glittering sparks.

"It's for your own safety. No more sharp objects allowed on interkingdom flights. If you've got a permit to devastate Kingdom A and you accidentally land in Kingdom B and scratch someone, you've violated the Accords and we'd have to kill you, so you see, it's all for the best."

"Fine, fine." Naphtheena chomped her toenails off. "Now conjure up that painting on the double so I can be on my—"

"Just as soon as you've done the same to the talons on your forepaws."

"Talons...off...my..." Naphtheena's cheeks began to swell and shift hue to a darker part of the spectrum.

"Mmm, it looks like we're going to have to do something about those fangs of yours as well." He waved his hands and a hideous appliance made of black gum appeared. "Just stick this in your mouth before you go through the Great Gateway and one of my colleagues will fix it in place for you with a sealing spell that is guaranteed to release its hold the moment your paws touch the soil of your destination. Well, virtually guaranteed. Since this is our first day, the thaumatic technology might have a few bugs in it, and maybe a scorpion or two, but you can always contact our main office with any complaints."

"I am not putting that loathsome lump of goo in my mouth," Naphtheena said. "And you can't make me."

"Certainly not." The wizard was unruffled. "Nor can you make us approve your request to fly to—" He peered at the open scroll before him. "—Yvitelli, was it?—" He looked up at the dragon with an amiable expression. "—ever."

Naphtheena's wings sagged. "I'll wear the dumb fang-capper. Now can we move this along? I've trimmed my hind talons, I'm going to nip off my forepaw talons—"

"Yes, yes." The wizard nodded. "And once you've done that, Master Runcible over there is going to have to run his hands all over your wings, to make sure you're not one of those dragons who have spikes growing on them. Terribly dangerous things, spikes. And then we'll have Master Dagmar—he's the skinny one at the end of the line—pass that special wand along every one of your scales. And *then* we'll just have you pop into the Booth of Revelation, so we can see if you've got anyone in your vestibular paunch, because we both know it's not conducive to a safe flight if you're carrying unaccounted-for weight."

"But this will take forever!" Naphtheena wailed. "And if you detain me past my assigned departure time, *you'll* be the ones to suffer for it!" An unusual swelling developed along her flanks. "I'll devour you!" More spark-flecked steam spurted from Naphtheena's jaws, to be casually deflected by the blandly smiling wizard. "And it will be *legal*!" Now vast clouds were erupting from other orifices, both fore and aft. "And do you know what? At this very moment I would happily give up any chance of ravaging the kingdom of Yvitelli just to have the supreme joy of turning you and all your colleagues into *brunch*!"

"Well naturally that's all true," said the wizard affably. "Provided that we were detaining you *without just cause*."

He passed a small leather folder to the simmering dragon. Naphtheena skimmed the contents. They were mostly boilerplate mumbo with a dollop of legalese jumbo, but dragons make very good lawyers and she extracted the gist readily: this new order of Grand Gateway wizards had received miraculously instantaneous imprimatur from both their Council and her Union.

"All right," she grumped as she returned the folder. "You can make me miss my flight window and get off scot free. I don't care. I'm a dragon. I've lived for thousands of years and there's plenty more where that came from. I'll simply re-file the parchmentwork and come back here another day. When I do, I'll make sure to leave myself an excess of temporal wiggle-room to jump through all of your hoops. I will get to Yvitelli, I promise you that. Maybe not today, maybe not tomorrow, but soon, and for—"

"Pardon me, but you're holding up the line," the wizard interrupted. "And you are doing so *without just cause*, taking up our organization's valuable time with your needless ranting."

"Then I'll step out of line and—" Naphtheena's pulse became so strong and rapid that it sounded as if she were harboring a village drum corps in her gizzard.

"I'm afraid we can't allow that. It would be construed as uspicious behavior. We'd have to take you into custody for a full investigation. Are you allergic to wolfsbane? We do have gloves that are coated with monkshood instead, but wouldn't it be simpler for everyone if you simply were a good little dragon and complied with the rules, used your permit to travel to Yvitelli, and got on with your life?" He glanced up at the sky, checking the angle of the sun, then returned his gaze to the scroll before him. "And sooner rather than later, before this does become a matter for *very* deep internal investigation."

A low, ominous rumbling began deep in Naphtheena's entrails as she frantically snapped off her talons while at the same time urging the backup wizards to get a move on with their hands and wands and whatevers. In fact, she was making such a racket that the wizard at the podium had to shout to make himself heard when he said, "Oh, and one more thing: you're going to have to put any gold coins you might be carrying into *this* bowl and drain yourself of any venom into *this* one, and it can't be more than three hogsheads' worth of liquid, and put your hind paws on those two outlines over *there*, and put your forepaws on *that*, and if you'd just remove your shoes—"

Naphtheena could have pointed out that, as a dragon, she never wore shoes. She could have, but by that point all of her logical faculties were engulfed by a tidal wave of wrath: compelling, unstoppable, inevitable and, in the parlance of the Extemely Common Lingo, mind-blowing.

Dragons' minds seldom blow alone. There was a loud report of a volume somewhere between *pop!* and *ka-PLOWIE!* The corps of officious wizards, the Grand Gateway, the waiting dragons, the barracks and even those hiding around the corner of same were all liberally splattered with bits of reeking azure dragon flesh. There wasn't an un-gaping mouth in the vicinity, with one exception:

M'sieu Bertrand flicked a shred of the late Naphtheena's pancreas off his tunic and smiled.

"It worked?" Trissa the enchantress goggled.

"It worked!" Prince Gomitino recovered from his initial shock and clapped his hands with glee.

"But of course," said M'sieu Betrand. "Logically, it couldn't help but to do so. After all, what did I tell you to summon by your spells, Ma'm'selle?"

"You said—" Trissa was still a little gobsmacked by what she had just witnessed. "You said to summon whatever cosmic force was exasperating, frustrating and maddening enough to make a dragon lose its temper, but you never *specified*—"

"Nor did I need to. Some choices are best left to the cosmos itself, is it not so? And I think you must agree that the cosmos provided just what we needed." He cocked his head at Prince Gomitino and extended one hand. "I believe fifteen per cent is customary, Your Highness, but in this case, wouldn't you say—?"

Which was how a humble Sesinaypazoonpeepian waiter came to rule over twenty per cent of the lovely little realm of Yvitelli, which he renamed the Duchy of Sayrvicompri, though he still charged Prince Gomitino extra for the dragon's biscotti.

Et voilá tout l'histoire.

Esther Friesner

Nebula Award winner Esther Friesner is the author of thirty-nine novels and over one hundred ninety short stories, in addition to being the editor of ten popular anthologies. Her works have been published in the United States, the United Kingdom, Japan, Germany, Russia, France, Poland and Italy. She is also a published poet and a produced playwright. Her articles on fiction writing have appeared in *Writer's Market* and Writer's Digest Books.

ITEM NOT AS DESCRIBED
BY J.W. ALDEN

From: Vaenala the Unbound <unbound1@hexmail.net>
To: Kobe Thompson <B14cKm4giXXX69@wahoo.com>
Subject: this will not suffice

Mr. Thompson,
    I received your parcel today. Considering the distance between us (by my reckoning, at least a thousand leagues as the crow flies), I feel honor-bound to thank you for the speedy shipping time. I'm afraid I cannot thank you for the contents of said package, however. This is clearly not the Lost Blade of Cragthor.
    Had you at least done your research, you might have known that Cragthor was very particular about his weapons and how they were made. For one, you would not have caught him dead wielding anything but Vorlexian steel, which bears the telltale ripples and mottles of ancient pattern welding. If Vorlexian hands wrought this blade, I'm a

halfling's uncle. It looks more like something out of a cutlery drawer. I suppose I will give you a point or two for attempting to recreate the runic markings left behind by the goblin blood Vorlexians dipped their weapons in, but for future reference: goblin blood is black, not red.

    Now, I am a sensible being, Mr. Thompson. I will give you the benefit of the doubt here. I will assume this was all a simple mistake on your part, and that you did not intend to defraud me. If I melt it down, I may even be able to get some use out of this cheap facsimile. As such, I am prepared to keep the item "as is" in exchange for a 50% refund. We can call it a day with no feelings hurt, no spells cast, and no negative feedback left on anyone's profile. I think this is quite reasonable. What say you, sir?

    ~ Vaenala

From: Kobe Thompson <B14cKm4giXXX69@wahoo.com>
To: Vaenala the Unbound <unbound1@hexmail.net>
Subject: RE: this will not suffice

    Um im pretty sure item was listed as replica like new without wrapping but will issue small refund if thats what u prefer i guess

From: Vaenala the Unbound <unbound1@hexmail.net>
To: Kobe Thompson <B14cKm4giXXX69@wahoo.com>
Subject: RE: RE: this will not suffice

Item Not as Described

Mr. Thompson,

    I told you I was willing to be reasonable about this, but if you're going to insult my intelligence further, we can put a stop to this little mummer's show right now. While your message doesn't inspire much confidence that you are fluent in the common tongue, I assume you can at least read the words that *you* wrote in your own auction listing. For your convenience, I'll paste the entire description here:

> LOST BLADE OF CRAGTHOR—GENUINE!!!
> Very hard to find one of a kind from cragthr who killed teh demons at seleros and still has there blood on it!! feel a power as you hold this mighty sword!!1! happy bidding this is a steal come on

    As you can see, the word "replica" appears nowhere in this description. You have the word "genuine" in the title, for hell's sake! I will admit your reference to Seleros should have tipped me off, as Cragthor never visited the lower wastes, to my knowledge. But that doesn't give you the right to defraud me. At least common brigands have the stones to take up arms when they want to rob you of something. While I might have flayed you alive had you gone that route, you'd at least have a slither of respect about you, if not honor.

    Now, you claim your intent to issue a "small" refund. But I've been very clear about what I expect from you if you wish a civil end to this little palaver. You will refund half my gold, sir, and not a sovereign less. If I have not received such from you within a fortnight, I shall take this up with a higher power. What follows, I wash my hands of.

    ~ Vaenala

From: Kobe Thompson <B14cKm4giXXX69@wahoo.com>
To: Vaenala the Unbound <unbound1@hexmail.net>
Subject: RE: RE: RE: this will not suffice

lol whatever

From: Bid-o-Mancy Customer Support <help@bidomancy.com>
To: Vaenala the Unbound <unbound1@hexmail.net>
Subject: RE: Item Not As Described (AUTOMATED REPLY)

Dear Ms. The Unbound,

    Thank you for contacting Bid-o-Mancy customer support with your issue. We're sorry there was a problem with your transaction. When you filled out our correspondence form, you indicated that item #931179, "LOST BLADE OF CRAGTHOR—GENUINE!!!" did not arrive in the condition described by the seller on the auction listing. Before we escalate this case to our resolution center, we'd like to ask a few questions about your transaction:

    Have you double-checked the auction listing to ensure you're not mistaken about the item's description? We've found that some users commonly mistake the "Like New" category for the "Brand New" category.

    Have you contacted the seller about your problem? We prefer to give our members a chance to resolve things on their own before we arbitrate a dispute.

    If you have, was the seller responsive?

    Please reply at your convenience. Your case will be assigned a customer support representative from

Item Not as Described

there. We apologize for any inconvenience you have suffered, and we hope to resolve your issue as soon as possible.

Thank you,
Bid-o-Mancy Customer Support
Twice Awarded "Best in Customer Service for the Dark Arts" by Yrrgoth and Associates

From: Vaenala the Unbound <unbound1@hexmail.net>
To: Bid-o-Mancy Customer Support <help@bidomancy.com>
Subject: RE: RE: Item Not As Described

Dear Customer Support Golem,

Have I double-checked the listing? In case you failed to notice, I am called Vaenala the Unbound, not Vaenala the Uneducated. The listing was a weeping font of lies from top to bottom, and that didn't change with a second reading.

And yes, I held parley with the blithering clod and got what I might have expected from one who would seek to prey on the Unbound One: pure idiocy. So no, "responsive" is not quite the word I'd use. I've forwarded a copy of our exchange along with this message. You be the judge.

~ Vaenala

From: Bid-o-Mancy Customer Support <help@bidomancy.com>
To: Vaenala the Unbound <unbound1@hexmail.net>
Subject: RE: RE: RE: Item Not As Described

Hi Vaenala,

This is Brian from customer support. I just wanted to let you know that I've escalated your case to our resolution center and you should be hearing back from us soon.

Also, it may interest you to know that our server handles all automated replies from us. Bid-o-Mancy strives to comply with the laws and legal restrictions of the realm, and as such does not employ golems of any kind.

Thank you,

Brian

Bid-o-Mancy Customer Support

Twice Awarded "Best in Customer Service for the Dark Arts" by Yrrgoth and Associates

From: Bid-o-Mancy Customer Support <help@bidomancy.com>
To: Kobe Thompson <B14cKm4giXXX69@wahoo.com>
Subject: Support Case #58632 (DO NOT REPLY)

Dear Mr. Thompson,

On Yogsmorn, Seventh Day of the Reaping, you sold item #931179, "LOST BLADE OF CRAGTHOR—GENUINE!!!" at auction. Unfortunately, the buyer has opened a support case regarding this transaction, which has been escalated to our resolution center.

Upon reviewing the transaction in question, as well as the subsequent correspondence between yourself and the buyer, we have ruled in the buyer's favor on this matter. A full refund has been issued from your account and the buyer may be supplied with a return label at your expense.

Item Not as Described

In addition, the customer service representative assigned to this case has found your auction listing to be in violation of Bid-o-Mancy's terms of service agreement. In accordance with the terms you agreed to upon the creation of your account, all auctions and transactions currently active on your profile will be suspended, your account and username will be banned from our services going forward, and the celestial firehounds of Lythrathyl will be commissioned to devour your earthly flesh. The amount of flesh to be devoured is based upon the severity of the violation as determined by the customer support representative assigned to this case. You will find a rough estimate of that amount in the box below:

[99 %]

If you have any questions regarding the resolution of this case, do not reply to this message. You may use the correspondence form on our customer support page (please supply the case number with any correspondence).

Thank you,
Bid-o-Mancy Customer Support
Twice Awarded "Best in Customer Service for the Dark Arts" by Yrrgoth and Associates

From: Kobe Thompson <B14cKm4giXXX69@wahoo.com>
To: Bid-o-Mancy Customer Support <help@bidomancy.com>
Subject: RE: Support Case #58632 (DO NOT REPLY)

wait what

From: Bid-o-Mancy Customer Support <help@bidomancy.com>
To: Vaenala the Unbound <unbound1@hexmail.net>
Subject: Support Case #58632 (DO NOT REPLY)

Dear Ms. The Unbound,

    Good news! The customer support representative assigned to this case has ruled in your favor.
A full refund, including the purchase price plus shipping has been credited to your account.

    In addition, the customer support representative estimates the seller is likely to perish from his or her injuries following standard punitive action. If you have any interest in obtaining the seller's remains for necromantic or alchemical purposes, you will have the exclusive opportunity to purchase them at a discounted rate following mystic appraisal. We hope this will serve as thanks for your patience in this matter, and that you will continue to use Bid-o-Mancy to meet your needs for the dark arts. Your business is importance to us.

    Thank you,
    Bid-o-Mancy Customer Support
Twice Awarded "Best in Customer Service for the Dark Arts" by Yrrgoth and Associates

Story Notes:

As you may have guessed, I wrote this story after having a bad experience on e-bay. After several not-so-helpful exchanges with customer service, I began to imagine all the gruesome ways I'd like to see the seller meet his end. When I realized the laws of this world could not grant the level of justice I desired, I figured I might as well invent one that would.

J.W. Alden

has been writing speculative fiction since he's been old enough to use a pen. He lives in South Florida with a cute girl and a bratty dog, and he's a graduate of the 2013 Odyssey Writing Workshop. You can read more from him at AuthorAlden.com.

STRANGER VS. THE MALEVOLENT MALIGNANCY

BY JIM C. HINES

Stranger shifted in the armchair and forced himself to make eye contact with his therapist: a decapitated head floating in an oversized jar of blue-tinged nutrient fluid. Long gray-blond hair drifted like tentacles. The base of the jar was decorated in a red and yellow floral pattern, reminiscent of the Hawaiian shirts Jarhead wore back in his full-bodied superhero days.

"In all my time on this planet, I've never killed anyone," said Stranger. "I've never *wanted* to before."

Jarhead's voice emerged, slightly mechanical, from a speaker below his chin. "Given your history with Scaramouche, it's no surprise she knows how to press your buttons."

Jarhead was a former speedster, a superhero from the seventies whose career on the east coast had come to an abrupt end when his nemesis strung a high-tensile wire across the road at neck height. Only the hyperquick actions of Jarhead's sidekick Robogirl had allowed him to survive... if you could call it survival.

"When do I get to talk? I've got traumas of my own, you know!"

Stranger did his best to ignore the taunts, which was difficult, considering they came from within his own bowel.

"It's talking to you again, isn't it?" asked Jarhead.

"It's been particularly irate today."

The blue-gray skin of Jarhead's forehead crinkled in thought as his eyelids lowered, curtaining his colorless eyes. "A tumor with anger issues. You know, this would be easier if it would come out and talk to me directly."

"Tell that hairy bowling ball that if I could uproot myself and move around, I wouldn't still be living halfway up your alien ass!"

"I don't think that's going to happen," Stranger said.

"It was worth a shot." Jarhead's bubbling sigh filled the room. "Start at the beginning. You said you learned of Scaramouche's escape at your press conference..."

STRANGER HAD LAIN awake all night in his apartment, trying to find the right words for his announcement the next morning. And then someone—he didn't know who or how—had broken the news online around 3:00 A.M.

The result was a crowd four times the size he had expected, pressing around the pavilion by the river in Lake City Central Park. Cameras and microphones tracked his descent like weapons, and the questions erupted before he finished climbing the makeshift stage.

One man managed to make his voice heard above the rest. "Your tumor currently has more than a dozen Twitter accounts. The most popular has sixty-thousand followers. Can you confirm whether any of these are official accounts?"

"What's a Twitter?"

Stranger adjusted the polarization of his helmet's faceplate to better block the afternoon sun. One of the experimental meds in his latest round of chemotherapy had induced extreme photosensitivity. Only two years earlier, he had gone toe-to-toe with a villain wielding a fusion-powered plasma blaster. Now, even five minutes in the sunlight was enough to make his skin blister and peel. "My most recent scan showed seven tumors. The largest and primary is located in the lower portion of my bowel. I assure you that none of them are on Twitter."

"Don't ignore me, dude! I want a Twitter! Where can I get one?"

Another reporter spoke up, and Stranger stifled a groan. Thomas T. Thorton had always hated him, producing story after story that warned against the dangers of letting a superpowered alien walk among good, decent human beings. "Do they talk to you?"

"Don't let him make you nervous. It helps if you imagine every microphone is actually an enormous dildo."

"The primary tumor does, yes," said Stranger. "What it doesn't do is shut up."

"In other words," Thorton continued, "you're officially talking out of your—"

Stranger's silent command caused the microphone—dammit, now he was visualizing dildos—to twist out of Thorton's grip. As the microphone tumbled to the grass, it spoke in a tinny voice only Stranger could hear. "Sorry about that, sir. He's just digging for snappy one-liners. He's worried your cancer will make you more sympathetic to his audience, and his ratings will drop."

By the time Thorton recovered, Kelly Kane from the *Lake City Sentinel* had stood to ask, "What treatment options are you exploring?"

The sensors in his mask allowed Stranger to see the heat in her neck and cheeks, though she kept her expression professional. For ten years she had been a friend. She wanted to be more, and perhaps they could have been, if Stranger had found human females the slightest bit attractive. Only two breasts? And on the chest, of all places?

He had explained his powers to Kelly in their first interview, how he could whisper to objects in his native tongue and persuade them to obey his wishes. That was the night she gave him his superhero name, after an old Robert Heinlein novel. Heinlein's stranger in a strange land didn't have super-strength or invulnerability, but the name worked well enough.

"After consulting with Doctor Y, I've chosen to discontinue treatment."

His words stunned the crowd into silence.

"That's right, baby!" the tumor crowed. *"Get me a cape and mask. Me and my minions are invincible!"*

He wanted to pull Kelly aside, to apologize for . . . he wasn't sure what, exactly. For having cancer? Why should he feel guilty about that?

"Ha! I may be a lowly butt tumor, but that doesn't mean I can't mess with your mind."

Eventually, Kelly whispered, "How long?"

"Tell her it's not the length that matters, it's how—"

"According to Professor Edison, six months, one week, and three days." Trust the man who could peek through time to eliminate any ambiguity about your prognosis.

"How could this happen?" asked another reporter. She sounded affronted, as if Stranger's disease caused her great personal offense. "You're supposed to be invulnerable."

"I don't know. Maybe it's all the times I've been shot by death rays, gamma beams, laser weapons, and worse. Not to mention disarming nuclear weapons, flying toxic waste into the sun, and spending ten years on this planet eating food whose compatibility with my biology is iffy on the best of days. Seriously, what do you people put into those microwave burritos?"

"Will your tumor take questions?" asked Thorton.

"Ooh! Tell him I'll give him an exclusive, but only if I get approval on any photos. Maybe he could use the colonoscopy shot from three weeks ago? Or do you think I looked too puffy in that shot?"

The radio built into Stranger's helmet saved him from having to answer. "I'm sorry, I have to go. It seems that Scaramouche has escaped from Edgewood Asylum. Again."

Thank the gods. He spoke to the air around him. Wind filled his cape, giving it a dramatic flutter. The air became his elevator, cradling his body and lifting him up and away.

He missed his old skintight costume, feeling the warmth of this world's sun on his body, the air rushing past as he flew—

"Quit your bitching. I live where the sun never shines, remember? And the only time I feel the wind is when you break it."

"Edgewood Asylum is the dumbest institution on the planet." Bubbles dribbled up from the corners of Jarhead's mouth, something that only happened when he was truly pissed. "Crazed supervillains turn cockroaches into giant mechanized war machines or travel back in time to kill the inventor of bacon, and what do we do? *Lock them all up in the same place to compare notes!*"

This had been Scaramouche's fourth successful escape. Fifth if you counted the time she programmed a copy of her own mind and uploaded it to Facebook. Thankfully, e-Scaramouche proved to be just as erratic as her creator, and Stranger had been able to trap her in a neverending game of Bejeweled.

"I'm sorry," Jarhead continued. "But you can't rehabilitate the woman who tried to assassinate the Prime Minister of Australia with a radioactive platypus. How much have we spent on room and board and therapy for those clowns? If anyone deserves a death sentence..."

His final words hung in the air. Stranger watched the blinking LEDs on Jarhead's circulation regulator, remembering the sadness on Doctor Y's pale face as he pronounced Stranger's own death sentence.

"Ooh. Awkward..."

"Right. Sorry," said Jarhead. "So you flew to Edgewood."

STRANGER'S STOMACH GURGLED as he approached the main entrance, a steel door six inches thick, guarded by twin laser turrets. After a voiceprint check, the door swung open, and he strode inside to greet Doctor April Alexander, administrator of Edgewood Asylum.

"Thank you for coming so quickly." Doctor Alexander spoke in a whisper, as if this were a church or a funeral home. She avoided looking at his face. "I'm sorry about... you know."

"From this day forward, I will be known as That Which Shall Not Be Named!"

"We're on full lockdown," she said as she led him inside. "Everyone else is secure. Scaramouche was the only one to escape."

"How?" Stranger asked.

"She..." Her face reddened. "She talked one of the guards into releasing her. The guard died in the escape. I don't suppose—"

"I can't talk to the dead." Stranger sighed. All the precautions in the world couldn't protect against human frailty. How long had Scaramouche worked to select which guard would be most vulnerable to her manipulations, and to slowly warp her victim's mind with carefully chosen words?

Each cell was customized to the powers of its inhabitant. Magman lived in a walk-in freezer with precisely controlled oxygen flow to keep him from igniting. Verdana's cell was irradiated twice a day to prevent her from using her mastery of plants to create a mold-based weapon. Again.

Scaramouche's cell was unusual in its normalcy. She had no powers beyond her deranged mind, and yet she had proven herself time and again to be one of Edgewood's most dangerous supervillains.

"Cool new threads." Across the hall, the Halloween Princess pressed up against the window of her cell. "Tough break, man."

Stranger stopped. "What do you mean?"

"The cancer. That sucks, dude."

For a moment, he thought he had stumbled into another of those obnoxious parallel universes, one where supervillains sympathized with their foes instead of celebrating their demise. "I put you in here after you tried to unleash a plague that would have wiped out ninety percent of humanity."

Halloween shrugged. "Sure, but this is *cancer*."

"Me and my boys, we're the trump card of terror. Steamroller ran over your dog? Cancer! Nemesis stuffs your girlfriend into the fridge? Cancer! Michael Bay announces another Transformers *movie? Cancer, baby!"*

Stranger threw up his hands and entered Scaramouche's cell.

"How can I help?" asked Doctor Alexander.

"I need quiet." He listened to the room's contents, inviting them to share what they knew.

"She read me last," proclaimed a textbook about magnetic nanoparticles. An *Archie* comic piped up to say, *"Bullshit! She always took me along when she used the toilet."*

"That was two days ago," said the stainless steel toilet in the corner. A translucent panel separated it from the rest of the room, providing minimal privacy. *"Poor woman was constipated from the meds they fed her to keep her from going manic."*

"She left you a message." The words came from the pillow on the floor. Scaramouche had neither blankets nor a cot, presumably to keep her from creating some sort of evil mattress-based superweapon. "She asked me to tell you that you were almost out of time."

"How did she know?" Socialization was kept to a minimum at Edgewood, but somehow the inmates always kept up on the latest gossip.

"Don't ask me. I just hope the next inmate has better hygiene. Scaramouche would forget to shower for weeks at a time. Do you know what it's like having that nest of greasy, sweaty hair press down on you every night?"

"Out of time." He turned the phrase over in his thoughts, but before he could figure out the clue, a noise like a T. Rex gargling boulders erupted from his stomach.

Oh, gods. Not now. Not here. He froze in place, muscles clenched, but all his strength wasn't enough to fight against his own body.

"Don't blame this one on me!" his tumor yelled. "This is what you get for trying to kill me!"

"What's wrong?" Doctor Alexander started toward him.

"Stay back!" He used his powers to fling her out of the room, then slammed the door. He ducked behind the partition.

"Wait, what are you doing?" the toilet cried. "What's happening?"

Stranger's belt flew from his costume, and his pants dropped as he flung himself onto the cold, metal seat.

"It's a bird. It's a plane!"

Stranger pressed a hand to the wall as his insides exploded.

"It's Super *Shit!*"

"I'M SURE DOCTOR ALEXANDER understood," said Jarhead. "The side effects of chemotherapy aren't pretty."

Stranger's face burned. That hadn't been the first such incident, but always before, he had been able to reach somewhere safe and private. "I blew a hole the size of a basketball through the toilet and the floor of Scaramouche's cell. I left a crater two meters across in the sublevel below."

"I see." Jarhead pulled his lips tight, struggling not to laugh. "And how did that make you feel?"

"Fuck you."

"I'M SO SORRY," Stranger said for the fourth time. "I'll find a way to pay for the repairs."

His tumor hadn't stopped babbling. *"Did you hear when that shit went supersonic? We should weaponize this! What kind of range do you think we can get? We'd have to modify your suit, but—Ha! Your suit butt!"*

"It's all right," said Doctor Alexander, though her face was pale, and her eyes were still watering. "Our insurance covers acts of superpowers. Even . . . even this."

"Imagine dropping a bunker-buster like that on just one villain's hideout. Every bad guy in the city would either surrender or run for the hills. Nobody's going to stick around and risk that. *It's the fecal equivalent of the nuclear deterrent!"*

"I think I need to turn this over to another hero," Stranger said.

"No! We can do this! Just you and me, Tumor and his sidekick, Brown Thunder!"

"This isn't your fault."

Her sympathy made him feel worse. He swallowed an unexpected lump in his throat. He couldn't control his own body, couldn't control his emotions . . . the only consolation was that his helmet hid his anguish. "What if someone had been working in the sublevel?"

"You've still got a bit of gas in here. Stop clenching and let it fly, man! Wait—I've got it! This is brilliant! Methane's flammable, right? If we install a rear-mounted pilot light, you could fight evil with your superpowered flamethrower!"

"Nobody knows Scaramouche as well as you do," said

Doctor Alexander. "You said she left you a message. No one else could have heard that. We need you."

She was right, damn it. "Scaramouche said I was almost out of time." Time... "The university."

"What?"

Stranger was already rising into the sky. "She's going after Professor Edison at Lake City University."

For the past two years, Edric Edison had been working on what he called "magnetic time." He argued that true time travel was currently impossible, due to the immense computational difficulties in navigating both time *and* space simultaneously. Travel backward even a single minute, and the entire universe moved around you, leaving you sucking vacuum. But if you treated an object as four-dimensional, an unbroken solid stretching through time, you could yank a future or past version of that object into the present. As long as you had the original to use as an anchor.

How many past and future Scaramouches would she create? She would delight in the paradoxes, and an army of sociopathic geniuses would be unstoppable.

Police cars blocked the street in front of Edison's building. A crowd pressed around the wooden barriers by the entrance. They exploded into cheers when they spotted him.

He landed harder than he had planned, cracking the blacktop. Damned peripheral neuropathy. At this point, he doubted he'd ever get full feeling back in his extremities. He searched for the nearest uniformed officer. "What happened?"

"Professor Edison is gone, and his lab was ransacked," stammered a young rookie whose nametag read *Conroy*. "We're glad you're here, Stranger. You look good. I mean, you don't look *sick*. Not that I'm a doctor. And I know your costume hides everything, but ... you just don't look like someone who's dying."

"Tell him about the superpoop!"

"We love you!" shouted a man near the back of the crowd.

"We know you'll beat this!"

"You're so strong!"

"Strong?" Stranger turned to face the woman who had spoken. "You think these malicious lumps of flesh cannibalizing my body make me *strong*?"

"*Temper, temper!*"

"Not the cancer," she said. "The way you're facing it. Your courage and dignity are an inspiration to the whole city."

Stranger strode toward her. "You all know I disappeared for two weeks in March." He heard his voice rising, but he couldn't stop his anger any more than he could have held back his eruption at the asylum. "I gathered a sphere of air around myself and flew to the dark side of the moon. Do you know what I did there?"

The crowd shifted uncomfortably.

"I cried like an Earth baby. And then I punched the fucking moon. Do those sound like the actions of a strong, courageous, dignified man?" He stomped toward the entrance. "I need to question Edison's lab."

"There's more," the police officer said, weakly. Stranger sighed, knowing from experience what he was about to say. "Scaramouche has also kidnapped Kelly Kane."

JARHEAD PURSED HIS LIPS. "Some would say the courage isn't about your breakdown, but about your choice to come back afterward."

"Where else was I supposed to go? My own world blew up, remember? Besides, the moon's boring. Nothing happens there but the occasional meteoroid strike. You want to know what a conversation with the moon sounds like? 'Ouch. Ouch. Ouch.' It gets old fast."

"Have you considered a brain-jar? It's not as bad as you'd think." Jarhead began to pace back and forth on the desk, carried by the spider-like metal legs on the base of his jar.

"Even if we could cut off my head, and even if your technology could be adapted for alien biology, it's too late.

The cancer metastasized through my body. It would just follow my head into the jar and kill me there." Stranger shifted in his chair, trying to find a position that didn't aggravate the aches in his joints. "Everyone wants to help. Scaramouche is the only one to come up with a solution that might work . . ."

THE AIRPORT WAS EMPTY when Stranger arrived. Police and airport security had pulled everyone back a full five hundred yards: the government's minimum recommended distance for a potential superpowered showdown.

In one hand, he clutched the wooden puzzle box he had found in Professor Edison's office. Scaramouche had defaced the intricate multicolored woodwork with the word *Pandora* scrawled in blue Sharpie marker. "Repeat the message, please."

The box was happy to oblige. *"Terminal six. Hope to see you soon."*

His tumor chuckled. *"'Terminal.' Just like you. I like this woman."*

Stranger swooped toward the terminal, where he spotted two figures sitting in a luggage truck beside an abandoned passenger jet.

Scaramouche sat waiting, her legs extended and crossed on the dashboard. A white mask hid her face—the mask of comedy, not tragedy, which was reassuring. When Scaramouche wore her other mask, the body count skyrocketed.

Behind that mask hid the mind of a genius. As Doctor Mona Merlo, she had earned PhDs in psychology, physics, and law. Her masks also hid the horribly scarred results of a scheme gone wrong, something involving a nanoexplosive, a trained ferret, and a microwave. Merlo's brilliance was matched only by her randomness.

"Stranger!" Scaramouche jumped to her feet. "Long time no see! How's my favorite butt-bleeder?"

Kelly Kane was chained to the passenger seat. Scaramouche had used multiple chains, making it harder for Stranger to use his powers to free her. A metal tank sat in the first of three luggage carriers hitched to the tiny truck. Explosives covered the tank like oversized, blinking pimples.

"*Sulphuric acid,*" said the tank. "*Strong enough to burn the eyes right out of her head. If I move, the bombs go off. And the boss can set them off by remote. Oh, her seat's wired, too.*"

"Are you all right?" he asked.

Kelly grimaced. "It's not like this is my first kidnapping. Be careful. She's even more manic than usual."

Her pulse and respiration belied her outward calm. Trying to keep his own anger under control, Stranger held the wooden box out to Scaramouche. "All the evils of the world escaped from Pandora's box, until only hope remained. Hope for who?"

"For you, of course." Scaramouche brought a cup of Starbucks coffee to her mask. She fitted the straw through the mouth and sipped slowly. "You and I go way back, Stranger. You're like the husband I never had."

"You had a husband. You mutated him into a gorilla."

"Details. The point is, I can give you something the doctors can't."

"What's that?"

"A choice. Two, in fact. Cancer is such an ugly, boring death," she said. "You deserve better."

"*I resent that. Punch her in the face!*"

"You're going to do me a favor and kill me? No thanks." Stranger concentrated on the chains, asking them for their weaknesses.

"Oh, but it would be a glorious death in the arms of the woman who loves you." She laughed. "Don't look at me like that, K.K. Everyone knows. In supervillain circles, there's a running bet as to what would happen the first time you two kids did the deed. I've got five grand that says the first super-orgasm would kill her."

"What's the other choice?" Stranger snapped.

She shrugged. "I could just cure you."

"Don't listen to her, boss! It's a trick!"

Of course it was a trick. And yet... "What's the catch?"

Scaramouch took another sip of coffee before answering. "You have to help me kill the Stranger."

"You're going to need to explain that one," said Jarhead.

"Professor Edison's time magnet." Stranger stared at the carpet. "Scaramouche couldn't really cure my cancer. What she could do was reach into the past and pull a younger version of me—a cancer-free version—into the present. Combine that with any halfway decent mind-swapping device, and voila. I'm young and healthy again."

Jarhead whistled. At least, Stranger assumed that was what the sound was supposed to be. It came out more like a dolphin's clicking laughter translated through a synthesizer. "Ingeniously cruel. How did she respond when you refused?"

Stranger didn't answer.

"You *did* refuse, right?"

"You're insane."

"That's beside the point," said Scaramouche. "What's important is that you survive. And since you'll know your younger body is susceptible to cancer, you can start screening earlier. You didn't discover the tumor until our shootout at the ice cream factory, right?" She giggled. "I thought I had finally built a bullet that would work on you. Hit you right in the ass. Made the whole 'getting-the-shit-kicked-out-of-me-by-cartons-of-ice-cream' thing totally worth it."

Stranger wasn't exactly bulletproof, but bullets liked him. They tended to lose their way and tumble to the ground when fired in his direction. At point blank range, they simply refused to leave the gun's barrel. "You want me to sentence my past self to *this*?"

"I want to offer your past self the chance to save your life." Scaramouche's frozen, grinning face tilted to one side. "Or are you saying the younger you wouldn't sacrifice himself to save a fellow hero?"

"The paradox—"

"Timeline split, just like the Parallel Universe War of '09. Or the evil Gold Panther and his ridiculous goatee. Don't sweat it. The universe is very bendy. It will be fine. Probably."

Stranger struggled to focus through the mental haze that clung to his thoughts. "That's what you really want. To create an alternate timeline. One where Scaramouche never had to worry about the Stranger."

"It was either that or steal some fossils and try to raise an army of dinosaurs. I may do that anyway, because who doesn't love dinosaurs, right?"

Stranger studied the tank again. The acid wouldn't hurt him, but it would almost certainly kill Kelly. He couldn't suppress all of those individual explosives at once.

"What's it going to be, John?"

It took him a second to realize Scaramouche had called him by his human name. "I'm not—"

"Stop it." Scaramouche waved a gloved hand. "Voiceprint matching. Facial comparison software on the mouth and chin your old mask left exposed. General build and body language. Not to mention 'John Knight's' convenient Powerball win years back. Yet, despite your millions, you kept your job in the newsroom. All the better to keep tabs on the city, right? Until recently, when you—I mean, he—went on longterm medical leave."

Kelly was staring at him. "John?"

"How could you *not* know, Kane?" Scaramouche asked. "You're supposed to be a reporter!"

"If you knew, why didn't you say anything?" asked Stranger.

"This was more fun." Scaramouche waved a hand impatiently. "Go on, show her. You're dying anyway, right?"

With a sigh, Stranger removed his helmet.

"Whoa." Scaramouche jumped back. "Never thought anyone could make me feel pretty. When did the alien acne start?"

"Side effect of the treatment." He touched the swollen lumps. Uneven stubble covered his scalp and much of his face.

"Why didn't you tell me, John?" asked Kelly.

Stranger managed a small, self-deprecating smile. "I was afraid some psychopath would use you against me."

"You've tried to kill him so many times," Kelly said to Scaramouche. "Why would you save him?"

"Because this is a ridiculous way to die!" Scaramouche shouted, suddenly furious. "Killer robots, psychotic alien gladiators, zapped into the seventh dimension of Hell, *that's* how people like us are supposed to die. If nothing else, we should tumble over a waterfall to our deaths together like Sherlock Holmes and Moriarty."

"I thought Holmes survived," Kelly said.

"Shut up. The point is, fuck cancer. Cancer's not even an ironic death. It's just stupid!"

Stranger had never been able to outthink Scaramouche. "If you let me die—"

"Then they import a new hero." Scaramouche snorted. "I can't stand temps. They don't understand our *routine*." She tapped a control on her wrist, and the explosives began to beep in unison, a chirping chorus of impending death. "I don't have all day. I have yoga at four thirty."

Stranger sagged against the truck. He couldn't let Kelly die. "You win."

"The hell she does!" The tumor's outrage bubbled through Stranger's thoughts. *"Nobody defeats Tumor and the Fecal Tornado!"*

Scaramouche giggled as she retrieved the time magnet from another trailer. The pistol-sized device resembled a radar gun.

"I'm sorry, John," said Kelly.

Scaramouche sang in Italian as she calibrated the time magnet. "October third of 2002, wasn't it? You were in a coma after moving the moon back into its proper orbit. If I pull you through from that day, the young you should sleep through the whole mind transfer."

"*Dumbass.*"

Stranger clenched his jaw. "*If you have something to say...*" "*Forget the acid tank. Just stop scarface from triggering it.*"

"I can't control people. I'm not telepathic."

"*Double dumbass. You're talking to me, aren't you?*"

"You're a tumor, not a person, and I can't control you."

"*That hurt. You can't control me because I'm superpowered. Scaramouche isn't. More importantly, the meat in her skull isn't.*"

The words hit him like a sucker punch from Gargantua. No matter how twisted Scaramouche might be, she was also brilliant enough to make this so-called "cure" work. That hope had wormed its way into Stranger's heart, poisoning his thoughts just as his tumors had done to his flesh. With Kelly in danger, he had no choice. He *had* to accept Scaramouche's offer, because it was the only way to save an innocent life. If that meant killing an alternate version of himself, so be it. But if there was any alternative...

"*Damn you.*" He couldn't decide who was more cruel: Scaramouche, for offering hope, or his tumor, for taking it away.

Stranger concentrated, trying to imagine Scaramouche not as a person, but as a collection of flesh and blood and bones. A body, complex and beautiful and fragile. A biological machine controlled through the junction of electrical cables to the brain. He focused on that pulsing lump of electrochemically-active meat and whispered, "*Stop.*"

Scaramouche collapsed like a discarded Muppet.

Stranger studied the controller on Scaramouche's wrist. "*How do I use you to deactivate the bombs?*"

"What did you do?" Kelly whispered. "She's not breathing."

"She's not doing anything," Stranger said. "I shut down her brain."

"You killed her?" She sounded horrified.

"It was my tumor's idea." He finished disarming the trap, then snapped the chains holding Kelly in place. He picked up the time magnet. His hands shook. Clenching his jaw, he crushed the device to scrap.

"Can you revive her?"

"*Don't do it! Wait another twenty seconds, and she's a rutabaga for life!*"

With a sigh, Stranger willed Scaramouche's brain to *live*.

"So you beat the villain, saved the girl, and mastered a new aspect of your powers," said Jarhead. "Sounds like a win to me."

"It was. I think I owe her more than I realized."

"Why is that?"

"*You owe me, you ungrateful alien superdouche! If I'd known what you meant to do next, I never would have taught you that trick!*"

"Because after I returned Scaramouche to Edgewood, I started thinking. If I could force her brain to shut down, why couldn't I do the same to an ordinary human tumor?"

"*I saved your life, and in return, you declared war on my brothers and sisters.*"

"I thought you couldn't control the cancer."

"I can't control *mine*." He sat back in the chair. "How many people do you think I could help in six months? And when my own tumors finally begin to win, I thought I'd take a nice, long flight into the sun."

"Suicide?"

"No." For once, the tumor was mercifully silent. "Just a hero and his arch-nemesis tumbling over the waterfall."

Story Notes:

Jim would like to thank author Jay Lake for his help and encouragement on this story, as well as for his honesty and openness in sharing the ugly details about living—and dying—with cancer. Well fought, sir.

Jim C. Hines

is the author of the Magic ex Libris series, which has been described as a love letter to books and storytelling. He's also written the Princess series of fairy tale retellings and the humorous Goblin Quest trilogy, along with more than forty published short stories. He's an active blogger, and won the 2012 Hugo Award for Best Fan Writer. You can find him online at www.jimchines.com.

HOW TO FEED YOUR PYROKINETIC TODDLER

BY FRAN WILDE

Department of New Health Services, Parenting Manual #415

With the recent epidemic of *pyrokinesis-novus* affecting children worldwide, parents who are eager to move from the newborn-feeding stage should consider the following guidelines and questions, developed to help promote healthier eating, better feeding socialization (in light of the current food-lobbing craze), and more confident, calmer parenting.

Suggested Equipment:
- Oven mitts.
- Metal spoon and bowl (no plastic!).
- Flame-retardant diapers, bib, and seat.
- Dining space free of loose fabric, curtains, and lint.
- Welder's mask (optional).

Signs a child is ready for solid foods: Pincer-grasps objects, makes chewing motions, and remote-singes milk or formula. Caution: You may be ready for your child to begin eating solid food long before they are. Do not rush this stage.

What should I feed my toddler? Healthy eating must begin while children have limited ignition capacity and their aim remains unfocused. Children should be able to self-feed and make good choices before full pyrokinetic abilities develop. Suggested beginner foods include mashed items that taste better when warm or toasted: pumpkin, corn, peas, and potatoes.

For older toddlers, consider reward systems that keep tempers from flaring. Vitamin-added mini-marshmallows and tater tots are a fun treat for the whole family.

Creating a calm dining environment: The process of establishing toddler likes and dislikes is admittedly riskier than in past generations. A safe environment is paramount: remove all fabric from the dining space before seating your toddler in their fireproof high chair. Remember to keep your voice level or upbeat at all times. A patient parent can slowly introduce new foods and guide a toddler's curiosity without undue scorching.

Suggested feeding methods: (1) Scoop and run: Spoon a small portion of food onto the metal utensil and place it on your toddler's lips. Step back quickly. Repeat as necessary. (2) Distraction (requires two adults): Have one parent make funny sounds from afar to distract the toddler's aim. Proceed with scoop and run. (3) For picky eaters: Brightly colored, FDA-approved, non-flammable extend-a-spoons are available from Disher-Brice and Fabbo.

Dining out with toddlers: Today's family restaurants are either completely fireproof or equipped with the latest family-friendly extinguishers. These venues will now only accommodate groups of six and fewer. Do not allow children to run among the tables or chase the wait staff, and be sure to leave a large gratuity. Do not expect to be welcome at any, now rare, historic restaurants, heavily-tapestried venues, or cafés featuring wooden decks. Avoid gasoline-powered food trucks at all costs.

In an emergency: This manual can be used to extinguish small fires.

Success gallery: (photo) Betsy Van Morris of Glen Cove, NY, feeding Sue-Ellen, age two, while wearing the experimental scorch-guard parent-cover, in clown print.

✧ ✧
Remember, you are your child's best advocate and resource.
Teach them responsible eating, before it's too late.
✧ ✧

Parents of younger children and tweens: Please see manuals #4332 and #7554.

Parents of teenagers: Please phone the Department of New Health Services with your success stories as soon as possible. Our thoughts are with you.

Fran Wilde

writes speculative fiction and fantasy short stories and novels. She can also tie a bunch of sailing knots, set gemstones, and program digital minions. She rarely ties gemstones, programs sailing knots, or sets minions. Hardly ever. She's on the Twitter (fran_wilde), and can be found talking about food and genre fiction (nothing flambé yet!) at www.fran-wilde.wordpress.com.

A STIFF BARGAIN

by Matt Mikalatos

I woke to the sound of my own name, though it was not yet time to rise. I reached for the comforting feel of my coffin lid and discovered to my dismay that I was lying on a feather mattress, covered by a quilt which must have weighed at least ninety pounds. I had forgotten that I had moved into a boarding house.

"Isaac van Helsing," the voice said again.

I pried my eyes open. Standing at the foot of my bed was my former servant and thrall, Richard. This surprised me, as he was dead.

He thrust out his lower lip, pouting. "You murdered me. Your loyal servant!"

Richard had recently tried to murder me. He had pinned me, sucked my blood to become a vampire and left me to die at the claws of a rather nasty zombie bear. He was a vampire for about thirty seconds before he stupidly walked past a sun lamp I had set up. The last time I had seen him, it had been while emptying out my Dust Buster. I cleared my throat. "You were never particularly loyal."

"Semantics," Richard said. "And now, I've returned as a ghost. For sweet revenge!" With a flourish, he lifted one transparent hand and yanked back the curtains. On reflex, I raised my hand to shield myself from the sunlight, but a weak grey light filtered through the window. It was dusk. Late dusk, at that. Richard cursed.

I lowered my hand and rolled my eyes. "Ah," I said, tonelessly. "The sunlight. It burns."

"Don't mock me! It was daylight when I got here. It's difficult to wake you. You sleep like the dead."

I pulled on my jeans, then my shirt. I padded barefoot toward the kitchen, Richard floating beside me. "This is all your fault," he said. "I don't have a job now. How will I make a living?"

I rolled my eyes. "You're dead. You don't need to make a living." I could hear Mother Holmes, the owner of the old boarding house, clanking pots and humming to herself. She refused to treat me like a vampire, choosing instead a smothering maternal attitude of smug, but loving, superiority.

"Good evening," I said, and Mother Holmes turned, her face wrinkled as an ancient apple. She plopped a bowl of stew on the table in front of me. The smell of garlic wafted from the bowl, burning my eyes and blistering my skin. I pushed it away. "Mother Holmes, as I've told you three nights in a row, I cannot eat human food."

She scowled. "You pay for room and board, and that is precisely what you will get."

She spooned a bit of stew into her mouth and looked at Richard. "It's good to see you again, dear. What are you up to these days? You look much too thin."

Richard gave me a long stare, then turned to Mother Holmes. "I plan to haunt Isaac for a century or two. Maybe murder him if I get a chance. Outside of that, I'm not really sure."

A hearty knock came from the door, and I gladly leapt from my chair to answer. Mayor Rigby stood outside, his hat in his chubby hands and an apologetic smile on his face. "Good evening, Mr. Van Helsing," he said.

He stepped quickly inside and I closed the door behind him. He nodded to Mother Holmes and dropped his hat. His sweaty, nervous manner practically shouted "prey," and I licked my lips without thinking. "Is there a problem, Mr. Mayor?"

"Nothing you can't handle," he said, counting out three hundred dollars in bills and laying them on the table.

Richard floated over. "Is it the squirrels?"

I gave him an irritated scowl. "Be silent, this is business for the living. The dead are best seen but not heard."

Richard mumbled something about how I was undead, and I made a mental note to find a good exorcist. The mayor put his finger on the bills. "This is only the up-front money, of course."

I nodded. This was our current arrangement. I removed supernatural horrors from his community (myself excluded) and he paid me. I then paid Mother Holmes and remained, as always, one of the rare vampires unable to afford a castle or underground grotto. I was never good with money. Still, my current modest room was a considerable upgrade from my previous home: a black, windowless cargo van with a coffin screwed into the floor, currently parked in front of Mother Holmes's house. "Is it," I asked, "the squirrels?"

"No, no," the mayor said, annoyed. "They're a minor inconvenience. Hardly worth the money."

I had no idea what was going on with the squirrels, and must admit to a feeling of relief. I had no desire to chase rodents through the trees, supernatural or not. "What seems to be the problem, Mr. Mayor?"

He looked at his feet and flushed. "It's the leader of our neighboring town. Her name is Katie Lou Riley. Every week Ms. Riley calls and leaves disturbing messages on my voice mail . . . truly disturbing messages. She threatens that she will come and take over our fair town's government. I was hoping you could persuade her to stick to her own town."

I cocked my head and looked at him carefully. "That's all? You're not holding anything back?"

The Mayor coughed delicately into his hand. "Well. She does have certain...powers."

"Like?"

"Oh, I don't know. Mind control. Things like that."

I shrugged. As a vampire I could hypnotize people, control animals, turn into a wolf or a bat, and live forever, so long as I didn't get a wooden piercing, eat garlic, or wear cross jewelry. Some mayor with mind control powers shouldn't be too much to worry about. "I'll take care of it," I said.

Richard floated through the table. "I'll come with you. To watch your back."

I narrowed my eyes. "Watch my back?"

"In case there's a chance to slip a knife into it."

I couldn't stop him, so he floated alongside me as I drove the cargo van to the next town. As we crossed the town limits I felt a deep shiver go down my spine. I pulled the van to a stop outside of city hall, but it was nearly ten at night. All the offices were closed.

I rolled down the window. A rousing chorus of song came from a nearby church, and lights blared from the windows. Richard and I exchanged glances and we made our way toward the church.

"Something's wrong," I said, as we got closer. A band of people burst from the church, beating spoons against pans and shouting like maniacs.

Richard grinned, showing his ghostly teeth. "They're going to kill you, I just know it."

I snatched a townie out of the dancing, shouting mob and yanked him toward me. "I'm looking for Katie Lou," I said. His eyes lit up and he cheered.

"He's one of us, boys," he shouted, and the crowd let out a huzzah.

I scratched my cheek. That was puzzling. "Where is she?"

"She's sleeping. She's a ... what's the word?"

Another person in the crowd shouted, "Narcoleptic!"

A third person said, "Well, not exactly. She just sleeps a lot."

I drew myself to my full height, puffed out my chest and bared my canine teeth. "Then let us wake her!"

The crowd, strangely, did not appear terrified. Instead, they let out a terrific cheer, and swept me toward the church. I fought against the dark tide of the crowd, because a vampire cannot enter consecrated ground. I would catch on fire and burn to death, a rather unpleasant way to go. Richard knew this, and it was with obvious pleasure that he began to shout, "Yes, yes, everyone into the church."

I struggled against them, but there were too many, and in my panic I couldn't turn into a bat before they washed me over the threshold. I screamed. But I did not catch fire. I looked down at my cold, pale hands.

Richard squealed and flew around my head shouting, "Call the fire department!" until he realized I was unharmed. He settled glumly beside me. "Never mind."

I sighed. "I expect you to be pleased by my death, Richard, but gloating is beneath you."

He rolled his eyes. "You never really knew me, did you?"

The church looked much like any other church. A small stage near the front with a podium and the black maw of a baptismal font behind it. A neat row of pews lined up like ribs. One thing seemed to be missing. No crosses anywhere. Not over the door posts, not on the stage, not on the hymnals or in the brick work. I hadn't caught on fire because this was not consecrated ground. A tingling sensation traveled across my scalp. The crowd lined into their seats, still beating on pots and pans, blowing trumpets, having loud conversations on their cell phones. I gripped a pew. If Katie Lou could not be on consecrated ground, she was more than just some woman with mind control powers.

A man in a white suit came jogging from the side of the church and onto the stage. "Good evening, everyone!" They all cheered. "Ten years ago I got a woman pregnant and when Katie Lou saw our daughter, well, she decided that this was the sort of baby she would like to eat. Katie Lou said to serve the baby up on her ninth birthday. That's today! Happy birthday." More cheering! He gestured to the side stage and three men brought up a small girl in a white robe, bound tightly with ropes.

My blood started to boil. Well, technically not my blood, but I was the one who had it last, so, finders keepers. No one hurts kids, not when I am around. I became a vampire when I was only eighteen, helping my father in the family vampire hunting business. And there was no way that an insane town mayor was going to eat a little girl while I watched.

"Never!" I shouted.

Everyone stopped. The man in the white suit looked at his assistants, as if they might know the answer to his questions. "Who is this, now?"

"I'm Isaac Van Helsing," I said, my voice trembling with emotion. "And I'm a vampire!" I dropped my jaw and did my best impression of a rattlesnake. I was pleased to hear gasps from the crowd.

The next thing I knew, I was bound to a long wooden plank by heavy metal chains. Richard floated nearby, his head propped on his hand. My head throbbed intensely when I moved it. "What happened?"

Richard grinned. "Someone shot you with a tranquilizer gun."

I frowned. "That works? On vampires?"

"Just kidding. You went into a trance and walked onto the stage and they tied you up. I guess Katie Lou is going to eat you, too." He pointed at White Suit, who was riling up the crowd. "That guy says she likes you."

I shook the chains. I didn't have enough leverage to break them. The little girl was five feet away from me, her face battling between resignation and mild terror. "Don't worry," I said. "I'm going to get you out of here. What's your name, young lady?"

She looked at me uncertainly. Her bangs were cut unevenly, and she looked tiny and helpless in her white robe. "The Sacrifice."

"No, dear, your name."

"That is my name."

I growled. "That is not okay." A growing sense of dread washed over the church. I looked back at the baptismal font. Cold, clammy air came from it. I tasted salt water on my tongue. "If I only knew who Katie Lou is," I said. "Maybe we would have a chance." I turned my attention to White Suit. He was holding a ream of paper over his head with one hand, the other holding a bottle of Elmer's glue.

"Now is the time to wake her from her slumber," he shouted. "Pen and glue!"

The crowd echoed him with fervent delight. A black light came on, and people's clothes started to glow. I could feel a presence, itching at the back of my mind. Richard shimmered, the beginnings of a psychic storm picking at the edges of his existence. "I'm glowin' off Katie Lou Riley!" White Suit shouted.

Wait. Pen and glue. I'm glowin' off Katie Lou Riley. Why did that sound so...familiar? It was like hearing someone speak with a heavy accent. I knew I should understand, but I couldn't quite figure it out.

The Sacrifice gave a little scream. "I can feel her coming! If you're gonna do something, it's got to be quick!"

White Suit laughed and held his hands over his head. "We're going to get fat again!"

I swallowed, hard. Those last few words, I thought I knew them. And now they were saying the whole thing, over and over: "Pen and glue! I'm glowin' off Katie Lou Riley! We're going to get fat again."

A horrific nausea gripped me. I knew what they were saying. I screamed for Richard. He looked over at me, unconcerned.

"Richard, you have to get us out of here. Untie the girl, get the key and get me out. Right now, Richard, right now, right now!"

Richard looked down at his fingernails. "Why so worried, boss? You can handle anything. Ha ha ha."

I tried not to scream. I could feel her now, rising toward us. My brain started a primal keening, like a monkey alarm clock inside my head. The chanting echoed around the room.

The Sacrifice started rocking back and forth. "She's awake!"

I took a deep breath. "Richard, these idiots aren't pronouncing it correctly. Her name isn't Katie Lou Riley. And stop looking at your fingernails, you're a ghost, we all know you don't have dirt under there."

Richard stuck out his tongue. "Being insufferable is not likely to get you much help. Besides, I can barely move a curtain, I certainly can't break the girl's ropes." He nodded apologetically to the girl. "I would if I could. No one likes to see a young girl eaten, even for a good cause."

I ground my teeth. "I didn't want to tell you this, but it's entirely likely that you can possess human hosts. Lots of ghosts can."

"I can... what now?"

"Steal their bodies."

Richard cackled with glee and immediately disappeared. The girl had gone rigid with terror. I reminded myself to take deep breaths. I thought I could see the first tentative bit of Katie Lou pushing its way onto the stage. The White Suit loomed over me, a knife in one hand and a wooden stake in the other. "You were right about the bodies," he said with Richard's voice. "Tell me what's going on and I'll cut the girl free."

"Richard, Katie Lou's sheer psychic backwash could cause you to cease to exist. If you're not going to save me and the girl, save yourself!"

Richard laughed. "You're actually scared." He looked back at the townspeople, chanting and moving into a religious frenzy. "I thought we came here to get rid of a prank caller."

I struggled against my chains. They didn't budge. Richard White Suit dangled a key over me, laughing. I tried to turn into a mist, or a bat, or anything. A rabbit would be fine! But the psychic trauma of Katie Lou's arrival had effectively neutered me. "It's not Katie Lou. Put the pieces together, Richard. I don't want to say her actual name. But she sleeps a lot."

Richard snorted. "Narcoleptic, I know."

"She's really terrifying."

"That doesn't narrow it down much."

"She enjoys blood sacrifice."

Richard shook his head. "I don't get it."

"Imagine the name... Katie Lou... sound like anything else?"

"Nope. Nothing."

I screamed in frustration. "They're not saying 'Katie Lou Riley' they're saying 'Cthulhu R'lyeh.' They're trying to say Ph'nglui Mglw'nafh Cthulhu R'lyeh wgah'nagl fhtagn."

Richard White Suit's jaw dropped. "Cthulhu? The 'elder god' of terror who will one day rise up and wreak havoc on the universe?"

"So they say."

Richard grabbed the sacrificial knife, his hands trembling, and sliced the ropes off the girl. She jumped up and rubbed her wrists. She didn't hug him or move near him, probably evidence of the troubled relationship between her and her father, who had raised her as an appetizer for the elder god. Richard turned to me, the stake in his hand. "I'll make this quick."

I scowled at him. "Take your time, Richard. Might as well enjoy yourself."

"I'm in a bit of a hurry. I don't want to be here when Cthulhu arrives."

"He's not going to stop until he gets his bloody sacrifice to lull him back to sleep!"

"I thought 'Katie Lou' was a she?"

"It is an ancient alien god who hibernates beneath the

ocean. We haven't had a good look at the reproductive organs yet."

Horrific squid-like tentacles burst through the floor, knocking Richard to the side and grabbing me around the chest. The Sacrifice tried to run, but the tentacles grabbed her legs, and then Richard, and dragged us deep below the church building. I fell through darkness and slammed into a wide slate platform hard enough to break the chains on my arms. Richard landed on me next, followed by the girl.

The tentacles recoiled into the black water below us. "Somehow they've moved Cthulhu here beneath their town! What a terrible idea."

"Your phone is ringing," Richard said.

The girl was holding onto my leg, panting. I pulled my phone out and saw a series of horizontal marks with something like letters hanging off of them. "It's Cthulhu." I put one hand on the girl's head and held the phone to my ear.

A feminine, but guttural, voice said, "Cthulhu . . . is bored. And hungry."

"I see. Um. Is there any chance we could entertain you with something other than constant blood letting?"

There was a long silence. "No."

"Cthulhu, look into my mind and search for something called 'HBO.'"

I felt the dirty water of the elder god's mind wash through my head. "Yes. Bring Cthulhu this... HBO. Also. An 'easy chair.'" I felt its attention turn to the Sacrifice. "And bring also... marshmallow Peeps. An abundant supply. MAY THE WATERS BENEATH THIS TOWN BE COVERED IN PEEPS!"

"Release us and all of this will be yours."

"Very well."

"Also you have to stop prank calling Mayor Rigby."

"No. He must live with... the call... of Cthulhu!"

"He's an ordinary man who can't handle your great presence."

Cthulhu laughed, and the horrific psychic backlash caused all three of us to fall to our knees. "He is no ordinary man. Cthulhu must remind him that his refrigerator is running and that he must catch it."

"The thing is, he's paying me six hundred bucks to get your calls to stop."

"Cthulhu has reasons for the suffering inflicted on this Rigby."

Bargaining with an elder god is dangerous business. I didn't want to find myself inside a tentacled maw, but then again I needed that six hundred bucks to pay rent. "Why, O Great Tentacled Monstrosity, must you torture this poor soul?"

"Rigby is his last name. His first name is... Zog-Yesseriyal!"

"Soggy cereal?"

"Zog-Yesseriyal! Brother of Cthulhu! The crusher of dreams! The serpent-skirted shouter on the hill! The churner of stomachs!"

I put my hand on my head. "You mean to say that Rigby is one of the elder gods?"

"The horror of lower southeast Burbank! He-who-wakes-me! Devourer of my leftovers! The crosser of the invisible territorial line in the back seat of the family car!"

"I take it you have a grudge against your brother?"

"He-who-makes-tortilla-chips-go-stale!"

"Enough already. I get it."

"There are more names."

I paced the slate platform. Richard and the girl still stood frozen, pushed against the back wall. "There must be some way to get you to stop harassing Mayor Rigby."

There was a long pause, and then Cthulhu inserted a bargain into my mind. She would never call Rigby again if I agreed to it. I considered carefully. Stepping between warring interstellar creatures was dangerous. I reluctantly agreed, and the elder god showed me a narrow stone stairway. I pointed it out to the girl, and she went up first, her legs shaking. I followed, Richard at my back. I was surprised that the elder god had agreed to my bargain without demanding actual blood from anyone.

We walked much of the way in silence. As we neared the top, Richard said, "I saved us by making a mental bargain with Cthulhu."

I narrowed my eyes and turned toward him. "I made a bargain, too."

"What was your bargain?" Richard asked.

"Richard, you shouldn't make deals with creatures like that unless you're extremely careful," I said.

We came up into the church. All of the cult members were lying on the floor, as if they were marionettes without strings. Richard grinned and moved close to me, the stake raised in his hand as he lunged for my heart. "I promised him the blood of all the cult members! And I will give him yours as a bonus!"

Richard knocked me backward and I fell to my back. I could have thrown him off easily, but the girl had fallen beneath me, and I was struggling not to harm her. The stake touched the skin of my chest, the full weight of Richard's body

A Stiff Bargain

pushing it in. My muscles strained to hold him back. "There won't be any Peeps!" I shouted. "Imagine a Peepless existence!" Richard's face twisted into a scowl. "At least respect me enough to shout final words that make sense."

I smiled at Richard. "This should make sense to you: the body you're in belongs to one of the cult members you promised to Katie Lou."

Richard's face fell. "And the girl!"

The girl shook her head. "Having grown up as a sacrifice I was never a fan of Katie Lou. I'm Presbyterian."

"Me too!" Richard shouted. "I'm not part of the cult!" The building shook, and tentacles wrapped around Richard's torso, yanking him back toward the abyss. "Nooooooo! I'll be back, Van Helsing! I will be avenged!"

I snatched the Sacrifice into my arms and sprinted outside. Enormous, unwholesome appendages smashed into the perverse church, eventually drawing the entire building down into the hole. The girl wept, her head against my chest, and I stroked her hair gently. "Don't worry. You're safe now. You're safe."

She put her hand in mine. "Now you're my father," she said.

I didn't know what to say to that. I imagined that Mother Holmes would be glad to have another boarder, and perhaps she would adopt the girl. She didn't have a mother, or any possessions to speak of, but we did go by her house and I wrangled her father's easy chair into the back of the van for a later delivery.

We arrived at Mother Holmes's house almost an hour before sunrise. She made the appropriate clucking sounds and gathered the Sacrifice to her ample bosom. "What's your name, child?"

She cuddled in close and said, "My name is Safe."

Mother Holmes hustled her toward a washroom, a comforting stream of verbiage surrounding them like a cloud. I made sure the blinds in my room were closed tight and lay on my bed, still in my clothes, on top of the quilt, too tired to turn off the light. It had been a long day. After some time I could hear Mother Holmes and the girl in the kitchen, the latter gladly slurping up stew. Mother Holmes said, "You're nothing like your father!"

I felt something strange... a small warmth in my chest, the corners of my lips tugging upward. I reached for my cell phone and put the caller ID blocker on before dialing Mayor Rigby. He answered on the third ring.

"Mayor Rigby," I said, muffling my voice. "Your goat is eating everything in my garden."

Rigby, still struggling toward wakefulness, said, "I don't have a goat."

"That's okay," I said. "I don't have a garden." I hung up quickly. Now I just had to short-sheet Rigby's bed, booby trap his office with Dixie cups full of water and write CTHULHU RULES on his windshield with whipped cream, and my bargain with Katie Lou would be finished. No doubt she would eventually get more followers and send them to harass Rigby another way, but I had earned my six hundred bucks. That was the last prank call. And if Katie Lou tried to back out of our deal I could always cut off her HBO and Peeps.

My phone buzzed. Caller ID made it clear which terrible deity was on the phone. I was tired, and I debated sending it to voice mail, but picked up at the last second. "Hello?"

"Where are Cthulhu's Peeps? Cthulhu has eaten all of her minions and is hungry."

"Tomorrow," I said, yawning. "I'll bring them tomorrow."

A satisfied rumbling came over the phone. "Van Helsing."

"Yes?"

"Is your refrigerator running?"

I sighed. "No. It's standing in the kitchen. Go to sleep." I clicked off the phone, turned it to silent and closed my eyes.

Sometime just before I drifted off, Mother Holmes came and pulled my quilt up to my chin.

Half awake I asked, "The girl?"

"She's clean, with a full stomach and a smile on her face, sleeping in the room down the hall."

"That's a good thing," I said, and slipped Mother Holmes the three hundred dollars for the girl's rent. I felt her warm lips on my forehead. She turned out the light and closed the door behind her, and I slept and dreamed and did not wake, not until night came again.

Story Notes:

When the first *Unidentified Funny Objects* anthology called for submissions they specifically said that vampires and zombies would be a tough sell, so I wrote a story about both ("The Working Stiff"). I enjoyed the characters so much, I wanted to write about them again even though two of them were dead. This story came about after reflecting on how difficult it must be for centuries-old creatures to deal with the enormous culture shift around them. Also, phones were a lot more fun before caller ID. And, let's be honest, the idea of aliens coming to earth and setting themselves up as cult leaders might have been scary once upon a time, but it's pretty hilarious in the 21st century.

Matt Mikalatos

was brought up on a steady diet of monster movies, comic books and high-fat foods, practically guaranteeing him a vocation as a speculative fiction writer. He is the author of the novel *The Sword of Six Worlds*. You can learn more about him on his blog (www.mikalatos.com) or on Twitter (@mattmikalatos).

THE GIRL WITH THE DAGON TATTOO

BY JOSH VOGT

" Welcome to Innsmouth Ink and Piercing Pit. Wot's your poison, pretty thing?"

"I'm here for a Dagon tattoo."

"Can't do that."

"What? It's listed as a discount special right there in your window."

"So it is. But that's wot you'd call an inside joke. Like them Cthulhu cupcakes the bakery sells down the street. Nobody eats them and gets transported to extremes of ecstasy and horror. Just frosting tentacles and candy googly eyes, y'know? Bit o' local color to make dumb tourists chuckle. Er . . . no offense."

"I'm not a tourist. As a blessed follower of Father Dagon, the visions led me here; so I know you can inscribe the true sigils and incantations on my flesh."

"Ah. You's one o' them? Figure yourself a chosen chum? There's a laugh."

"Listen here—"

"Ain't got time for every wannabe princess of Pisces. Go snog some seaweed, eh?"

"Zip your frog lips and look at this."

"... where'dya get that?"

"Not so smug now, are you?"

"I ain't funnin', missy. Folks 'round here don't take kindly to strangers flashin' symbols of the Esoteric Order."

"I know that. Do you think I'm an idiot?"

"Ayup."

"Shut up. I wouldn't show this without being certain you can provide what I need. Now, are you going to cooperate or keep acting like a bumpkin?"

"Let's say that Dagon tattoo's a thing after all. Still plenty o' reasons I ain't gonna so much as sketch a scale on your skin. For starters, I ain't got the right... y'know... necessities."

"Such as?"

"Gotta use nuttin' less than a hunnerd percent squid ink. That and fishbone needles."

"I've brought my own supplies. Everything needed, including a ceremonial dagger and dose of opium for yourself."

"Well, aint' you Little Miss Think-of-Everythin'. How'd you get all this?"

"I told you. I'm blessed by Father Dagon himself. I performed the proper supplications on the beach and the tide washed in the required bounty."

"Erm... has you profaned yourself before loathsome monuments under a gibbous and waning moon?"

"I make a habit of it."

"You meditate on the nature of them nameless things that sleep in the darkest watery chambers beyond all comprehension?"

"Just yesterday."

"You dream of long-drowned horrors when the stars aligned in their indescribable orbits?"

"Months ago."

"How's about ph'ngluing your wgah'nagl?"

"You made that one up. And don't be crude."

"Gluh. Fine. But there's another problem. You ain't the right shape."

"If you're daring to comment on my figure—"

"Look, missy. To get a Dagon tattoo good and proper, you gotta be a certain make n' model. I ain't just talkin' flippers and scales. You got pulsating gills? No? And how're you gonna fit an epoch's-worth of diabolic chants on a body that ain't treacherously vast? The full text of Cthäat Aquadingen don't exactly make for a tramp stamp, y'know."

"Oh. I ... didn't think of that."

"Here's the thing—I could cram in a few bits and pieces, but it'd be like puttin' a star chart on a postage stamp. And if the images aren't fully etched, you'd suffer all sortsa nasty side effects."

"I'm committed to showing my devotion to the god of the ocean floor. I don't care about the consequences."

"'Specially if one of them consequences is lookin' pretty spiffed up to your Dagon fan club back at the Miskatonic University, hm?"

"How did you know about that?"

"Only so many places you could snitch an Order medallion from. You'll be handin' that over now, by the way."

"Back off or I'll ceremonially remove your fingers. I'm giving you two options. Refuse me and I'll march straight to your Order temple and confess that you tempted me with secrets about the Dagon tattoo. I hear they aren't kind to those who reveal sacred arcana to outsiders."

"You wouldn't dare."

"Try me. Second option—we compromise and find a way to condense some of the larger tattoo portions. I'll pay you and surrender the medallion peaceably."

"You wanna compromise in renderin' the infinite and detestable likeness of Father Dagon?"

"I'll even toss in a baker's dozen of those cupcakes from

down the street. A treat for us to... chuckle... over and set aside any hostilities."

"That your daft idea of sweetenin' the deal?"

"Call me daft again. See what happens."

"... look, mebbe I could write 'I Heart Dagon' in eldritch hieroglyphics and dress it up a bit with nightmarish symbols that incite madness in any who gaze upon them. Unless your friends can read a language that was dead before the stars were born, they won't know the difference."

"That'll suffice. I do insist on still using the squid ink and fishbone needles."

"Why not? Gots to be authentic, right? I'm gonna get prepped, but this lovely chat has riled my appetite and I don't like to work hungry. How's about those cupcakes? Be sure to get the fresh ones. None of their half-price, day-old batches."

"What's wrong with those? Stale?"

"Nah. They just tend to hatch in your mouth instead of your stomach."

Josh Vogt

A full-time freelance writer and editor, Josh Vogt has sold work to *Paizo's Pathfinder Tales*, Grey Matter Press, *Orson Scott Card's Intergalactic Medicine Show*, *Shimmer*, and *Leading Edge*, among others, and is working to get his fantasy novels to readers. When not writing, he's rotating through an array of odd hobbies to stave off existential despair until he can get back into a story. You can find him at JRVogt.com, Write-Strong.com, or on Twitter @JRVogt. He is made out of meat.

IMPROVED CUBICLE DOOR

by M.C.A. Hogarth

"I can't work with Don anymore," Candace said. "And frankly, I'm not the only one."

I stopped hunting in my desk drawer. From the shape of the shadow next to my file cabinet, she had her hands on her hips—never a good sign. I turned to face the door into my office. "This sounds serious."

"Have you walked past his cubicle lately?" she asked.

"I've had meetings," I said. That really wasn't an excuse. Spend enough time in back-to-back meetings and you start hoping that your direct reports will devote enough points to precognition to figure out what you need without you telling them.

"Come with me," Candace said.

I shrugged and followed her. My office was one of several that bordered the walls. The interior of the floor had been cut up into a maze of cubicles: sometimes literally, for the departments that had cause to keep all but the most ardent of petitioners at bay. As was illogical but typical, the twelve people I managed were on the other side of the building. I didn't know what to expect, and Candace didn't help with her silence. We turned the corner row and I stopped.

"Is that ... ?"

"Yes," she said with distaste. "He cast Improved Cubicle Door."

I approached Don's cube warily. The hedge of thorns that blocked entry into his tiny domain actually extended a vine my way as I stepped within range. I stepped back out again. Quickly.

"Have you tried calling him?" I asked.

"He doesn't answer," Candace said. "He's not answering anyone's calls. No one's emails either."

"A mobile hedge door," I said, exasperated. "That's taking it too far. I don't mind it if you guys want a half-size door for privacy, but this thing's a safety hazard. God knows what our customers think of it."

Candace said, "Morale's degrading, too."

I stiffened. "How badly?"

She shrugged. "I can't even speed up the network connection anymore. My mana store's as weak as it was when I was unemployed."

Now I was seriously concerned. As the department's best project manager, Candace had developed an enviable mana sensitivity. Where her stores went, everyone else's followed.

"Thanks for bringing this to my attention," I said. "I'll do something about it."

"Thanks, Jin."

I studied the twining thorns for a few moments longer, then retreated. I couldn't deal directly with the door, not without preparation anyway. What if I failed to tear it down? Talk about a morale-killer. A manager's supposed to have more power than his employees, or it says something about the quality of the command chain. I don't get much mana from doing projects as an individual contributor anymore. All I've got is what's passed down to me by directors who deem our department is doing its part for the company's bottom line. All of which means I can't afford to look weak.

So, first things first. I renewed the privacy wards on my office and closed the door on the curious world, then tried calling Don on speakerphone.

Ring. Ring. Ring. Voice mail. Don never bothered to personalize his message. Maybe I should have seen that as a sign. Still, he had to be working, or he wouldn't have the power to cast a spell the level of his guardian thorns. I picked up the crystal paperweight I'd gotten as a management award and ran my fingers over it while murmuring the arcane syllables that would bypass Don's password.

The voice mail dropped me into Don's inbox. "You have two hundred twenty-seven new messages."

I almost dropped the paperweight. My finger trembled when I hit the button for the first message, dated two weeks ago. An irate woman accused Don of never getting back to her on her very important contribution to the excess inventory project. The one after that made a similar complaint about the warehouse maintenance project. I fast-forwarded to the last few and winced through the stream of invective. Some had gone so far as to formally curse the department, which might explain some of the problems Candace had reported with the mana store.

Something like this *should* have come to me. The only way I wouldn't have heard of it was if Don had arranged it.

We've fired people for casting Deceive Manager before. It's a hard thing to prove, but if you can ...

I hadn't signed up for this headache. Don had never performed gracefully for us, but he'd done the job. As much as I wanted to know what had happened, the fact that it had took precedence. I needed to straighten him out right now or begin the major ritual of summoning HR, which would require libations and paperwork and far more energy than I had to spare.

It was time to dig to the bottom of this.

"You wanted to see me, Boss?" Don drawled from the door.

"Ah, I see you received my message," I said.

"It was kind of hard to miss," he said. "The phoenix did some damage to my cube door, by the way. Set fire to it."

"They tend to do that," I said, suppressing my glee. I'd hoped sending my summons with a phoenix would take care of that problem.

"Lucky I had that thirty-two ounce Mountain Dew from the gas station," Don continued. "Put that sucker right out before it could set fire to the building."

So much for that. "Don, I have some concerns."

"You wouldn't send a phoenix for a casual get-together," he said. "Can I sit?"

I stared at him as he dropped into the chair in front of my desk. I hadn't expected the problem to be this bad. "I've been getting some complaints."

"Complaints?"

"Your inventory projects are hanging loose in the wind, Don. What's going on?"

"Oh, it's all exaggeration," Don said. "You know how it is with Operations. They're convinced that all we do all day is sit around and eat donuts."

"Is that what you're doing?" I ask. "Sitting around and eating donuts? I've done some asking around, Don. You haven't attended a meeting in two weeks."

"I scry them," he said with a wave. "If they look like they need PM guidance I dial into the bridge."

"Don, the meetings are down the hall. People walk from other buildings to our conference rooms because we're the project management department. It's courtesy to walk the forty feet to the room and sit in a chair."

"If I walk forty feet to the room and sit in a chair I can't keep track of anything else," Don said. "If I sit in my cube and scry the meeting, I can be working on a dozen other things at once."

"And just what are these dozen other things you're working on?" I ask.

"Office productivity projects," Don said. "I want to make our department more effective."

I let a disapproving silence rest between us. Don seemed unfazed by it. "I appreciate your interest in maximizing our productivity, but I really need you to be more aggressive in your management of the inventory initiatives. Those will do a lot more for the bottom line than any plan you have for reducing forms we have to fill out which we don't own anyway."

He shrugged. "Whatever you say."

"I'll want a status from you at the end of the week," I said. "Thanks, Don."

"You're welcome," he said and strolled out.

Office productivity projects. Right. I believed that one. I needed to know exactly what Don was using all his spare time on. I pulled the wide-brimmed coffee mug from the bookshelf, the one with the company logo embossed on it, and blew the dust from inside. I was only halfway through my morning coffee, but speed was of the essence. If Don got back before I could fix the eye on him I'd lose any chances of riding him past his cube wards. I dumped my four dollar latte into the scrying mug and cast the spell.

There was Don, taking the long way back so he could scope out both break rooms. I watched him snitch a pecan brownie from the plate the office assistant had brought before meandering back toward my group. There was the door . . . damn, the phoenix hadn't done enough damage to the thing. It should have been crispy and instead it was only singed at the top. A few curlicues of smoke rose from one of the vines, fortunately missing the sensors on the ceiling. Mountain Dew was vile stuff. I would have half expected it to fuel the fire, not put it out.

The vines parted for Don and I leaned toward the mug.

And then . . . I saw my face. Somehow he'd managed wards that could detect pre-existing spells and block their effects on their targets. No employee should have that much mana. You could win the Employee of the Year award and still not have the mana store to finesse wards like that. If I had any doubts that Don was up to no good they'd vanished with his image in my mug.

I went to the break room for a cheap refill, leaving the company mug behind. Scrying always dropped things to room temperature and changed them just a little; it made for nasty coffee and unpleasant water. It also defizzed soda. For once, though, I didn't begrudge the mug the cost.

Don had a deadline. I didn't expect him to meet it... which meant I had to lay some very important groundwork. Four days was cutting it fine, but Giselle was known for her quick turnarounds.

It was time for me to send a meeting request to my director.

"JIN, JIN. Good to see you as always. What can I do for you?"

She was smiling—that was good. That meant I hadn't flubbed my offering to her administrative assistant. I could never remember which chocolate generated more mana for James, white or milk. He was also picky about incense.

"Thanks for seeing me," I said. Giselle was a busy woman and preferred straight talk. I got to the point. "I'd like to request additional mana."

"Your mana allotment did get to you this pay period, didn't it?"

"Yes," I said.

She picked up a pen and turned it in her hands. "Should I ask?"

Better to just tell her now. "I have an employee to deal with. He has mana he shouldn't while doing less work than he should be."

"What's your plan?"

It didn't seem a good idea to admit I didn't have one yet. I improvised. "My first meeting with him wasn't productive. I gave him a deadline to meet. If he doesn't, I want to get into his office and see if I can't find a mana stream."

One of her brows lifted. "A mana stream. You think he's double-dipping?"

"I can't be sure until I look," I said, "but if he's not doing the work, he's got to be getting the stores from somewhere."

She looked more interested—not good. I liked Giselle but I preferred her benign neglect, since she had a tendency to become incendiary when drawn out. Literally. "Just how much mana does he have that he shouldn't?"

"His cube has a door made out of tentacular vines," I said.

She put the pen down. "I'll give you a week's worth of mana. If it turns out you don't need it I'll want it returned."

I said thank you and withdrew, not altogether liking the twinkle of interest in her eyes. Yet another reason to hope Don got his act together. I should be so lucky.

". . . AND I'LL HAVE a talk with him," I said.

"You'd better!" my guest said as he stood. "If you people aren't going to take this initiative seriously we're going to have to take it up the chain. This is important business, though you wouldn't know it the way Don's treating it."

"I'll take care of it," I said, again.

My visitor wasn't appeased, but was also too busy to hang around. I was glad to see his back; the director of business operations from the Field department wasn't a man I wanted angry with me, and definitely not someone I wanted talking to Giselle. Friday had come and gone and Don had defied me and the people angry with him were finally coming straight to my office instead of trusting that their emails and phone calls would reach me.

Candace was waiting for me outside.

"Do I even want to know?" I asked.

"I hope so," she said. "Jin, I'm mana-less, and so is everyone else."

"I'm hoping this is a joke," I said.

She handed me her employee ID card, the one you swipe to get through security checks. I turned it in my fingers. It didn't fizzle, it didn't jump and it certainly didn't sing. When I shook it, there wasn't even enough left over in it to rattle. "What the hell?"

"All of us are empty," she said. "There's not a drop left between the group of us to cool a can of Coke. And that's not all. It didn't just drain away—it was taken."

"Let me guess," I said. "Don has something to do with it."

"Come look," Candace said.

I followed her, wondering what horrors I would find. I didn't have to finish the walk to see. The door of thorns had become a tower of thorns. I stood at the base of this monstrosity and said, "Is your cube in there?"

"I assume," Candace said. "I rescued my computer and set up in the conference room, along with Luis and Marcy."

Don's fortress of thorns spanned a four-cube block and met the lowered ceiling. He'd been artistic, I had to give him that— the fabric panels typically used for cube walls were still part of his cube-fortress, they were just connected by dense meshes of vine and leaf. Philodendron leaves, of course, since nothing else grew this far from a window. Ivy maybe.

There was no door into this domain. I wondered how he got in.

"Well then," I said. I sighed. "Let's meet in the conference room."

"I'll round up the rest," Candace said.

"WE WANT TO HELP," Prandesh said. A row of grim faces trained gazes on me from around the conference room table. Three computers were scattered on the sideboard, so poorly fueled they needed wall cables to pull data from the network. The muffins I'd hastily procured from the cafeteria in the main building had barely been touched: never a good sign.

"I appreciate that," I said, hands flat on the table. "But you have work to do."

"Yeah, and we can't do it," Candace said. "Don's stolen all our power! Have you ever tried to work the old-fashioned way? You can't get anything done."

"It can't be that bad to work without magic," I said. "The computers can still get on the network."

"The only reason we found those cables is because Don isn't managing his excess inventory project," Luis said. "I remember what it was like to work without magic, Jin. It's not pretty and it's not productive. You want us to move forward, our best bet is to help you take care of the Don situation."

"Don's not a situation anymore," Candace said. "He's a challenge."

"Definitely a challenge," Marcy said.

I sighed. "All right. I was planning to infiltrate his cubicle fortress alone, but if you feel that strongly about backing me up you can come. We'll make a quest of it."

"All right!"

"We're behind you all the way!"

"Let's meet at the fortress around four forty-five," I said. "That should give him time to clear out, assuming he's cutting out early."

"I'd be shocked if he's even showing up at all," Candace muttered.

Me too. In fact, I was counting on it.

FIFTEEN MINUTES BEFORE close-of-business I arrived at the door to Don's fortress to find my group awaiting me, each armed and armored. The weapons were eclectic. Luis had a T-square half his size that he claimed had been with him since his student days in engineering, and from the nicks and scuffs on the thing I believed it. Candace's laser pointer was probably the deadliest of the bunch; it was CFO Manning's preferred weapon in arcane duels and I'd seen him cut most of the top officers' shields into ribbons with it. But the assortment was good, from Marcy's telephone cord whip to the variety of cable-crimpers and punch-down tools on Mike's belt.

I'd brought an old standby.

"Is that a magic wand?" Marcy asked.

I grinned and turned the transparent wand upside down so she could watch the colored glitter in it flow to the opposite end. A child's toy, properly enchanted, served just as well as a more obvious object as long as you believed. I was good at believing, and better at enchantment. My pockets were always filled with small and seemingly innocuous objects.

"Now to pick the lock," I said, turning to the seething mass of vines. "Watch my back."

"On it, Boss."

I approached the vines with my wand outstretched, side-stepping so as to give them as little of me to attack head-on as possible. The wand's repulsion spell gave the tentacles in front of me pause, but my back prickled when I realized just how *deep* the layer of plant protection went. I wasn't more than two steps in when I heard the hiss of the laser pointer searing off a vine, then the thwack-whack of Luis's T-square going into action.

Finding the "door" to the cubicle took me a nerve-wracking few minutes as the vines bounced off my shields. I could fortify them with the extra mana Giselle had passed me but I didn't want to use it so soon. Who knew what Don had set up inside the fortress? I hunkered down to examine the lock, then whipped out my case of computer tools. As leaves and thorns rained down around me beneath the furious blows of my group, I tried screwdriver after screwdriver in search of the proper length and size and magical resonance. None of my normal tools worked.

But that's why I carried my "special." I hadn't needed to use the long T-15 Torx screwdriver since I'd ditched my ancient SE/30, but that lovingly maintained tool had so often appeared on the scene whenever someone finally gave up on getting to the impossibly distant case screws that it had acquired some of the power of miracles. When I slotted it into Don's lock, the door gave and the tentacles withdrew to a safe distance.

"Wow," Candace said, her voice shaken. Plant ichor stained her company polo sap green. "Is it safe to go in?"

"No," I said, putting my set of picks away. "But we're going in anyway. Be on your toes, people."

We filed into Don's fortress, weapons at the ready. The rustling I thought I heard resolved into a slow ticking.

"Watch out!" I said, and we threw ourselves to the ground as a volley of mechanical pencils thunked into the opposite wall.

"Hey, those could have hurt us!" Marcy said, indignant.

Prandesh rose to his feet and tiptoed to the opposite wall. He pushed his glasses down his nose and squinted. "They're mana suckers," he said, pulling one free. "Looks like the standard spell. Trigger, action, fuel source, and fuel shunt."

"Give me that," I said, suddenly suspicious. Prandesh handed it to me and I started taking the spell apart. What I wanted to know I found out soon enough. "The fuel shunt leads to the fortress," I said. "He's got lines into the thing."

"I can't imagine him doing it any other way," Candace said. "You'd need a constant mana stream to keep this thing operational."

"I mean direct lines," I said. "No firewalls."

Silence. Then, "That's stupid," Mike said. "Who'd allow unprotected mana streams into a continuous enchantment?"

"Someone sloppy," I said. "Someone who makes mistakes." I looked around for the first time: the four-cubicle space was now a vine-encircled courtyard leading to an antechamber for a stairwell, a black, unlit stairwell. I sighed and pushed myself up. "Let's hope he keeps making mistakes."

"He can't possibly work up there," Candace said.

"Like a kid with a treehouse," Luis said.

I shook my wand until it started glowing, then headed up the stairs. They were sticky.

"Enchantment?" Prandesh wondered. "Or did he just not clean up after a spill?"

"This isn't a single spill," Marcy said. "Yuck."

"Stop!" I said. Beneath the arcane light of my plastic wand glowed a trip-wire. "He's got a trap set up here. Anyone good with fiber optics?"

"Let me up," Marcy said. "I did a stint managing the new fiber ring installs beneath the campus."

We pressed ourselves flat to the walls so she could advance and study the light. After a moment, she said, "If we interrupt it, it will definitely go off. But I also get the feeling that if we cancel it, it'll still trigger."

"So what do you suggest?" I asked.

She shrugged. "Back up." We shuffled backward. She stood a few steps down and whipped it with her spiral phone cord.

"Protect Jin!" Candace shouted. She knocked me down, and several more bodies piled on me before I could even assess the result of Marcy's act. I should have seen it coming, really—Marcy had an impulsive streak. A real go-getter, Marcy, but nothing scares her and she sometimes overestimates her abilities. I wondered wryly if I should mention this in her performance review.

Crushed beneath three people, two of whom stunk of plant ichor, I reflected that this was not how I'd planned to spend my Tuesday evening. Then again, anything was better than rush hour traffic.

One by one, my people slid off me. "Everyone intact?" Candace asked.

"Yeah. Damn, though! I'm almost sucked dry!" Mike said. "That was actually pretty clever."

I sat up. The stairs were covered in a river of gleaming paper clips. As I watched, the mana they'd drawn off my group sank into the stairs.

"That must have taken him forever," Prandesh said, picking up one of the discharged ones. "Enchanting that many paper clips? Do you have to do them one by one?"

"With enough brute force you could do it by the box," I said, checking myself for bruises. I'd probably have a few mothers blooming on me soon enough. "Just be glad they weren't binder clips."

"Those would have hurt coming down," Candace said. "Marcy—"

"I found out what it did, didn't I?" Marcy said, testily.

"Let's just keep going," I said, squeezing between them.

It only felt like an eternity getting to the top of Don's plant-and-fabric fortress, but soon enough I found myself on the threshold to his sanctuary.

"Did anyone bring test equipment?" I asked.

"I've got a kit," Mike replied.

"Come on up, then."

Mike wormed his way forward and pulled a test kit from his belt. He hunted for a place to stick the leads, then shrugged and dug them into the fabric wall. He flipped a few switches, then said, "I don't have enough juice left to make it go, but it's ready."

"Here, I'll do it," Candace said, leaning past me to tap the kit. It glowed blue in the corner-of-the-eye vision of arcane sight.

"You're not using personal energy, are you?" I asked, startled.

"We all are, Boss," Mike said. "Don made off with the company stuff... Well, how about that. No traps."

"That doesn't make sense," I said. "Did he honestly believe we'd be stopped by a handful of mechanical pencils and a case of paper clips?"

"I bet he wasn't expecting all of us at once," Mike said, packing up the kit. "Why would he?"

"The vines would have kept most people out anyway, except possibly a VP," Candace said.

My people spread out behind me as I walked into Don's second-story cube and sat at his computer. Now, at last, I could use a few judicious bits of Giselle's offering, if not the way she would have expected. Power that flows from higher up always has the signature of the person who handled it last until attached. Usually I got my mana with my direct deposit slip, glowing on the paper and already keyed to me for easy use ... but in borrowing extra, I'd forced my management to use a temporary vessel for it. Those vessels, bland, frequently cleansed and often interchanged, maintained the charge from the person who touched it last.

A director's signature was a handy way of convincing a computer to authorize a remote computer management request.

"Would you look at this?" Prandesh said. "He's got cable flags. A whole stack of them."

"This looks like a cannon," Luis said.

"What, was he planning to pepper people with 'Buried Cable' flags from above?" Candace said. "This is so completely out of hand!"

"I'll say," I said, as I found what I sought. "Don's moonlighting for Nemesis."

Utter silence. I took out my Jumpdrive and plugged it in.

Then Candance: "He's working nights for the competition? That's—"

"—in violation of his employee contract, yes," I said. "Which means I get to challenge him to a duel."

"Oh, wow," Marcy said, in a low voice.

"I haven't seen a duel in years," Luis said.

"I haven't seen one ever!" Marcy said.

And no wonder. HR required its management to ascend a ladder of increasingly rigorous action to reprimand and eventually fire an unruly employee. But violation of the competition clause—that was grounds for an immediate duel. If I won, Don was out of the company. If Don won, I'd get a reprimand and additional management training ... but Don would still get fired. This was the end of the line for him.

"Hack me a hole in the foliage," I said. "I'm transmitting this data to HR."

"Without a ritual?" Candace asked.

"The competition clause violation goes through emergency channels," I said.

"Right," she said, and started burning a hole for me.

"What happens after they get it?" Marcy asked.

"I leave Don my calling card," I said.

As the challenged party, Don got to choose the dueling place and I got to choose the time. I sent him email before leaving: eight tomorrow morning, when I'd be at my sharpest and almost everyone else would be half-asleep.

He'd responded curtly, and chosen exactly as I'd hoped: we would meet at his fortress.

I sat at my desk in my workroom at home, rolling the wand between my palms. I'd seen my share of corporate duels, both on the lower rungs of the ladder where it was exclusively a matter of firing someone, and on the corporate officer level, where it involved the distribution of resources or the direction of high-level company initiatives. I'd long admired the CFO's touch with those laser pointers, and of course the Chief of Operations's command of golf clubs left a man in awe.

But the CEO impressed me the most. The man never appeared on the field of honor with the same weapon twice. He seemed to choose his approach based on who'd called him there... and given that his rightful opponents included a stream of indignant investors and company shareholders, the fact that he could fight with almost any approach... well, I wanted to be that man someday. He was full of surprises.

I had a surprise or two of my own. The corporation gifted management personnel with a new magical shield with each level they ascended. As a manager, I had a nice flexible sheath to augment my personal protections, and it had stood me in good stead when deflecting attacks, curses, and the normal tectonic activity of a division crammed with departments struggling for the same resources. It also helped me push off attacks from my own direct reports; they all knew I had it.

What they didn't know was that a glitch in the promotion process had netted me not one, but two management shields: the one I'd earned by moving into the process management department as its new lead, and an extra I'd earned while still in Operations as night shift supervisor. A supervisor's thin shield could become astonishingly tough under repeated customer attack, and I'd spent a good year fielding the most unhappy people, calling in at 3 A.M. in a panic over a frame failure.

Don had done half my work for me by choosing the place. Time for me to do the other half. I settled down to craft a few new spells and put the finishing touches on my strategy.

"I'M SO SORRY it had to come to this," Don said.

"That's my line," I said, casually.

We stood inside his thorn-lined courtyard. The vines had been forced into abeyance so that the rest of the group and a good part of the floor could crowd around and watch. A duel is splendid entertainment for a monotonous week.

"Is that your weapon of choice?" he said, eyeing the fire axe I'd removed from the wall.

"Yes," I said. "What's yours?"

"I prefer missile weapons," he said, lifting a rubber band ball seething with energy.

For a moment I reconsidered my plan. He could make fast work of my defenses with enough of those bands. But no, it was a good strategy. The company hadn't hired me for my stolid work ethic alone. If I wanted to make it all the way up the ladder I had to show off my brains.

"I'm ready," I said to the woman garbed in black. Not just a black pantsuit, understand, but black heels, black hose, black gloves. She wore a black hood, drawn so low over her face I could only see her lips—no lipstick, just these pale coral things that faded into her face. Even the card-holder with its pulley and drawstring, clipped to her lapel, was made of black plastic.

HR folks were creepy.

"I'm ready too," Don said to her.

She nodded, a slow, considered movement. A shimmer rose around the courtyard and the hair on the back of my neck stood on end. Part of the procedure in duels involved cutting off the dueling area from external sources of energy. I grinned at Don's sudden frown, and fingered the handle of the axe. He'd forgotten about that, or never read about it.

"Begin!"

I sprang, not at Don but at the walls. A sweep of my axe cut four tendrils of vines. They regenerated on my upswing.

"Hey, over here!" Don said, and a rain of rubber bands bounced off my manager's shield. I ignored him and kept chopping at the greenery. The crowd couldn't decide whether to cheer or boo, but I kept at the task. I'd done too many stints in corporate magic theory to be wrong. How many certificates had I hung in my cubicle as a young call center tech? I'd gone to the most ridiculous classes just for a change in routine.

Using Magic as an Enhancement to Remote Troubleshooting.

Magical Test & Accept Procedures.

Arcane Solutions to Personnel Problems.

Unauthorized Use of Arcane Energies.

Troubleshooting Blocked Mana Streams.

Proper and Improper Employee Conduct.

I hacked off tentacles. I swept thorny vines from their tentacular bodies. I split open the connections between cubicle walls and watched the vines sluggishly reweave them closed. Don pelted me with rubber bands, striping open holes in my shield that began to close more and more slowly.

"This is it, Jin," Don said. "I'm going down anyway, but I'm taking you with me." A giant pink band split open the final crack in my managerial protections.

Revealing my supervisor's tough skin.

"Damn it!" Don said, and renewed his attack.

I grinned and renewed mine.

"Jin, what are you doing!" Candace called from outside. "Go after Don!"

"With an axe?" someone hissed. "If they actually hurt one another's bodies, that's big trouble!"

I wanted to tell her I knew what I was doing, but I couldn't afford to distract Don, not when he was doing so well in that frenzy.

I chopped off a vine . . . and it didn't grow back. I grinned and swept the axe in a long arc, knocking down one of the fabric walls and taking half the hedge with it.

A rubber band pinged off my body and fell at my feet. I turned to Don, axe in hand.

He was staring at the band. A properly charged missile weapon penetrates the magical defenses; it does no harm to the physical body.

"Go on," I said. "Try again."

He flicked another band at me. It bounced off my stomach. "What the hell?"

I waved a hand at the fortress. "You've been feeding this thing with your mana stream from your night job, but HR closes off all external energy shunts at a field of honor. Since you're lazy and not much of a theorist, you didn't bother to see what store-bought spells default to when they're supposed to be fueled by external lines and those lines get clogged or closed."

"The caster!" someone said behind me in wonder.

"No!" Don said, throwing down the ball. He looked at his hands, but nothing in them glowed. "NO!"

"I'm sorry, Don," I said. "Your own lack of foresight defeated you."

The HR advocate lifted a hand and centered it over Don, evaluating my claim. "You are without power," she said to him after a few moments. "You have lost. This duel is ended."

Don's hands balled into fists.

"Pack your things," the woman said. "You'll be escorted off the premises at lunch."

I lifted my axe and the crowd cheered. My group swarmed me, babbling their congratulations.

And then they parted like a wave for Giselle.

"Jin!" she said, and her eyes were considering. "That was a nice job."

"Thank you, ma'am," I said. "Oh, by the way, here—" I took out a company keychain, still mostly full, and offered it to her. "I only used a little."

She smiled and arched a brow. "Would you like to keep it?"

"Of course!" I said, startled.

She sketched a privacy shield before continuing. "It's obvious why I should be pleased with you. Tell me why I shouldn't."

I flushed. "I let this matter with Don progress to a point where I had to fire him." Giselle nodded. "Good answer. I don't think Don could have been salvaged, so I'm not all that unhappy he's gone . . . but I hope you don't exercise the nuclear option with every employee who plays hooky on company time." She smiled. "There's your bonus. Do something worthwhile with it."

I watched her go, speechless. Shaking myself, I looked through the crowd for Don—up the stairs, no doubt. Mindful of Giselle's admonition, I followed him and found him in front of his computer.

"Why'd you do it?" I asked, after we stood in tense silence for a while.

"I wanted a door," Don said with a shrug. He resumed packing.

"Everyone in my group's allowed to cast Cubicle Door," I said.

"A *real* door," Don said.

"Only management gets offices," I said.

Don snorted. "Yeah. That's the problem."

I spent a long time, considering that.

"ALL RIGHT," I said, "Open your eyes!"

My people greeted the sight of their new cubicles with a

series of completely satisfactory gasps and exclamations. The sun shone on fabric walls, cast from the giant floor-to-ceiling windows that lined the edge of the building ... but the retractable roofs and full translucent doors with the sliding sun-shields allowed each person to control just how much light they got. As an extra bonus, the line of cubicles was adjacent to my office ... and right next to one of the copy rooms, the one that often netted the best baked goods.

"Oh wow, Jin," Candace said. "This is a lot of trouble!"

"You have no idea," I said with a laugh. "I thought Facilities was going to clock me when I put in the move request. Still, the area next to Don's fortress isn't going to be useful for at least a few weeks, so I had a slightly easier time of it."

"This is wonderful," Candace said. "Sunlight and a roof! It'll be like having our own little offices."

"That's the idea," I said. "Hey, guys?"

Most of them turned to look at me.

"Just do me a favor and answer the door when people knock?"

They laughed and went back to excited talking and moving of boxes. I couldn't think of a better use for my bonus; a happy employee is a productive employee. I went for coffee, still grinning.

Story Notes:

It always bewildered me that few people seemed to see the potential for magic in a modern office. Here was a world with its own language, its own rituals, even its own mazes...! Twisty little passages through endless gray cubicles, all alike, reminding me of the first RPGs I ever played on my green-and-black Apple IIe screen, where dungeons looked like endless blank corridors with tiny square rooms that might contain pixelated monsters and the possibility of treasure.

Nothing as bland as a cubicle farm could fail to hide a dragon or two. "Improved Cubicle Door" was born out of that instinct for magic and my lifelong love of RPGs. I even gave the result to my coworkers. The HR director wanted to know why she got cast as the creepy one, and where she could get a cloak of her own.

M.C.A. Hogarth

Daughter of two Cuban political exiles, M.C.A. Hogarth was born a foreigner in the American melting pot and has had a fascination for the gaps in cultures and the bridges that span them ever since. She has been many things—web database architect, product manager, technical writer and massage therapist—but is currently a full-time parent, artist, writer and anthropologist to aliens, both human and otherwise.

ON SAFARI

by Mike Resnick

It was a sunny summer day on Selous, as it always was. The sky was a perfect blue, the grass was green, and you could smell excitement in the air.

"Just think," said Anthony Tarica, as he and his companion stepped through the hatch of the ship and began walking down the ramp to the ground. "We might have won a negatronic washer and dryer instead."

"Poor Roberts," agreed Linwood Donahue, following him down the ramp. "If he'd sold just three more units, he'd have replaced one of us here." He snickered. "I hope the poor sonuvabitch has a lot of laundry."

"I can't believe we're really here!" enthused Tarica. "All my life I've wanted to go on a real safari."

"I wonder how they could afford it," said Donahue. "I mean, a safari has to cost a lot more than a washer and dryer."

"Why worry about it?" said Tarica, taking a deep breath and scenting adventure. "We're here for the next five days, and that's all that matters."

They cleared customs and walked out of the tiny spaceport.

They looked around, but there were no people in sight, just a few parked vehicles.

"That's funny," said Tarica. "I'd have thought there'd be someone from the safari company here to meet us."

"Yeah," said Donahue. "What do we do now?"

"If you gentlemen will step this way," said a cultured masculine voice, "I will attend to all your needs."

Tarica looked around. "Who said that?"

"I did."

Tarica and Donahue exchanged looks. "Am I going crazy, or did that safari vehicle just speak to us?" asked Donahue.

"I most certainly did," said the vehicle.

"I never saw a talking car before," said Tarica. "Oh, back home mine reminds me to fasten my seat belt and take the keys out of the ignition and not to try to beat the yellow light, and it castigates me when I go over the speed limit, but I've never actually had a conversation with one."

"I am Quatermain, your fully-equipped safari car and guide, trained in every aspect of safaris and safari life. I have an encyclopedic knowledge of the flora and fauna of Selous, I know every watering hole, every secret trail, every hidden hazard. I come equipped with a mini-kitchen in my trunk, an auxiliary trunk for your luggage, and a supply of water that will last for the duration of your safari. Furthermore, I am capable of erecting your rustic tent at day's end, and of protecting your safety at all times. I run on a small plutonium chip, and will not run out of energy for another 27.348 Earth years." One of the trunks popped open. "If you gentlemen will please deposit your luggage in here, we can begin our exotic adventure."

"Right now?" asked Tarica, surprised.

"Have you a problem with that?" responded Quatermain.

"No," said Tarica hastily. "I just expected that we'd spend a day unwinding in some luxury lodge before we set out on the actual safari."

"Luxury lodges are incompatible with safari experience," replied Quatermain. "If you gentlemen will climb into my back seat, we can be off on the adventure of a lifetime."

"Do you do this every day?" asked Donahue, as he joined Tarica on the back seat and the door automatically shut and locked.

"Yes, sir," responded the car. "This is old hat to me, but each excursion is still thrilling, because each is unique."

"Have you ever lost a client?"

"No, sir," said Quatermain. "I always know right where they are."

Tarica pulled out a cigar. "Well, I can't tell you how much I'm looking forward to this."

"I'd prefer that you didn't smoke, sir."

"But you've got an ashtray built into the arm rest here, and I assure you my friend here doesn't object."

"It's bad for your health, sir."

"I've been smoking for thirty-five years," said Tarica, "and I'm in perfect health."

There was a brief humming sound.

"I have just given you a level three scan, sir," said Quatermain, "and you have incipient emphysema, an eight percent blockage of the arteries leading to your heart, adult onset diabetes, and an undefined gum disease. You really must take better care of yourself, sir."

"I feel fine," said Tarica.

"I could give you a print-out of the scan, sir."

"All right, I'll take better care of myself."

"You could begin by not lighting that cigar, sir," said Quatermain. "I notice you're still holding it."

"Aren't you supposed to be looking for animals?" complained Tarica.

"I can see in every direction at once, sir."

Tarica sighed and put the cigar back in his pocket.

"I'm sure you'll be much happier for doing that, sir."

"You have two more guesses," growled Tarica.

They rode in silence for a few minutes. Then Donahue asked Quatermain how to open the windows.

"Why bother, sir?" replied the car. "I am equipped with the most modern climate control system. You name the conditions and I will accommodate you."

"But I'd like to feel the wind in my face," said Donahue.

Suddenly a blast of cold air hit his face.

"Simulated wind at 32 miles per hour, 82 degrees Fahrenheit, 7 percent humidity," announced Quatermain. "Would you like any adjustment, sir?"

"I'd just like some fresh air," complained Donahue.

"All right," said Quatermain. "Just let me slow down first."

"Why?"

"Even a small insect could damage your eye at the speed I was going," answered Quatermain. "It will take us an extra hour to reach the closest of the great herds, but your comfort is more important than an extra hour of daylight."

"All right, forget it," said Donahue. "Close the windows and get back up to speed."

"You're sure?" asked the car.

"I'm sure."

"You're not just doing it to make me feel better?"

"Just speed up, goddammit!"

They drove for twenty minutes in absolute silence. Then Quatermain slowed down to a crawl. "Bluebucks at nine o'clock," it announced.

"It's three-thirty," said Tarica. "Do you expect to wait five and a half hours for them to show up?"

"Nine o'clock means to your left, sir," explained Quatermain. "Three o'clock is to your right, twelve o'clock is straight ahead, and six o'clock is straight behind us."

"And I suppose twenty o'clock is some bird that's directly overhead?" asked Donahue with a smug smile.

"I don't call that by an o'clock, sir."

"Oh? What *do* you call it?"

"Up, sir." A brief pause. "Daggerhorns at two o'clock."

"There must be a thousand of 'em!" said Tarica enthusiastically.

"1,276 by my count, sir," said the car.

"Drive a little closer. I'd like to get a good look at them."

"I think this is as close as we should go, sir."

"But we're still half a mile away from them!" complained Tarica.

"783 yards from the nearest, to be exact, sir—or 722.77 meters, if you prefer."

"Well, then?"

"Well what, sir?"

"Drive closer."

"My job is to protect you from danger, sir."

"They're grass-eaters, for God's sake!"

"There are two cases on record of tourists being killed by daggerhorns," said Quatermain.

"Out of how many?" demanded Tarica.

"There have been 21,843 safaris on Selous, comprised of 36,218 tourists, sir."

"So the odds are 18,000 to one against our being killed," said Tarica.

"Actually, the odds are 18,109 to one, sir."

"Big difference," snorted Tarica. "Drive closer."

"I really advise against it, sir."

"Then take us back to the spaceport and we'll get a vehicle that caters to our needs."

"You don't *need* to see a daggerhorn close up, sir," noted Quatermain reasonably. "You merely *want* to."

"The spaceport or the daggerhorns," insisted Tarica. "Make your decision before they all move away."

"You are adamant?"

"I am."

"Very well," said Quatermain. "Shields up! Screens up! Laser canon at the ready!" It began playing a male chorus singing an invigorating martial song.

Tarica and Donahue peered out through a suddenly-raised titanium grid that covered the windows. The daggerhorns continued their grazing, paying no attention to the approaching vehicle.

Suddenly Quatermain's voice blasted out at 300 decibels through the external speakers. "I warn you: I am fully armed and will not let any harm come to my passengers. Go about your business peacefully and make no attempt to molest them."

The second they heard the speakers all grazing stopped, and the entire herd suddenly decided it had urgent business elsewhere. A moment later Quatermain and its passengers were all alone on the savanna.

"Invigorating, wasn't it?" said Quatermain in satisfied tones.

"I'm starting to understand why the corporation could afford this particular safari company," muttered Tarica.

"Tailswinger at nine o'clock," announced Quatermain.

"Where?" said Donahue, who was on the left side of the vehicle.

"Well, actually it's about 1400 yards away, and is totally obscured by branches, but my sensors detect its body heat."

"Well, let's go over and look at it."

"I can't, sir."

"Why not?"

"There is a female tailswinger in an adjacent tree, and she's nursing an infant."

"We're not going to steal it," said Donahue. "We're just going to look at it."

"I really can't disturb a nursing mother, sir," said Quatermain.

"But you had no problem disturbing twelve hundred daggerhorns," complained Donahue.

"None of *them* were nursing, sir."

"Fine," muttered Donahue. He tested the door handle. "Oh, well, as long as you're stopped, unlock this thing."

"Why, sir?"

"We left the spaceport before I could stop by a bathroom and I've got to pee." He tried the door again. "What's the problem? Is the door stuck?"

"Certainly not, sir," said Quatermain. "I am in perfect repair."

"Then let me out."

"I can't, sir."

"Nothing's going to attack me," said Donahue. "You scared all the animals away, in case you don't remember."

"I agree, sir. There are no potentially dangerous animals within striking distance."

"So why won't you open the goddamned door?"

"Uric acid can do untold harm to any vegetation it comes in contact with, sir," said Quatermain. "We must keep the planet pristine for future adventurers. Surely you can see that, sir."

"Are you telling me that all those daggerhorns we saw never take a piss?"

"Certainly they do, sir."

"Well, then?"

"Unlike yourself, *they* are part of the ecosystem."

"I don't believe this!" yelled Donahue. "Are you telling me no one you ever took out had to relieve himself?"

"If you will check the pouch just ahead of you, sir," said Quatermain, "you will find a small plastic bag."

"What if he needs a big one?" asked Tarica.

Another humming sound.

"I have just scanned his bladder, sir, and it contains only thirteen fluid ounces." A brief pause. "You really should cut down on your sugars and carbohydrates, Mr. Donahue."

Donahue muttered an obscenity and reached for the bag.

It was ten minutes later that Quatermain announced that they had come to a small herd of six-legged woolies.

"They look just like sheep," observed Tarica.

"They are identical to Earth sheep in almost every way," agreed Quatermain. "Except, of course, for the extra legs, and the heart, lungs, spleen, pancreas, kidneys, jaw structure, and genitalia."

"But besides that..." said Donahue sardonically.

"Note the billpecker perched on the nearest one's head," said Quatermain. "It forms a symbiosis with the wooly. It keeps the wooly's ears clean of parasites, and the wooly provides it with an endless supply of food." Suddenly the wooly bellowed and shook its head, sending the billpecker shooting off into the air before the shocked bird could spread its wings.

"Its ear is bleeding," noted Donahue.

"Very nearsighted billpecker," said Quatermain knowingly. "It is my opinion, not yet codified in the textbooks, that this is actually a triple symbiosis. The billpecker is a bird with notoriously poor vision, and the blood it inadvertently draws due to this shortcoming actually attracts bloodsucking parasites. Without the blood, no parasites. Without the parasites, no billpecker. It works out very neatly."

"Without the parasites there's no need for billpeckers," said Tarica.

"All the more reason for parasites," answered Quatermain, leaving Tarica certain that there was something missing from the equation but unable to put his finger on it.

"It will be dark in another forty-five minutes," announced the vehicle. "I think it's time to choose a place to set up the tent."

"How about right here?" said Donahue.

"No," said Quatermain thoughtfully. "I think seventy-five feet to the left would be better."

"We're in the middle of an open plain. What the hell's the difference?"

"A meteor fragment landed there 120,427 years ago. One has never landed here. The odds of a second fragment landing in the very same spot are —"

"Never mind," said Donahue wearily. "Set it up where you want."

Quatermain drove seventy-five feet to the left, and the tent constructed itself as if by magic. "I will be the fourth wall," announced the vehicle. "That way I can continue seeing to your comfort."

The two men exited through the right-hand door and found themselves in a rustic but spotless tent that possessed two cots, plus a table and two chairs.

"Not bad," commented Tarica.

"There is also a portable bathroom just behind this door," said Quatermain as a small door began flashing.

"When's dinner?" asked Tarica. "I'm starving."

"I shall prepare a gourmet dinner, specially adjusted to your individual needs. It will be ready in approximately two minutes."

"Now *that's* service," said Donahue. "Maybe we misjudged you."

"Thank you, sir," said Quatermain. "I do my best."

"Yeah, it was probably just a matter of getting used to each other," added Tarica. "But what the hell—a gourmet dinner on our first night on the trail!"

"We are not on a trail, sir. We are on the Maraguni Plains."

"Same thing."

"No, sir," said Quatermain. "A trail is a—"

"Forget it," said Donahue.

"I'm sorry, sir, but it is embedded in my language banks. I cannot forget it."

"Then stop talking about it."

"Yes, sir." A brief pause. "Please take your seats at the table. Dinner is ready."

The two men sat down, and a moment later a long mechanical arm extended from the vehicle and deposited two plates.

Tarica looked at his dish. "That's an awfully big salad," he remarked. "I'll never have room for the main course."

"Not to worry, sir," said Quatermain soothingly. "This *is* your main course."

"I thought we were having a gourmet dinner!"

"You are, sir. On your plate is lettuce from Antares III, tomatoes from Greenveldt, radishes from far Draksa VII, mushrooms from—"

"There's no meat!" thundered Tarica.

"Your cholesterol reading is 243," answered Quatermain. "I would be ignoring my responsibilities if I were to prepare a meal that would add to it."

"Your responsibilities are to take us to animals, damn it!"

"No, sir. My contract stipulates a total experience. Clearly that includes nourishment."

"What about me?" said Donahue. "There's nothing wrong with *my* cholesterol."

"You are friends with Mr. Tarica, are you not?" asked Quatermain.

"So what?"

"Clearly you would not want to cause your friend emotional distress by consuming an 18-ounce steak smothered in caramelized onions while he was obligated to eat a salad with fat-free dressing."

"It wouldn't bother me a bit," said Donahue.

"This false bravado cannot fool me, sir," said Quatermain. "I know you do not want your friend to suffer."

Donahue saw that it was an unwinnable argument and took a bite of his salad.

"That washer and dryer is looking mighty good to me," said Tarica. "Hey, Quatermain—are there any animals around?"

"No, sir, not at this moment."

Tarica got to his feet. "I think I'll take a walk. Maybe I can work up an appetite for this junk." He walked to the doorway and fiddled with it for a moment. "How the hell do you open this thing?"

"I'm sorry, sir," said Quatermain. "But it is not safe for you to go out."

"I thought you said there weren't any animals in the vicinity."

"That is correct, sir. There are no animals in the vicinity."

"Then why isn't it safe?"

"There is a six percent chance of rain, sir."

"So what?"

"The last ninety-four times there was a six percent chance of rain, my clients left the tent and came back totally dry," explained Quatermain. "That means statistically you are almost certain to be rained on."

"I'll take my chances."

"I cannot permit that, sir. If you get rained upon, there is a 1.023 percent chance that a man of your age and with your physical liabilities could come down with pneumonia, and our company could be held legally culpable, since our contract states that we will protect your health and well-being to the best of our ability."

"So you won't let me out under any circumstances?" demanded Tarica.

"Certainly I will, sir," said Quatermain. "If the chance of rain drops to four percent, I will happily open the door to the tent."

"Happily?"

"Yes, sir."

"You have emotions?"

"I have been programmed to use that word, sir," responded Quatermain. "Actually, I don't believe that I have any emotions, hopes, fears, or perverse sexual desires, though of course I could be mistaken."

"Can you at least pull back the roof so we can enjoy the sounds and smells of the wild?" asked Donahue. "You can put it back up if it starts raining."

"I wish I could accommodate you, sir," said Quatermain.

"But?"

"But flocks of goldenbeaks are constantly flying overhead."

"So what?"

"You force me to be indelicate, sir," said the vehicle. "But when you stand beneath an avian..."

"Never mind."

The two men finished their salads in grumpy silence, and went to sleep shortly thereafter. Twice Quatermain woke Donahue and told him to turn over because his snoring was so loud it was likely to wake his friend, and once Tarica got up and trudged to the bathroom, which he used only after demanding that Quatermain avert its eyes or whatever it used to see inside itself.

Morning came, the two men had coffee (black) and low-calorie cheese Danishes (minus the cheese and the frosting), and then climbed back into the vehicle. The tent was disassembled and packed in less than twenty seconds, furniture included, and then they were driving across the plains toward a water hole where Quatermain assured them they were likely to encounter at least a dozen different species of game.

"We're in luck, sirs," announced Quatermain when it was still half a mile away.

"We are?"

"Yes, indeed," the vehicle assured them. "There are silverstripes, spiralhorns, six-legged woolies, Galler-Smith's gazelles, and even a pair of treetoppers, those fellows with the long necks."

"Can you get us any closer?" asked Tarica, without much hope.

"Yes," answered Quatermain. "They are all on the far side of the water hole. I foresee no danger whatsoever. In fact, with no avians in the area, I feel I can finally accommodate your wishes and put my top down."

The vehicle drove closer, finally stopping about one hundred feet from the edge of the small water hole. The two men spent the next twenty minutes watching as a seemingly endless parade of exotic animals came down to drink.

Suddenly Quatermain shook slightly.

"Did you backfire or something?" asked Donahue.

"No," answered the vehicle. "I am in perfect working order."

"There it is again," noted Donahue.

"Yeah, I feel it too," said Tarica. "A kind of thump-thump-thump."

Suddenly there was an ear-shattering roar. Most of the animals raced away from the water hole. A few froze momentarily in terror.

"What is it?" asked Tarica nervously.

"This is your lucky day, sirs!" enthused Quatermain. "You are about to see a Gigantosaurus Selous."

As the vehicle spoke, a huge creature, 25 feet at the shoulder, 80 feet in length, with canines as long as a tall man, raced up the water hole, killing two silverstripes with a swipe of its enormous foreleg, and biting a treetopper in half.

"My God, he's awesome!" breathed Donahue.

"Maybe we should put the top back up," said Tarica.

"Unnecessary," said Quatermain. "He's made his kill. Now he'll stop and eat it."

"What if he wants to eat *us*?" whispered Tarica.

"Calm yourself, sir. He is hardwired to attack his species' prey animals, into which category safari cars and humans from Earth do not fall."

The gigantosaur glared across the water hole with hate-filled red eyes, and emitted a frightening roar.

"I'd back up if I were you," urged Tarica.

"He's just warning us off his kill," explained Quatermain.

"He's not eating," said Donahue. "He's just looking at us."

"Hungrily," added Tarica.

"I assure you this is all in keeping with his behavior patterns," said Quatermain.

"Uh ... he's just put his front feet in the water."

"He has no sweat glands," said the vehicle. "This is how he cools his blood."

"He's halfway across the water hole!" said Tarica.

"He has a long neck," answered Quatermain. "Wading into the water makes it easier for him to drink."

"He's not drinking!" said Donahue. "He's coming straight for us!"

"It's a bluff," said Quatermain.

The gigantosaur emitted a roar that was so loud the entire vehicle shook.

"What if it's not?" screamed Tarica.

"Just a moment while I compute the odds of your survival."

"We haven't *got* a moment!" yelled Donahue.

"Checking..." said Quatermain calmly. "Ah! I see. The shaking of the ground dislodged a small transistor in my data banks. Actually, the odds are 9,438 to 1 that he *is* attacking us. That's very strange. I've never had a transistor dislodged before. The odds of it happening are—"

"Shut up and get us out of here!" hollered Tarica as the gigantosaur reached their side of the water hole, leaned forward, and bared its fighting fangs.

"Shall I back up first or put up the top first?" mused Quatermain. "Ah, decisions, decisions!"

Tarica felt something hit the top of his head. He looked up and found himself staring into the hungry eyes of the gigantosaur, who was drooling on him. It opened its enormous mouth, lowered its head—

—and the top of the vehicle slammed shut. There was a bone-jarring shock as the gigantosaur's jaws closed on Quatermain. Three teeth were broken off, and the creature roared in rage, releasing its grip. Quatermain backed up quickly, spun around, and raced off in the opposite direction.

"Well, that's that!" said Tarica, pulling out a handkerchief and wiping the drool from his face and head.

"Not quite," noted Quatermain. "The gigantosaur is in full pursuit."

"You've already told us you won't run out of fuel for decades," said Donahue.

"That is true."

"Then there's no problem."

"Well, there is one little problem," said Quatermain. "My right rear tire is dangerously low, and of course if it goes flat I will have to stop to change it."

"Why did I work Super Bowl Sunday?" moaned Tarica. "I sold five units during the game. Why didn't I stay home and watch like any normal man?"

"I didn't have to sell nights," added Donahue. "I could have sneaked off to the waterbed motel with that sexy little blonde from the billing department who was always giving me the eye. She was worth at least four sales."

"Relax, sirs," said Quatermain. "The gigantosaur has stopped to kill and devour a purplebeest. We are totally safe." There was an explosion as the tire burst. "Well, 13.27 percent safe, anyway."

"I'm starting to hate mathematics," said Tarica.

"I don't suppose one of you gentlemen would like to help?" suggested Quatermain.

"I thought you could change it yourself," said Tarica.

"I can. But when unassisted, it takes me four hours and seventeen minutes. The gigantosaur, should he choose to take up the pursuit again, can reach us in three minutes and twenty-two seconds."

"Why would he?" asked Donahue. "I mean, he just made a kill, didn't he?"

"He made some kills at the water hole," said Tarica. "Maybe he's not hungry at all. Maybe he just likes killing things."

"Open the door and tell me where the jack, wrench, and spare are."

"Those are obsolete," said Quatermain. "Get outside and I will instruct you. My tool case is in the trunk."

Donahue and Tarica were outside, standing before the remains of the back tire, tool kit in hand, half a minute later.

"All ready?" asked Quatermain. "Good. Now, which of you is better versed in quantum mechanics?"

The two men exchanged looks.

"Neither of us."

"Oh, dear," said Quatermain. "You're quite sure?"

"Quite," said Tarica.

"How about non-Euclidian mathematics?"

"No."

"Are you certain? I don't mean to distress you, but the gigantosaur has finished his meal—I believe it took three bites, though there is a 14.2 percent chance that it took four, given his missing teeth—and he will be upon you in approximately fifty-three seconds."

"Oh, shit!" said Donahue. "Let us back in. At least you're armored."

"Please replace the tool kit first," said Quatermain. "We can't leave it here for some unsuspecting animal to injure itself on."

Tarica raced to the back of the vehicle.

"Open the goddamned trunk!" he bellowed.

"Sorry," said Quatermain. The trunk opened, Tarica hurled the tool kit into it, and it slammed shut.

"You shouldn't have yelled so loud," said Quatermain, as the ground began to shake. "The sound of the human voice seems to enrage the gigantosaur. He will be here in nineteen seconds."

"Let us in, damn it!" yelled Donahue, tugging at the door.

"I am afraid I can't, sir," said Quatermain. "I am obligated to protect the company's property, which is to say: myself. And the odds are 28.45 to one that you both can't enter me and close the door before he reaches us."

Tarica looked behind him. It seemed that the entire world consisted of one gaping gigantosaur mouth.

"I hate safaris!" he yelled, diving under the vehicle.

"I hate safari cars!" screamed Donahue, joining him as the gigantosaur's jaws snapped shut on empty air, sounding like a clap of thunder.

"What are we going to do?" whispered Tarica.

"I'll tell you what we're *not* going to do," replied Donahue. "We're not going to crawl out from under this thing."

They lay there, tense and silent, for half a minute. Then, suddenly, they became aware of a change in their surroundings.

"Do you notice it getting lighter?" asked Tarica.

"Yeah," said Donahue, frowning. "What's going on?"

"Do not worry about me, sirs," said a voice high above them. "I am virtually indestructible when my doors and trunk are locked. Well, 93.872 percent indestructable, anyway. Besides, it is a far better thing I do today than I have ever done."

They looked up and saw Quatermain sticking out of both sides of the monster's jaws. The gigantosaur tensed and tried to bring his jaws together with full force. Six more teeth broke, he dropped the vehicle (which missed Tarica and Donahue by less than two feet), and raced off, yelping like a puppy that had just encountered a porcupine.

"If you gentlemen will lift me off my side," said Quatermain, "I will change my tire and we will continue the safari as if nothing happened."

The men put their shoulders into the task, and a few moments later Quatermain was upright again.

"Thank you," said the vehicle. "Please re-enter me now, while I go to work on the tire."

They climbed into the car, and the door closed and locked behind them.

"Four hours and seventeen minutes and I'll be as good as new," said Quartermain. "Then we'll travel to the Marisula Delta and explore an entirely different ecosystem."

"Let's just travel back to the safari office," said Tarica. "I've had enough."

"Me, too," added Donahue.

"You want to end your safari four days early?" asked Quatermain.

"You got it."

"I am afraid I cannot accommodate you, sirs," said Quatermain.

"What the hell are you talking about?"

"Your company paid for five full days," explained Quatermain. "If you do not experience all five days, we could be sued for breach of contract."

"We've experienced five days' worth," said Tarica. "We just want to go home."

"Clearly your travel has left you mentally confused, sir. You have actually experienced only 21 hours and 49 minutes. I am not aware of confusion taking this form before, but I suppose it can happen."

"I know how long we've been here, and I'm *not* confused," said Donahue. "Take us back."

"Yes, sir."

"Good."

"As soon as the safari is over. My tire will be ready in four hours and thirteen minutes, and then we will proceed to the Marisula Delta."

Tarica tried the door. "Let me out!"

"I am afraid I cannot, sir," said Quatermain. "You might try to find your way back to the spaceport. If you do, there is a 97.328 percent likelihood that you will be killed and eaten, and should you make it back intact, there is a 95.673 percent chance that a breach of contract suit will be brought against my owners. Therefore, I feel I must fulfill our contract. Sit back and try to relax, sir."

"We'll starve."

"Not to worry, sir. I will be able to feed you right where you are."

"We can't sleep in this thing," complained Donahue.

"My understanding of human physiology, which I should note is encyclopedic, is that when you get tired enough you can sleep anywhere." A brief pause. "All your needs will be provided for, sir. I even have a one-month supply of plastic bags."

It was five days later that Quatermain pulled up to the spaceport.

"Serving you has been a true pleasure, sirs," it intoned as Tarica and Donahue wearily opened the door, raced around to the back, and grabbed their luggage. "I hope to see you again in the near future."

"In your dreams!" growled Tarica.

"I do not dream, sir."

"*I* do," muttered Donahue. "And I'm going to have nightmares about this safari for the rest of my life."

A squat robot, looking for all the world like a fire hydrant on wheels, rolled up, took their bags from them, and led them to a small waiting spaceship.

"This isn't the same spaceliner we took here," said Tarica dubiously. "It looks like a small private ship."

"Your Stellar Voyages ship is not available, sir," said the robot, as it placed their luggage in the cargo hold "This ship was supplied, gratis, by the safari company as a sign of their appreciation."

"And to dissuade us from suing?" asked Donahue.

"That, too," agreed the robot.

The two men climbed into the ship and strapped themselves into the only two seats provided.

"Welcome, gentlemen," said the ship as the hatch closed and it began elevating. "I trust you enjoyed your once-in-a-lifetime safari experience on the planet Selous. I will be returning you to Earth. I come equipped with all creature comforts except sexual consorts"—it uttered an emotionless mechanical chuckle—"and have a gourmet kitchen at your disposal."

"What happened to the ship we were supposed to be on?" asked Tarica.

"I regret to inform you that it was destroyed in an ion storm just as it was entering the system," answered the ship.

"Uh... we're not going through that same storm on the way out, are we?" asked Donahue.

"Yes, sir," said the ship. "But there is no need for concern, sir. I am a new model, equipped with every conceivable safety device. I am far more maneuverable than a—" The ship shuddered for just an instant. "Just some minor space debris. Nothing to worry about. As I was saying, I am far more maneuverable than a spaceliner, and besides, this is my home system. Every ion storm during the past ten years has been charted and placed in my data banks."

"So you've flown through them before?" said Tarica.

"Actually, no," said the ship. "This is my first flight. But as I say, I am fully equipped and programmed. What *could* go wrong?"

Tarica cursed under his breath. Donahue merely checked to make sure there was a small paper bag near his seat.

"I am sure we're going to get along splendidly together," continued the ship. "You are Mr. Tarica and Mr. Donahue, am I correct?

"Right," said Tarica.

"And my name was clearly discernable in bold letters on my nose as you entered me," said the ship proudly.

"I must have missed it," said Tarica. "What was it?"

"I am the *Pequod*."

Donahue reached for the bag.

Story Notes:

This story is a tribute to a dear friend, and a one-time collaborator, the late Robert Sheckley. It's exactly the kind of story he was doing in the 1950s, before he began experimenting—which reached its apex in *Dimension of Miracles*—with a form of humor that only worked as science fiction.

Mike Resnick

is, according to *Locus*, the all-time leading award-winner, living or dead, for short science fiction. He is the winner of 5 Hugos, a Nebula, and other major awards in the USA, Japan, Spain, Poland, Croatia, Catalonia, and France.

Mike is the author of 71 novels, close to 300 stories, and three screenplays, and is the editor of 41 anthologies. He recently took on the editorship of the Stellar Guild line of books and *Galaxy's Edge* magazine as well.

HOW YOU RUINED EVERYTHING

by Konstantine Paradias

The first step toward realizing it's your fault that everything's gone wrong is admitting that you were, at the time, the only man with a functioning time machine.

The second step is, of course, admitting that you stole it from its original owner, by bashing his head in with a shovel when he wasn't looking. And that you left the poor bastard unconscious out in the rain, telling yourself that you'd be back fifteen seconds of real time later to help him using copious applications of your now almost inexhaustible capital, considerable connections, and a first aid kit.

Because what you were going to do was step into that time machine, go back to the past, and make your life so much better. Armed with the knowledge of other people's financial and personal successes, you would venture into the times of the monkey-men (or your dad's) and there proceed to build yourself a financial empire.

The third part toward accepting how the entire mess might actually be your fault, is realizing that you don't know the first thing about driving a time machine. That, as you look at the series of knobs, flashing lights, levers, revolving spigots, glass tubes, masses of wires and circuitry with the complexity of fractals, you don't think: *Dear God, what is this thing?*

Instead, you say: "Yeah, I got this."

As you start pressing buttons and flicking unlabeled switches and turning spigots and prodding screens, listening to impossible gadgetry rev and whirr and roar beneath the dashboard and inside the unknowable bowels of the machine, you don't-for-one-moment-stop-to-consider: *I have no idea what I'm doing.*

Instead, you say: "Alright! Rev it up!"

As the time machine screeches, roars, and a previously obscured dial pops out of the dashboard, proceeding to spin and whistle madly, your instincts (honed by a steady diet of science fiction books and serials) tell you that this is obviously the date dial, through which you can adjust your destination. You're so busy winding it, flipping it to your date of choice that you don't stop for one moment to consider that: *None of those numbers are dates. And that smaller dial, why is it pointing to Mil?*

You just say: "Come on, baby! 1960, let's go!"

So the time machine roars once more, shudders like a cheetah in heat and then it jumps. You find yourself in a forest with pine trees tall as houses blocking your view. It jumps again and you're on a hill, overlooking a glade, where men in long robes wave sickles and gnash their teeth at the sight of you. You jump again and this time you're in a jungle. Then you're in a marsh. Then you're standing beneath the shadow of a great mountain. Then you just jump and jump and jump and jump...

When the time machine screeches to a halt so sudden that it sends you flying, you find yourself landing in the middle of a field of tall grass, beneath a sky that's baby-room-wallpaper blue. The air smells clearer, fresher, yet still alien. You take a whiff, look at the empty fields around you that stretch on forever, and as you notice a group of upright monkeys, you think: *This doesn't look like Woodstock at all.*

The upright monkeys approach and you're naturally scared. You never liked monkeys, anyway: they're like caricatures of people, all hair and big stupid eyes and mouths full of sharp teeth. One of them (the biggest and bravest of the bunch), reaches out his long, misshapen hand to touch you. He's unarmed, but you've seen *2001: A Space Odyssey*; you know it's only a matter of time before he finds a big enough bone to smash your ribs.

The rock's in your hand before you know it. It's jagged and it barely fits in your palm, therefore perfect. You whack the upright monkey with it, because you'll be damned if you let another one of those things bite you in the ear like that circus one did, when you were six. The upright monkey squeals, snarls. and claws blindly at empty air, so you crack it on the head again and again. When it's down, you sit on its chest and keep bashing it, until it's good and quiet. Not once, at any point do you stop to think: *Jesus Christ, what am I doing? What if I'm altering history?*

What comes out of your mouth is: "Yeah! Yeah! Get some! Get some!"

So you throw away the rock. The upright monkey ladies begin to swoon for you once they're done soiling themselves in terror. The monkey-men begin to divvy up the corpse to offer to you, their new master. Long story short, you end up spending the night with them, showing off that trick you learned with your lighter back in college. Somehow (and not in any way that you can actually describe), a great fire breaks out that consumes the entire valley of tall grass, and you run back to your time machine.

Panicked, you press buttons again, flicking every switch, but this time, you turn all the dials *away* from you. You sneak a look at the dial, which now reads: 1800 Mil.

As the time machine revs up and jumps, forward and upward, you never once stop to think: *Maybe I should stop. Maybe I* should try to go back and ask the man I brained for directions. Before I brain him, of course.

Instead, you say: "Onward and upward!"

When the time machine screeches to a screaming halt, you find your senses assaulted by an overwhelming smell of burning plastic before you open your eyes. Something flies by you, leaving behind only an afterimage of green light and a scent very much like battery acid. Something behind you explodes, just as you're beginning to rev up the time machine. A cold metal hand wraps around your arm. You follow it and find yourself staring into a pair of frosted-glass eyes, set above something that looks like a speaker.

"Throk'to akh-ha?" it blares.

"Aaaaah!" you retort.

The metal thing with the speaker for a face raises its other arm, producing something that looks like a prop gun from a Flash Gordon flick, when a ragged man jumps from cover and cuts its hand clean off with a sword made out of light. The dial of the machine spins and stops short of *180 Mil* as you slap the big red button at the center of the dashboard and you're ejected across time with a severed robot arm that bleeds black liquid onto your lap.

When you finally stop, you're standing beside a podium. A short man with tiny, beady eyes and a toothbrush-wide moustache looks at you, his hand frozen mid-salute. There's a red band wrapped around his arm that looks awfully familiar.

"*Was is das?*" the man on the podium asks with a voice you've come to recognize after countless of hours of playing *Call of Duty*.

Somehow, the Flash Gordon prop's in your hand and you pull the trigger. Green light shoots from the tip and strikes the familiar man, reducing him to a pile of dust in an instant. As the Gestapo officers rush toward you, machine guns in hand, you're thinking: *Damn! I just killed Hitler!*

You say: "Hot diggity damn!"

You pull the lever, not really checking the dial. One of the officers shoots at you and you see the bullet slowing down mid-flight, stopping and then returning back to the barrel, swallowing up the flame that had just propelled it through the air. You jump, and in the time it takes you to blink, the time machine has landed in the middle of a park, in a place that smells like freshly bloomed anemones, with just a dash of hash.

You look around and all you can see are hippies, jangling their guitars to the non-tune of Yoko on the radio, turned to almost-music by the genius of John Lennon. The hippies run, of course. They head for the hills, their reefers forgotten in the grass. Only one girl's left, staring at you with wide-eyed wonder.

"Where the hell did you come from?" she asks, her voice sounding vaguely familiar. The way she's dressed, her clothes a mish-mash of beads and cotton threads, complete with a makeshift dreamcatcher hanging from her neck between her breasts, she looks like a pagan goddess, refitted for the twentieth century.

"I'm from the future" you tell her in your most suave tone. "Wanna hop on my time machine?" you give her a wink that you know is embarrassing, even under the circumstances.

"You're from the future huh, spaceman? Whose arm is that?" she asks, smiling as she looks at the severed robot arm still in your lap.

"Oh that? That's just a trophy taken from one of my many fallen foes. The future *is* a dangerous place, after all. Thank goodness for my ray gun, I suppose..." you say, reaching for it, when you realize it's not there anymore. Frantically, you pat down your jacket, your pants. You open dashboard drawers, spilling out yellowed papers and dog-eared notebooks with gilded lettering. Suddenly, it hits you: *The Nazis have the damn ray gun.*

You're desperately trying to consider the implications when the hippie girl walks up to you and her hazel eyes suddenly dawn in your field of vision. Her lips are the color of fresh cherries. She runs her hands through your hair and she doesn't just feel right. She feels divine.

"It's okay, you can show off later."

"Later when?" you ask, as she kisses you and you roll on the grass, your hands all over each other. The entire time, you're thinking: *Eh, why hurry? I've got a time machine, for Christ's sake!*

You're sharing a joint, when she says: "My name's Lily. *FFFF-tttp.*" she exhales, letting out a billow of smoke so white, you'd think her lungs had elected a new pope.

"You know, you look like a Lily. *FFFtttp,*" you say, blowing halfway-formed rings of smoke.

You look at her as she turns, eyes following the arch of her back as you're passing the roach, when you notice them for the first time: first, the tiny tail, wagging at the small of her back; second, the tiny patch of ink printed above it.

"You know, you're the first man I've seen who didn't have a tail. *FFFFtttp.*" she says, half-smiling, as she turns to ruffle your hair.

"What's that thing on your back?" you ask, as your brain slowly pieces together the design. It's a tattoo, shaped like a stylized swastika. *Please, let this be a post-modern statement* you pray.

"What, that? Oh, you like it? It's a Party thing. They were gonna put it on my palm like everybody else, but I thought why not try something new, you know? Why, where's your tattoo?" she says, between puffs.

"That's a Nazi-oh God."

"Oh please, don't tell me you're like one of those Jew-lovers? My fiancé went to one of their rallies once and they shipped him off to 'Nam to kill gooks all day." Lily responds, matter-of-factly.

"Fiancé? You have a boyfriend?" you exclaim and suddenly, the small details that had escaped you begin to sink in: the color of her eyes, her hair, the line of her neck, the sound of her voice, the derision in her tone. "Where did you say you lived?"

"Over in Jonestown, a ways off from the big city."

"And your fiancé's name's Kurt?"

"Mmm-hmm."

"And your maiden name's Popowitz?"

"Used to be. Daddy changed it to Lauk, after the war, to get on the Party's good side. How come you know so much about me?"

And suddenly, it hits you: this woman is your own mother, who's now a Nazi (like everyone else) because you gave them a ray gun in the first place!

The fourth part toward realizing how you've messed everything up is coming to terms with the fact that everything that's gone wrong is entirely your own damn fault. Also, that you need to stop and fix whatever it is you're doing, right now.

The fifth part toward realizing that everything is your fault is taking a deep breath and trying to think of a viable solution: finding the man who owned this machine and asking for his help is a solid plan. Thinking about going back in time to the point before he met you and thus risking a paradox, is not.

Guess which one you go for, as you run to the time machine, your clothes bundled under your arm, your own mother chasing after you, screaming: "*Juden*! Halt, *Juden*!"

You flip the dials and watch as the counter changes from *Mil* to *Cen* to *Dec* to *Yea* all the way down to *Day* thinking: *I can do this, I can fix this, I've got all the time in the world!*

And then your own mother throws a rock at your eye and you hit a switch by accident. The time machine revs up and you watch in horror as the dial flips from *Day* to *Ma,* same way kitchen dials do, switching from the lowest setting to the highest. Now the reading has changed, from 450 *Day* to 450 *Ma* and before you can utter a single word, you've already jumped...

...and landed in the middle of a desert. Then in a city made of rock and wood, where starved men and despairing women scream at the sight of you. Then in the middle of a jungle, set ablaze, beneath a sky the color of charcoal...

The time machine lurches for a final time, crushing something that screeches once as it snaps its neck. Terrified, you chance a look, fearing the worst. Thankfully, it is only a velociraptor caught in its dying throes, shaking its full, colorful plumage. With a great squawk, the majestic thing dies and you sit in your driver's seat, on the verge of tears. Not only because you have just had velociraptors ruined forever, but because you have also plunged history into a mess that you couldn't possibly get it out of. How the hell would you find the time traveler? And even if you did, how could you reason with him? How could you get him to stop you from making everything even worse? Why couldn't time travel be simple like in the movies, where history and time are just obstacles to be brushed aside at the hero's whim?

You're too busy feeling sorry for yourself and the entire universe, when more velociraptors burst from the foliage, seeking both to overpower and to devour the strange, weeping thing that just crushed their brother. They look like killer peacocks as they flap their tiny hands and shake their plumage, their claws aiming for your throat. You turn a lever blindly and watch them retreat back into the dense jungle, as you fast-forward yourself to safety.

When you think you've reached a safe place, you stop the time machine and climb off it without turning the dial. Choking back your tears, you sit beneath the shadow of a great oak tree, looking at the instrument that you have just used to doom everything. You get dressed, take a deep breath and start going through the drawers all over again. The majority of the manuals and notebooks have been left in the field where you'd met Nazi-Lily. If the time machine had ever had an instruction booklet, it has been lost along with so much else.

No way around it, you think. *I'll just have to find the time traveler myself.*

You're too busy stuffing what few papers are left back inside the glove compartment, trying to come up with a solid, viable plan that would allow you to restore history back to its original, less-terrible state, when you notice the shape of a man, creeping up behind you. You're about to turn, to talk to him, when you hear the distinct noise of a shovel being dragged across the ground and then swooshing through the air, going for your head. You needn't turn around to know exactly who he is.

"Oh, you stupid, stupid, bas—"

Whomp.

Story Notes:

"How You Ruined Everything" is the kind of story I've always wanted to write, but had never got around to (until now, that is). We're all plagued by the constant thought of how different our lives would be if we had made our choices differently, if we perhaps had had the guts to walk up to that cute girl in the coffee shop (or that guy in the gym) and had asked them out; what our lives would have been like if we perhaps had not opted for that Bachelor's degree in Philosophy or a BA in English. Other times, we might slap ourselves in the face at random intervals, thinking about how we ruined our chance at that Dream Job. Oh, how different, how much more joyous and fulfilling our lives would be, if we had a time machine to right old wrongs!

But it wouldn't. Because deep down, we know that our new choices would have spawned new regrets, new lines of hindsight and a secret longing for what we had BEFORE we fixed everything. We'd purposefully seek out to undo all the choices we made just so we could go back to our old path and lament our choices all over again. Human beings are an odd lot, really. Makes you wonder how the hell we made it so far in the first place.

Konstantine Paradias

is a jeweler by profession and a writer by choice. Plagued by an overpowering sense of hindsight, he finds himself constantly second-guessing his every choice and secretly knows that getting himself a time machine would be a pretty terrible idea. He vents his frustrations and dreams on his blog, Shapescapes, instead.

INSIDER INFORMATION

by Jody Lynn Nye

"Uh, oh," Detective Sergeant Dena Malone thought, as the five witnesses' faces lit up at her approach over a Japanese plank bridge. At first, all they would have seen was a small woman with razor-cut brown hair and pale skin, wearing a police uniform tunic. Then they recognized her. Dena felt her face grow hot. It seemed to take forever to cross the expensively landscaped and gardened roof of the ultra highrise, the largest green space she had ever walked on in the city. "Here it comes."

"Cool!" said a tall man with a tattoo that ran from his left temple to his jaw. "We get the reality show cop! How's your baby doing? Can we hear your Salosian talk?"

Dena felt the inevitable roiling in her belly as K't'ank shifted when he heard his name. The meter-long alien lived in her peritoneum, implanted there by the Alien Relations Department of Earth. She had been identified as an ideal host in spite of being pregnant at the time. K't'ank's optic nerves were connected to her own through her spinal column. Where most human beings might see a meter-long rose pink parasitic snake, Dena knew him as a scientist and a galaxy-class busybody. She had been fooled into thinking hosting K't'ank was a temporary arrangement. It wasn't. She reached for the platinum bracelet that provided the alien with his sole means of communicating with the outside world and switched it off.

"Malone!" K't'ank protested, his voice now only audible through bone conduction.

"Let's get the facts down first," she said, firmly, settling her wrists on her growing abdomen. As if it wasn't enough for a working cop to have to host a visiting alien, she was also five months pregnant. "Then we'll all have a nice chat. So, want to tell me what happened here?"

The five looked at one another, then over the side of the roof of Totality Software. Dena leaned over to see for herself. By squeezing her eyes, she activated the telescopic feature of her police-issue contact lenses, and zoomed in on the scene below. At the ground level, ninety stories down, occasionally obscured by passing air traffic in between, the coroner's staff was putting a white-covered body on a stretcher into the meat wagon. The blue lights on top began flashing, and the vehicle took off, angling upward toward the northwest for the morgue.

"Who is that?" she asked.

"Was," said the man with the tattoo, with annoying precision. He, like all his fellow Totality employees, wore a headpiece with a single gray lens that covered his right eye like a pirate's patch. "Art Smedley. Our CTO. Chief Technical Officer. He fell off the roof."

"Suicide?" Dena asked.

A woman with brilliant neon green hair and golden skin nodded her head sadly.

"I never thought he'd do it."

"Self-destruction?" K't'ank asked, though audible only to her. "Curious! With so many means of achievable death available to one in the normal course of human life, why choose terror and collision?"

"Hush!" Dena said. She gave the others an apologetic smile. "Had he been threatening self-harm?"

Suicide was a major crime in the city, and unsuccessful attempts were usually penalized with terms in locked mental therapy facilities as well as eye-watering fines. The successful ones couldn't be prosecuted, though they knew their families would have to pay the city for cleanup and nuisance costs. Dena hoped that would deter some of them from going through with it.

"I never heard him say he wanted to kill himself," the man protested. The ID he presented gave his name as Frank Perugio.

The green-haired woman's eyes flashed. Her card named her as Roshin Caitako.

"He did, though. To me. He didn't feel he could confide in *you*. Any of you."

"That's not fair, Rosh!" protested the other woman present, Magi Tene, a blonde of middle years clanking with computerized bangles and other gizmos. The two remaining males, who looked like father and son, added their protests.

"We need you to find out why he did it," the father said. He was Jerry Lopez. His son was Dario. Dena nodded.

"I'll need access to his personal computer—providing he didn't take it with him—and to go through his office. You folks realize that as of the time you called us, your computer systems went on lockdown. Nothing can be deleted until we've had a chance to look at it."

"We know!" the elder Lopez exclaimed, his brows drawn down. "Government invasion of privacy!"

"It's normal, Jerry! Come on, Detective, I'll sign you on," Perugio said. They headed toward the access tower. He gave her a sideways glance. "Uh, could we talk with Dr. K't'ank now?"

"Sure," said Dena, with a groan. She switched on the bracelet. K't'ank, never one to disappoint an audience, introduced himself.

"Most curious the way your cities are constructed," he said. "My planet-sharers are much more careful in the construction of their habitats. Are our lives more precious to us than yours?"

"Not at all!" Perugio protested. "We prize life and safety. Look at our rooftop! This is our living space. We spend hours out here every day. It's set up to protect us." Dena swept an eye around so K't'ank could take in all the features, a mix of cultures and eras. A croquet lawn sat beside a net-encased basketball court. The ornamental fountain she noticed on arrival was less than an inch deep, with sophisticated drainage preserving the water and preventing anyone from drowning. At the rear, behind the access tower, was a miniature arena, complete with electronic scoreboard and T-shirt cannons. It was fenced high so no ball, or ball player, could fall over the parapet just a few yards away.

"But consider the statistics," K't'ank said, and Dena knew he had them at his fingertips, so to speak. He spent most of his life on the Internet. "Harm comes to humans in many ways every day . . . ." The Totality employees listened raptly, leaving Dena to concentrate on observing the crime scene. She took recordings of her own of the rooftop, the access tower, and the corridor leading back to Smedley's office.

That sanctuary reminded her less of a Fortune 5000 company official, and more of a toy store. Smedley had at least one of every major nerd collector toy dating back over a century—static, animatronic, holographic, you name it—arranged on paper-thin shelves that lined every wall. Enviously, she touched the holocrystal display from *Star Trek 21*, the first movie in the second reboot, a limited edition collector's item. She noticed he owned copy #7 of 500.

Under all the clutter were equally expensive office furnishings. She sat down in the enormous black nylon sling behind the translucent desk. The chair automatically adjusted to her size and weight. It was, without a doubt, the most comfortable chair she had ever felt.

"It would be great to have a chair like this," she said, shifting to enjoy the way it cradled and supported her. "I wonder how much something like this costs."

"My late host had such," K't'ank said. "Eight thousand credits."

"Wow!" Dena said, appalled. She bounced in it one last time. "Well, I'd better appreciate it for the moment."

According to the security cameras and the communication records, Smedley had taken a personal call on his headset just before walking up to the roof and jumping off. No doubt about it. She replayed the video from several angles again and again. Smedley had been talking animatedly, paused at the edge of the parapet, then leaped off into nothingness. The cry he let out as he fell was audible on several recorders in the building. She cut off the replay before she got to Smedley's landing on the pavement. What she could see from the roof had been as detailed as she wanted to get. The coroner would let her know if there had been an organic reason for Smedley to want to terminate himself, like the onset of cancer or dementia.

"I'm just bothered by the cheerful bound into eternity," Dena said, frowning at the screen.

"Humans are strange," K't'ank said.

"Thank you, Captain Obvious. But what do you think about his behavior?"

"He deliberately takes the step," K't'ank agreed. "As if he was joyous to do so."

"Could he have been part of a cult?" Dena asked. "I agree with Perugio. I just don't figure Smedley for a suicide. He seemed so happy."

A scan of his personal files bore out her initial impression. Sifting through the remains of a life was tedious work. The personal stuff she could do, using an algorithm to pick up trends in the backlog of the victim's emails, notes, and diaries, not to mention online postings. When the program finished sorting, it would point out probability trees and anomalies. Smedley's professional life, however, required a specialist. She could not download all his files to the police computer yet; undoubtedly she required a password or an override by the company sysop. She could, however, access read-only files.

"He does not appear to be part of a collective personality," K't'ank said. "Greatly an individual dedicated to individuals."

"That's what I think, too," Dena said, pausing the video of Smedley just before he plunged over the side of the Totality building. "But he wasn't pushed. What happened there?"

The person on the other end of the call Smedley had been on when he died was a stockholder in Totality, Iris Bendix. Dena put in the code on her police handset, and connected. For the next ten minutes she listened to the woman at the other end downloading her shock and grief. In between wails, Dena made the right noises, and managed to work in a few words. When Iris stopped for breath, Dena interrupted in her calmest voice.

"Tell me about Totality," she said. "I see that you've owned a piece of it for years."

The distraction worked. "I've been on board from the beginning," Iris said, sounding as if she was pulling herself together. Dena ran the brief ID video on Bendix's file. A slim woman with smile lines but no other wrinkles. Long white hair. Former model, presently CEO of her own company.

"What do they do?"

"They make a total immersive environment," Iris said. "It's like having your own holodeck. Companies have been moving toward this for years, but never quite getting there. Totality did it."

Dena had a few headsets, helmets, vests, and bodysuits in her closet that had promised that holodeck experience. They didn't deliver, and had become obsolete almost as soon as she bought them.

"It's in the eyepatch?" she asked. "The gray eyepatch?"

"Yes. It projects a whole user experience into the eyes. One or both, depending on how you program it. It's fabulous. You've never tried it?"

"No, I . . ." Dena didn't want to admit that she and her husband couldn't afford the system on their combined salaries. Not yet, anyway. Maybe after the next raise. "Ms. Bendix, could it— I'm sorry to have to put it like this, but this is what happened— could it make someone walk off a cliff?"

She was afraid Iris would fold up again, but she remained calm.

"God, no! Totality has more safeguards than the Academy Awards voting system."

"I'll look into it. Thanks for your help."

"Anything I can do to find out what happened," Iris said. "Art was a great guy!"

THE PROGRAMMERS were eager to let Dena experience the Totality system. Six of them fussed over her in the white-walled, gadget-filled showroom, getting her preferences on fantasies or favorite programs down on a roll-up screen monitor, accessing her social media to download her friends list, and fitting the surprisingly light headset to her face.

The gray patch was translucent, but it bothered Dena to have something so close to her eye.

"Stop fluttering your eyelids!" Caitako said. "You'll forget all about it in a moment."

"I can't," Dena protested, batting away the technicians' hands until someone sat on her lap to stop her.

Then they turned it on.

"Oh, my everliving God!"

An endless plain of grass and wildflowers surrounded her. Birds flew, chirping musically. Huge, white, fluffy clouds rolled overhead. A gorgeous dark-skinned man, muscled like an ancient god, rode up beside her on a white horse. He plucked a bunch of grapes, glistening with dew, from a vine that suddenly sprang up from the ground and took one perfect, round purple globe from the bunch. He leaned over toward Dena with a knowing, wicked smile. She opened her mouth, waiting for the grape's cool, wet shape to touch her tongue.

"It is baffling!" K't'ank's voice interrupted her. She felt his tail whipping against her internal organs. "It is not natural! Stop the illusions at once!"

Dena blinked. Through the hazy image of the divine man and his horse, she saw the Totality employees and the lab.

"That is absolutely amazing," she said. "I felt as if I was there. Wherever there was."

"It's the greatest system we have ever made," Perugio said proudly. "We've sold over eight hundred million units."

"I do not like it," K't'ank said.

Dena removed the light band from her head.

"I can see how it would overwhelm reality," she said. "Is it possible there was a system malfunction that caused Mr. Smedley to see something that wasn't there?"

"Never. You get used to it in a short time," Dario Lopez said, polishing the eyepiece and putting the headset back into a pure white carton. "You're always aware of what's real and what isn't. It's why we made the background lens gray. It sticks out."

"Well, check the system and get back to me," Dena said. "I am finding no reason why Mr. Smedley would have jumped off a building, not when he had a set of mint 1977 Star Wars figurines to come home to."

"Will do, Detective," Perugio promised. He leaned toward her. "Um, Dr. K't'ank, can I, uh ... do you have email in there?"

"Most certainly!" K't'ank said. "I would be pleased to add you to my correspondents. I am very active in staying current with connections."

"It keeps him quiet at night," Dena pointed out dryly.

SHE TOOK SMEDLEY'S files home on a small drive, and went over them while her husband watched a couple of hours of television on their wall-sized screen. K't'ank shared Neal's passion for reality videos. Dena had learned to glance up every few seconds while she was doing something else so he could follow the program, without really seeing what was on the screen herself. The medical examiner's file had arrived during dinner. She studied it.

"Smedley's health was fine. He broke his wrist during high school, but since then, nothing. No cancer. No fatal disease. Nothing but a little myopia."

"Everybody has myopia," Neal Malone said, without looking away from the tri-vid screen.

"Yeah, I know. It couldn't have been an organic failure. But what? It has to be right in front of me. Something that drove him to not only kill himself, but do it happily."

"Look up, Malone, look up!" K't'ank said. "That terror is like one who lives on my world!"

A nightmare beast lunged directly toward them, opening a vast blue, fuchsia, and slate gray mouth lined with row after row of sharp teeth. She jumped backward, her heart pounding. It turned on its tail and swam away.

"Why do you flinch?" K't'ank asked. "You know what you saw isn't real."

"I hate you," Dena said. Her pulse slowed to its normal rhythm.

"That is not an answer!"

"Yes, it is," she said, and went back to her reading. She stopped. "Could it really be that easy?"

"What is easy?" K't'ank asked.

"Seeing something that isn't there?"

She attacked the company files, much less easy to sift through. The screen opened hundreds of cascading files that all looked alike except for a few lines of text and a 3D rendering spinning in a box, of anything from a console to a single circuit. Smedley's job as CTO was to collect documentation and coordinate applications to the Terran Patent Office, among other things. At any time, he had somewhere between sixty and two hundred applications under consideration, with more in various levels of appeal or approval. Not only that, there was correspondence from all around the solar system and beyond regarding rival applications. Some of them were for technology almost identical to Totality's. A few were almost word for word identical to ones submitted by Smedley from a company on Enceladus. They had been forwarded to him by Ms. Bendix. Dena called her again.

"Those set off alarm bells in my mind," Iris confirmed. "It looked like someone inside the company was taking Totality technology and trying to bring it to market first, but I don't know who that could have been."

"Who in the company would have provided the tech specs for the original applications?" Dena asked.

"All of them," Iris said. "They're all engineers. Brilliant ones."

"Were they all out to get Smedley, forming another company behind his back?"

"Why?" Iris asked, reasonably. "They're all rich. Art thought it was just one person. I think he was close. Someone needed more time. I bet they still do. The system shut down while I was talking to him."

"That was me," Dena said. "I mean, the police. You think the data lockdown interrupted the crime?"

"Yes. The information must still be in there somewhere. If they can get the lockdown reversed, even for a microsecond, you'll lose the evidence. What you need to ask is, who had one foot out the door?"

Dena closed the connection. The ocean program was over. Now Neal and K't'ank were rapt over a show about nanotechnology for surgeries. She had to watch the excision of microscopic organisms that were as gross as the sea monsters from internal organs. The baby shifted and rolled across her bladder. Oops! Time to run. She heaved herself off the couch.

"Not now!" K't'ank shouted. "They are severing a tumor from the liver!"

Dena moaned.

"So, who had one foot out the door?" Dena asked, hearing her voice echo off the ceramic walls of the bathroom. "All the programmers say they're happy, but everybody lies."

"The green male claimed things that no one else did," K't'ank said.

"Green male? What green male?"

"Caitako."

Dena rolled her eyes.

"Do not do that!" K't'ank protested. "It ruins my image of the room."

"Caitako is a woman. That's a she."

"No difference," K't'ank said imperturbably. Dena had been trying for months to get him to acknowledge Earth genders. She washed up and went back toward the living room.

"What did she say that no one else said?"

"That he confided he might kill himself."

"Yes!" Dena said, raising a fist triumphantly. "That's right. That's what I heard, but I didn't connect it. It does happen that a suicide will confide only in one person. But nothing else added up. So it has to be her. But how did she do it?"

"The Totality system must have been compromised," K't'ank said. "Humans are inaccurate."

Dena shut off her computer.

"We'll talk to them in the morning."

"We will." K't'ank sounded smug. "Now I would like to enjoy the program without interruption. Look, Malone! They are resecting the upper bowel."

When she reached the Totality offices the next morning, there had already been thousands of cyberattacks on the police lockdown program. The place was crawling with security experts, all of them arguing with the programmers over who was to blame.

She spotted the lanky Perugio over the heads of the others. He plowed his way through the crowd to her. He looked furious.

"I keep telling them that the Totality program couldn't have caused Art to jump off the building, but now they're talking about industrial espionage! How did Art killing himself get morphed into that?"

"I have just one question. Did the Totality system correct your vision?"

"No, it works with what you have," Perugio said, his anger shifting to puzzlement. "Why?"

"Because your friend Caitako has been ripping all of you off," Dena said. "I need to talk to her now. Where is she?"

"Uh..." Perugio checked his tablet computer. "Her card says she's up in the garden."

Dena spoke into her communicator. "Send up a skycar! The perp's on the roof."

Perugio stayed at her elbow as she ran for the access tower.

"Roshin would never hurt anyone. Art was her friend. I'm her friend."

"She formed a corporation on Enceladus and is trying to get your tech patented ahead of you. Smedley found that out, so she killed him."

"What? How?"

"I called the morgue," Dena said, watching the indicator on the elevator zoom from ground level toward the ninetieth floor. "Can the Totality system work in corrective lenses?"

"Sure," Perugio said. "It'd work in anything that has at least two gig of memory and imaging technology."

"Mine have sixteen gigabytes," Dena said, pointing to her own face. "I bet his were at least that good."

"Your what?" K't'ank asked.

"His contact lenses," Dena said. "She hacked his contact lenses! They made him see a roof that wasn't there."

The door slid open. The moment it did, Dena's vision blurred, but that was little compared with the effect on Perugio. He fell to his knees, clutching his eyes.

"What's happening?" he demanded. "Roshin! Why are you doing this? What did you do to Art?"

"Stay away from me!" Caitako's high voice floated toward them. Dena looked around, trying to spot her. The garden was overwhelming when she was trying to take it all in at once. Suddenly, it cleared. She could see the gingko trees, the fountains, the basketball hoop—and Caitako. The green-haired programmer huddled against the fence at the edge of the roof, a laptop clutched to her chest.

"Just stay where you are," Dena ordered.

She drew her service weapon and held it in both hands as she sidled out of the access tower. Perugio was no help. He felt around him as though he had been struck blind. Dena left him and started toward the Japanese bridge, keeping her eyes fixed on Caitako.

"Not there, Malone!" K't'ank shouted, as she felt for the first step.

"What's your problem?" she demanded.

"No floor between!" K't'ank insisted. "You are not seeing out of your own eyes."

"What? Of course I am!"

"No, you are not."

"I know what I see with my own eyes."

"Argue with me!" K't'ank said, sounding frantic. She felt his tail beat against her ribs. "Only, stop walking. Now! Stop!"

She did. The bridge looked fine. Caitako was a hundred feet

in front of her. She could break right or left, behind one of the many obstructions.

"Why are you so sure what I see isn't what I see?" Dena asked.

"Because you are the owner-operator. I am an observer. I use your sight as a newcomer. I know when the images you perceive are not as they were before. There is pixilation, extremely fine, an overlay to your normal vision, not even as it was before you entered the facility this morning. Your eyes are lying to you."

Dena reached for the handrail of the bridge. Her hand went right through it.

"Not my eyes," she said. "My lenses." Dena turned her head to try and dislodge the image, to cause a time delay of any kind. "She reprogrammed my lenses!"

"Take them off," K't'ank said. "The whole garden is full of lies."

"I can't. They cover my whole eyeball. I can't take them off here. It takes ten minutes to get them out. She'll get away! These are police issue! They were supposed to be virus-proof. Can you do anything?"

"I possess passive capability only," he said, "but I will call out when I believe the floor is not the floor."

"When you *believe*?" Dena asked, desperately. K't'ank's reply was calm.

"It is all we have."

"All right. I want her before she blanks the entire database of this company. Try to warn me before I step on something."

She moved through the weird terrain, her heart pounding. Every time she thought the footing was solid, K't'ank's shrill voice was in her ears, warning her off. She tried to step on safe zones, but the console in Caitako's hands kept the landscape moving.

"Stop it!" Dena shouted. "You're trying to kill a police officer!"

Caitako's eyes were huge under her fringe of green hair.

"I don't want to kill you. I just need more time. Let me into the system. Please! Just for a second. That's all I need!"

"I can't do that until I'm done with the investigation," Dena said. "What am I going to find?"

"Nothing! Stop looking, please! Go away! I just want you to go away!"

"You're greedy, Caitako," Dena said, moving inexorably toward her. "You wanted to take your work to market first. It wouldn't last long, but it would be a big psychological moment. Art caught you."

"It was my work!" Caitako shouted, pounding her own chest with a forefinger.

"But you signed a noncompete clause, Caitako."

"It's so unfair!" the programmer wailed.

"Go forward," K't'ank urged her.

Dena felt an uprush of wind and halted, quivering. An endless cliff lay before her.

"I'm on the edge!" she cried.

"Not so," K't'ank said calmly. "An air fountain is beside you. Solid stones. Four steps there, jump to the left for more solids. Jump farther!"

"You try jumping with a growing baby and a petulant alien throwing off your balance," Dena snarled.

Keeping the moving green blob that was Caitako in her peripheral vision, she tried not to believe in what her eyes told her was ahead of her. K't'ank guided her, even berating her impatiently when she hesitated.

"Why do you wait?" he demanded. "Move! Nothing is there!"

"Do you know how annoying you are?" Dena asked, stung into hopping forward over a pit of crabs snapping their claws. An immense thorn bush blocked her way. But to either side, massive squids waved threatening tentacles.

"Is that a rhetorical question?" K't'ank asked.

"Yes!"

"Step right and go forward again. Go!"

The thorn bush that Dena was certain existed kept its shape in her eyes even as she ran through it. Her mind played tricks on her, convincing her she felt the pull of the sharp talons in her skin. She winced. She feared for her life, for that of her unborn child, and for K't'ank, not necessarily in that order, but she had a job to do.

"Police! Put the computer down!"

Instead, Caitako jumped up and ran for the access tower. Dena ran to intercept her, wondering when the police chopper was going to arrive. Caitako made to the left for the miniature arena. Dena followed, through the images of moving vines, snapping jaws, and boiling vats of acid. It felt like being in the middle of a giant computer game. Caitako was getting away!

"Tell me what's real!"

"Nothing!" K't'ank insisted. "It is all thin air."

"Good. That I can handle."

Dena plunged forward, running between the raked rows of seats. Caitako headed toward a darkened archway at the far end. With her unwieldy center of gravity, Dena wasn't sure she could catch her before she vanished. She grabbed up one of the T-shirt cannons in the stands. Following the green blob through the waves of illusion fuzzing her vision, she fired.

The green blob dropped. Dena heard the clatter of the laptop hitting the ground, and the crackle of shattered circuitry. The nightmares cleared away, leaving the arena empty and one dishonest programmer a boneless heap on the ground, a pile of white T-shirts scattered over her. Dust covered the entire rooftop suddenly as the police chopper lowered onto the playing field. An officer swung out and took Caitako into custody. Dena breathed a deep sigh and sank onto the nearest seat.

"Thanks, K't'ank," Dena said.

"Come, we are partners," K't'ank said. "And if you were to die, I would have to find another host."

Dena groaned.

"Thanks a million for your boundless sympathy."

"It is my pleasure," K't'ank said, as usual missing her sarcasm.

"May I give the press briefing this time? It was my insight that caused us to solve the crime."

"Not a chance," Dena said, rubbing her eyes. "But I will let you make a statement afterwards. First, though, I want to get these lenses out. They're killing me!"

"Almost," K't'ank said. "But not quite."

Jody Lynn Nye

Best-selling science fiction and fantasy author Jody Lynn Nye describes her main career activity as "spoiling cats." When not engaged upon this worthy enterprise, she has published over forty books and novels, largely humorous, some in collaboration with noted writers in the field, such as Anne McCaffrey and Robert Asprin, and over 110 short stories. Her latest books are *Myth-Quoted*, nineteenth in Asprin's Myth-Adventures series; and *View from the Imperium*, a sort of Jeeves and Wooster in space.

THE HAUNTED BLENDER

BY K.G. JEWELL

On Thursday, I inherited my grandfather's haunted blender. He'd tried to make the perfect basilisk omelet, insisting on gathering his own eggs, and ended up stoned.

And not in a legal-in-Colorado kind of way.

On Friday, I made gazpacho in his memory. Or, I tried to, but the moment I pushed *puree*, all hell broke loose.

It was a minor hell, so reality wasn't torn asunder, but it made an unreal mess of my kitchen. Ectoplasm splattered across my countertops, and the disposal burped bubbles of sin. This mess wasn't something I could clean up myself.

I called my girlfriend, Lisa. A fortuneteller by trade, she knew people that dealt with this kind of stuff.

"Try *Glip's Exorcism and Dusting*. I've heard good things," Lisa said, rattling off a phone number. I jotted it down on the fridge, the numbers burning into the whiteboard with an acrid hiss. "Also, Mother and I are going to the cabin tonight to finish reading our books."

"What are you reading?" I asked, sulfuric smoke from the charring whiteboard burning my throat.

"Ted, Sunday is book club. You're hosting, remember?"

The book club. Right. Lisa's mom's book club was reading *About a Boy*, and wanted to discuss it in the home of an authentic bachelor. Lisa had volunteered my kitchen. My now-hellish kitchen.

I eyed my microwave. The window showed a looping clip from *Three's Company*. Every thirty seconds Jack Ritter's hand got caught in a toaster, and every time it happened my toaster giggled.

"Right. No problem." Well, my kitchen was a problem, but hopefully Glip would take care of it.

"Also, save some gazpacho for us. It's Mother's favorite."

"Mmmm." I hoped the sound was non-committal.

"Oh! It's my turn to suggest a book for next month. Have any ideas?"

"Nothing comes to mind." I'd just finished *Never Grow Up: Child Athletes Past Their Prime*, but that was more therapy, less entertainment.

"Well, if you think of anything, let me know. Love ya." She hung up.

I called Glip, the numbers on the fridge bursting into flame as I dialed. He picked up on the first ring.

"Ted! Lisa said you were going to call." Dating a fortuneteller has its upsides. "She warned me to charge for unexpected extra-dimensional complications." It also has its downsides.

"How quickly can you come over?" I asked, watching the disposal burp a purplish bubble with a striking red shimmer. Looked fairly carnal.

"I'll be over in the morning."

I ate dinner out.

GLIP TURNED OUT to be a wizened little old man carrying a leather satchel half as big as he was. When I opened the door, he stepped past me, sniffing the air.

"Gazpacho? You didn't mention gazpacho."

Apparently, neither had Lisa.

"Can you fix it?" I asked.

Glip ran his finger along my mantel, right below my second-place trophy from the 2002 Little League World championships—or, as my mom called it, my loser's place trophy.

Glip examined his finger in the light at the window. He frowned. "Gazpacho is a problem you have to fix yourself—I can just tell you what you are in for."

I didn't like the sound of that. I prefer to delegate my extra-dimensional complications. "What am I in for?"

Glip went back to the kitchen, setting his satchel on the table. From its depths he unpacked a half-dozen pots, a dozen unlit candles, and a red snakeskin purse. From it he withdrew a magic eight ball.

"Reply hazy, try again," Glip read. He settled into a kitchen table chair. "What makes the blender special?"

"My grandfather always said it was haunted by the ghost of tomato paste." I retrieved the olive-green blender from the counter where it still sat, full of crushed tomatoes and a mysterious mauve slime, and set it in front of Glip. A piece of masking tape stuck to the back read, FOR TED. "But I checked the wiki-daemonum before I started, and tomato paste spirits are benign and non-influential on this plane of existence."

Glip traced a symbol around the blender's base, then retrieved a mozzarella stick from the snakeskin purse and waved it over the blender jar. The cheese turned into a mouse and scurried away. Glip shook his head. "Tomatoes *past*. It's haunted by the ghost of tomatoes past, not tomato paste. One's benign and non-influential. The other is soul-devouring and poltergeistic."

Glip repacked his satchel. "I'll be back tomorrow. You make gazpacho." He pointed a candle at me. "The ghost is upset, and if I clean this before you work things out, you'll be calling me in half-an-hour with some new manifestation. You need to make gazpacho again, but this time make it right." Then he left, leaving a fifty-dollar invoice for "consultation."

I waved goodbye. I couldn't afford to hire him, but my faucet had just started to sing the theme song to *Different Strokes*, and the book club was coming in twenty-four hours. I couldn't afford not to hire him—Lisa's mother was excited about the event, and Lisa was close to her mother.

When I'd made the offending gazpacho, I'd worked off my mother's recipe, a terse note typed on a three-by-five card filed in a grey metal recipe box sent with me to 2009 spring training. I'd been cut from the team, but kept the recipes.

Her note read:

```
(Tomatoes + Bread + Onions + Cucumbers) *
Blender + Oil + Vinegar = Gazpacho
```

My mother was a left-brain thinker.

The blender came from my grandfather on my father's side, so maybe that side of the family's recipe held the solution. I dug out my father's cookbook, which had fallen behind the spice rack and smelled of turmeric. Originally a sketchpad, the book was bound with rough hemp ties, each recipe hand-written and illustrated with a flowing fountain pen. The gazpacho recipe was inscribed in the spiraling petals of a sunflower, the ingredients listed on its leaves.

Fadai Special Gazpacho
Start with tomatoes sliced from the vine with a silver scythe by a full moon. Add bread, baked on the glowing coals of a resurrecting phoenix. Mix in garlic crushed by the weight of humanity. Add onions chopped without tears. Blend. Add diced cucumbers. Add equal parts olive oil, infused with sighs of despair, and vinegar born of sour love. Chill on ice, then enjoy.

My father was a right-brain thinker.

The Haunted Blender

THE GARLIC, OLIVE OIL, and vinegar I found on Craigslist. It wasn't difficult—there is enough crushing humanity, despair, and sour love on the Internet to go around. The onions and cucumbers I got at Safeway. The bread, available via the Firebird-o-rama phone app, materialized the instant I clicked *buy*.

But the tomatoes required legwork. The celestial bodies were aligned—tonight was a full moon—but I didn't have a tomato hookup.

The farmer's market around the corner from my house was famed for its authentic ingredients. I generally avoided the scene, as my life was authentic enough already, but it was my best lead.

The market was well under way when I arrived, a crowd packed along the thirty-odd tables lining the platform of an old railway depot. A light drizzle kept the crowd under the platform's canopy.

A drooling undead attendant manned (zombied?) the first booth, selling organic compost labeled PERFUME FOR THE PREVIOUSLY-ALIVE. I passed up the opportunity, stepping around a young woman pushing a stroller. I pretended not to notice that the child in the stroller strongly resembled a kobold; parents don't appreciate when you point out things like that.

The second booth sold raw cheese and pickup lines. "Free sample?" asked the young cheesemonger. He wore a black turtleneck and a matching scowl.

"No thanks. I like my lines pasteurized," I said, elbowing past a teenager dumping change onto the table.

The third booth held more promise. Traditional vegetables lined the table; broccoli, carrots, brussels sprouts, and a whole basket of tomatoes. A note beside the tomatoes read CERTIFIED HUMANLY RAISED AND HANDLED. A woman in overalls sat in a rocking chair, chewing on a piece of straw and trying a little too hard to be authentic.

Maybe the book club could invite her to read *Catcher in the Rye*—a genuine phony.

"Can you get me tomatoes harvested with a silver scythe by a full moon?" I asked.

She pulled the straw from her mouth and twirled it, her eyes narrowing. "You don't seem like a silver scythe kind of guy."

"It's what I'm looking for," I said, miffed at her stereotyping. My flannel shirt and jeans were nondescript and timeless.

She chewed on her straw, then nodded. "Well, if you're into that stuff, I know some folks who'd love to fix you up."

She scrawled something on a scrap of cardboard. "Meet me at this address at sundown. Bring fifty bucks and your own silver scythe."

"Thanks." This gazpacho was getting expensive.

I BORROWED a silver scythe from a friend of a friend, whose daughter had been the Grim Reaper in a school play.

"Silver-plated," the friend of a friend clarified.

"Close enough," I said, hoping I was right.

The address led me to an abandoned lot squeezed between a car wash and a YummiMart. A spray-painted sign read URBAN FARM AND SPIRITUAL CENTER. A couple-dozen scraggly tomato plants grew in lines scratched in the dirt.

My new farmer friend pulled up in a pickup truck about an hour after sundown. She rolled down her window to take my cash and wave at the plants. "All yours," she said as she drove off.

The moon came up. I sliced free a tomato.

Something soft hit the side of my head. "Murderer!" screamed a voice. I turned, and another projectile squished into my forehead. My vision turned red.

"Get him!"

I ducked behind a tomato cage. Someone was throwing rotten tomatoes at me. I peeked. It wasn't someone, it was a crowd of someones, dressed in flowing silver robes and sandals, bearing signs reading PETANQUE STANDS WITH THE OPPRESSED.

I raised my hands. "Wait!"

The incoming tomatoes stopped. I stepped out from behind the cage, hands in the air.

"I think there's been a mix-up. Who are you?"

A silver-robed man stepped forward from the mob. His bald head gleamed in the moonlight. "We are the People for the Ethical Treatment of Animals, Nightshades, Quetzalcoatl, the Undead, and Elephants. We have witnessed your despicable act."

"I picked a tomato? So?"

The crowd booed, surging forward and surrounding me.

"Tomatoes are the most glorious of the nightshades. They are not for humans to torture and murder for entertainment," their ringleader said.

"Wait. You're throwing tomatoes at me because I was picking tomatoes?"

"These tomatoes, picked humanely, are giving their lives for the cause," he said, gesturing at his basket.

"Willingly?"

He turned and waved me off, saying, "Harvest him."

Hands grabbed me from behind. I struggled, but my head was wrapped in a towel smelling of camphor, and everything went black.

WET SANDPAPER rubbed my cheek. I opened my eyes to a black cat licking my face. I struggled to sit up. The moon hung lower in the sky, illuminating a small, grassy park. I didn't recognize the neighborhood. A figure, shrouded in dark red, stood behind the cat.

"Are you prepared to play for your fate?"

"Huh?" I scrambled to my feet. "What?"

"You have been delivered for judgment." The figure opened its palm, revealing a small silver glowing ball. It threw the ball some ten yards into the grass. "We now play petanque for your soul." Another ball, tomato-sized and glowing red, followed the silver one. The red ball fell a foot from the silver.

A small silver circle appeared around the figure's feet, and the figure stepped outside of it.

"Your throw."

Still a little lightheaded from the towel's fumes, I stepped into the circle. Three green balls sat beside two red ones.

"I'm supposed to toss my ball as close to the silver one as I can, right?" A coterie of old men played petanque, a lawn-bowling game, in front of the railroad depot on Sunday mornings, espressos in hand. Lisa had once asked if she could take a picture of their bocce balls, resulting in an brief education in French swear words and a lecture on the trivial, but apparently vitally important, differences between bocce and petanque.

"One should always strive to be close to the truth."

Was this game getting metaphorical? That's why I avoided literature in favor of targeted self-help. Too much metaphor is bad for one's health.

I picked up and hefted a heavier-than-expected green ball. I lobbed it, overshooting the target by at least two yards. The cat, sitting beside the figure, licked its paws.

"Throw again."

My next shot, an improvement, dropped beside the red ball and a nose closer to the target. I stepped out of the circle. Maybe I'd get out of this in one piece.

"Who are you?" I asked, as the figure stepped into the circle to throw.

"I am the ghost of tomatoes past. The time has come to end your family's careless blending of my nightshade brethren."

The phrase "soul-devouring and poltergeistic" echoed in my mind. What had my gazpacho gotten me into? The second red ball dropped behind the first. My second ball was still a nose ahead.

Then the third red ball dropped, chipping my lead off into a bush.

The cat purred. I shivered.

"I don't suppose I can cut a deal with you?"

"The time for deals is past."

I hefted the last green ball. I could do this. I imagined I was re-pitching the final inning of the Little League series, only this time Mom wasn't signaling me to walk the guy. I could do it my way. I threw my best fastball. The ball hit the target, knocking it up in the air. Clunk. The target ball fell against the green ball from my first throw.

"How about now?"

I WAS ALLOWED to go home. When I got there, I made gazpacho, my gazpacho, not my mother's, not my father's. I made it with beets. I didn't need nightshade oppression in my life. The soup came out great, although a little purple.

With my blender appeased, Glip cleaned the kitchen in no time flat. He finished just as the book club arrived. Glip stuck around, contributing unexpected literary insights. The book club was a success. Lisa gave me a smooch. Her mom asked for my recipe.

Next month the book club is reading *Fried Green Tomatoes*. I suggested they do it at Glip's house.

Story Notes:

The opening line of "The Haunted Blender" came to mind while I was watching a band my partner said reminded her of "Smelly Cat" from the TV show Friends. I'd thank them for the inspiration, but they might not appreciate the publicity. From that line grew the further adventures of the character introduced in "The Day the Repossessed my Zombies," my story in the first *Unidentified Funny Objects* anthology.

K.G. Jewell

lives and writes in Austin, Texas. He has never lost a cage match. His website, which is rarely updated, is lit.kgjewell.com.

THE RETGUN

by Tim Pratt

If you find yourself squatting over a pit toilet while wearing stiletto heels, you've made a few bad choices at some point during the evening. I could have taken off my shoes, but then I'd be barefoot, in the woods, in the half-light of a lantern dangling from a tree branch, standing in whatever you can expect to find on the ground around an artisanal hand-excavated poop hole.

Apparently there was a fashion for high-and-low cultural juxtapositions in this particular dimensional node, hence a full fancy-dress party being held in and around a homemade earth-and-sod house lit only by torches. The hors d'oeuvres were processed cheese foam sprayed on mass-produced crackers, served on silver platters passed around by leggy supermodels dressed in hair shirts and stinking rags, plus prune-wine brewed in a ramshackle still and passed around in crystal goblets. Let me tell you something: prune wine goes right through you, so I didn't even have to pretend I needed to use the facilities when the time came to get in position.

The pit toilet was well back in the woods, some distance

behind the sod house, but it nevertheless came equipped with a scrupulously polite bathroom attendant—he was standing on the lowest branch of a nearby tree—dressed in a green velvet tuxedo and prepared to offer towels, breath mints, and cocaine on demand. Interdimensional travel is often way more boring than you'd expect, but this was not one of the boring times.

Earlier, when I was mingling among the partygoers—the worst human beings this node had to offer—a guy wearing a moth mask had lunged over to me drunkenly, tried to touch my cheek and slurred, "Your skin...so beautiful...like porcelain..."

I'd knocked his hand aside and said, "My skin is like the stuff toilets are made out of?" Proving that I'd had a way overly optimistic idea about the quality of the local toilets.

My business done, I scuttled away from the pit, tugged my rather ephemeral underwear back up around my hips, and pushed down my iridescent black dress, wondering how long I could plausibly pretend to be adjusting my garments before the attendant got suspicious about my loitering. Then I heard the sound of a human badly imitating an owl, which was both a good and a lousy signal to use in this node, since owls had been hunted to extinction here in a weird sports-and-dining craze some years earlier.

I reached into my purse for a can of aerosolized knock-out gas and sprayed it into the toilet attendant's face. He fell over, spilling cocaine and mints everywhere. Before I could blow out the lantern, a man wearing a skintight rubber outfit that covered his entire body except his crotch and ass appeared from around a tree, coming to avail himself of the facilities, and I sprayed him, too. Luckily the nostril-holes, which were the only openings in his mask/hood combo, allowed sufficient airflow to knock him out, too. He fell upon the unconscious attendant in a way that formed a rather suggestive tableau, but I mean, how could he not?

Then I blew out the lantern, and my light-compensating contact lenses (acquired in a better universe than this one) kicked in, giving me creepy green night vision. I could clearly see my partner and our prisoner approaching through the trees. (Okay, *senior* partner, but I refuse to be called "sidekick" or "assistant" or "Gal Friday" or "padawan" or any of the other crap Kirtley tries on me).

Kirtley was presenting as female tonight, mostly, with blown-out blonde hair and significant bosoms, but with a little five o'clock shadow, too, just by way of fucking with the gender binary essentialists. Kirtley comes from a world where body modification is pretty much as common as dying your hair, and Kirtley claims not even to remember Kirtley's own original birth sex—if it even fell firmly to one side or the other—and always marks "Not Applicable" on forms that ask for gender, generally just prior to setting the forms on fire, because seriously, you think we go around filling out forms? (In case you're wondering, the only acceptable pronoun for Kirtley is "Kirtley" so get used to seeing that word. Kirtley Kirtley Kirtley.) Kirtley was frog-marching the party host, a brutal pink-haired warlord named Princess Stephanie, who'd dressed for tonight's celebration of conquest in a gown of shimmering green silk accented by a string of "pearls" carved from the bones of her vanquished foes. Stephanie was groggy, presumably drugged, but not so insensible that she couldn't carry her own weight, more or less.

"Portal, please," Kirtley said, and I tossed the marble into the pit toilet and counted "one-two-three."

The telltale "pop" of displaced air told me the portal was open, and when I looked into the pit I saw a shimmering blue horizon, thankfully *above* the level of the pool of pee-and-poop at the bottom of the hole. I jumped in, emerging in the wrong orientation and rolling through the tall grass as my momentum sorted itself out. I was followed a moment later by the jumbled tangle of Princess Stephanie's cattywampus limbs. Kirtley managed to sort of *sidle* through the portal and didn't even lose Kirtley's balance in the process. Annoying as hell, but Kirtley had been at the interdimensional-secret-agent thing a lot longer than I had. I'd get the knack of being smooth in all situations someday.

Kirtley reached through the portal and plucked the magic marble—which was neither magic nor a marble—then tossed it to me. I never understood how you could reach into another dimension and pull the doorway to that dimension *out*—it seemed like pulling a hole out of a hole—but whenever I demanded an explanation Kirtley just rolled Kirtley's eyes and said "Science."

Princess Stephanie groaned, and I pondered the array of movement-control techniques I had at my disposal, but there was no need: Kirtley was already pulling the retgun from its undimensional hiding place, drawing forth the long-barreled, absurd-looking weapon from its invisible holster in a fold of twisted space at Kirtley's hip. The basic shape of the retgun was consistent—grip, trigger, barrel two feet long—but everything else about it shimmered and shifted, from sci-fi ray gun to Old West shooting iron to steampunk cog-pistol to ritual sidearm of the Ballardian Bleakness Corp to model of a gun carved out of pale white soap. Princess Stephanie blinked up at Kirtley and said "Wha?" in a way that made me wonder how she'd managed to subjugate all those continents, but it'd probably been decades since she'd had to subjugate anything personally; once you reach a certain level, you've got people to do the subjugating for you.

"Boom," Kirtley said, and squeezed the trigger.

This time the retgun emitted a cloud of glitter and sparkles and confetti, hitting the princess full in the face. She sneezed, wiped sparkles out of her eyes, then stood up, groggily, and said, "Damn, I drank too much apple brandy last night. My husbands and wives are going to kill me." She gave us a little wave, said, "See you at the next hootenanny," and lurched off across the grass in the general direction of a sprawling farmhouse/compound on a hill. Already my memories of her horrible history of atrocities were starting to fade, replaced by memories of a drunk woman we'd met in a field. If we stayed in this node too long, her contagious backstory would infect my brain entirely, too, and I'd

forget all about her true history—though Kirtley was immune to having Kirtley's memories rewritten, as the one holding the gun.

"You give her a good life?" I asked. "Because she doesn't much deserve one."

Kirtley put away the retgun and snorted. "Yeah, I set the phaser to 'fun.' Nah, it's a fairly neutral bit of continuity. She's still Princess Stephanie deep down, no matter what she thinks her name and backstory are now, so she'll probably claw her way up to the position of First-Over-Wife in a few months, and from there to Head-of-Household, Island-Inclusive, but the damage she can do is pretty limited in this world. There are only about five thousand humans on this entire island, and the sea is full of 'monsters'—quasi-sentient area-denial weapons from a war centuries ago—so she won't be voyaging off to other continents and causing any trouble. Besides, a big group family will have plenty of infighting, backbiting, betrayals, alliances, lies, and scheming, so maybe that'll keep her occupied."

"Poor bastards." I looked up at the farmhouse and thought of them having to deal with the bomb dropped into their lives that was Princess Stephanie, and worse, having her wormed into their memories and personal histories like she'd been there all along.

"The good of the many outweighs the whatever." Kirtley spat, grinned, and said, "Let's roll on out of here."

I tossed the marble and opened a portal to our interdimensional spy/crime-fighter lair, because my life was just exactly that cool.

That was the last of the good old days. Just before the Prime Army came to screw everything up with the truth and its consequences.

THERE WAS A GUY sitting in Kirtley's chair right in front of the meta-map console, dressed in a suit of lightweight armor that was heavy on the chrome ornamental spikes, his face painted with red and black tiger-stripes. He flipped through an old-school cardboard folder in his lap for a moment after we popped through the portal, then glanced up at us like we were shifty salesmen interrupting his important spreadsheet bullshit or something.

"Mmm," he said. "There you are. I am a Profound Imperator of the Prime Army." He inclined his head toward me. "You are Consuela Inez Gonzalez, AKA 'The Gen To End All Gens,' correct?"

I glanced at Kirtley, who was frowning but not throwing slurry bombs or unleashing a brace of collapsible mecha-ferrets, and I decided to keep things civil instead of plucking any of the grape-sized hallucinogenic grenades from my purse. "I don't know who that Consuela person is, but yeah, I'm The Gen."

He made a mark in the folder, then glanced at my partner/mentor. "And you are . . . oh, I can't possibly read off all these aliases and pseudonyms and code names and call signs and noms de guerre. Save that for the trial transcript. What name are you using these days?"

"Kirtley," Kirtley said curtly. (Sorry, sorry. I promise not to do that sort of thing again.)

"Ah. We don't have that alias on file. Thank you. You know how the Prime Army values the completeness of its records."

"You should leave," Kirtley said, and took out the retgun. "Unless you want to be ... oh, how about our butler?"

"We could totally use a butler," I said. "I am really sick of having to do all the butling around here myself. I buttle my butt off." Kirtley says wordplay is the lowest form of humor and I say what the hell does Kirtley know and then I kick him in the shins.

The Profound Imperator looked around our totally sweet cave, lit by floodlights set at dramatic angles among the stalactites, the whole place stuffed with high-tech gear liberated from a thousand dimensions, and did a full lip-curling sneer. "This cluttered void doesn't need servants. It needs to be filled with concrete. It's a sinkhole waiting to happen. But that's moot. The two of you are now in the custody of the Prime Army, answering for crimes that include—"

"You have no authority here," Kirtley said.

"Wherever I go, I carry the full authority of the Prime Army. Which is actual authority, backed by actual force, unlike your own. Now, please, allow me to read the charges—"

"Butler it is." Kirtley squeezed the trigger, and the retgun emitted a sound like a dinner bell ringing, and I waited for the memories to flood in, reminding me that this tiger-faced dude was our butler, had *always* been our butler, complete with colorful and plausible backstory about why he was dressed like such a moron, probably as some sort of penance or because he'd lost a profoundly ill-considered bet.

Instead the Profound Imperator just yawned, totally ostentatiously, complete with patting his mouth with the palm of his gauntleted hand and then stretching his arms over his head. "Please. The retgun's powers depend on displacement, Kirtley. You can't endow me with psychically contagious backstory —

unless there is a complete absence of contradictory information in the local node. In any informational conflict, the facts as they exist in reality will always win out over your feeble attempt to retroactively weave me into the local continuity. And since this world is *filled* with records about me, and populated by scores of my inferiors and servants and subjects and employees and helpmeets and slaves and assistants, who all have very clear memories about me, your feeble attempt to press-gang me into your pathetic ego circus is pointless."

Kirtley didn't freak out or anything, but the impenetrable façade cracked a little. The retgun disappeared back into its invisible holster. "We've only been gone for two *days*," Kirtley said. "You can't possibly have that much infrastructure in place here already—"

"When the Prime Army decides to occupy a node, we don't delay. This world is rich in timber, fossil fuels, and delicious megafauna. I haven't been able to get mammoth steaks in the capital for *weeks*. And with no noticeably sentient land-dwellers to oppose our arrival? It's low-hanging fruit. That this node happened to contain your hideaway was merely a happy accident." The Professional Impenetrator stood up, and I stepped back, because that guy was at least seven feet tall. "A word of advice, 'Kirtley.' If you're ever a wanted fugitive in the future, you might try hiding in a world with some *other* sentient creatures and technological artifacts? The energy signature of your little bat-cave here was visible on our first cursory scan. You'd have been better off hiding in the sewers beneath a teeming metropolis."

"Run," Kirtley said, and *then* Kirtley hurled the mecha-ferrets and triggered the sonic screamers in the heels of Kirtley's boots and activated the collapsible ceiling and the biometric conditional trapdoors and called down the cyber-bats from their hidden ceiling holes and launched the remote flashbang flares and all that other stuff. It was like an earthquake in a blender in an ambulance with a shrieking siren in a volcano at a rabies-infested petting zoo and we ran like hell and hit the escape chutes (I'd always hated polishing the slides, because I never saw the point, but here we were, Kirtley's bullcrap validated once again).

We landed on the spongy bed of moss outside at the base of the slide and found ourselves surrounded by a full metric cohort of the Prime Army, complete with bioengineered venomous weevil-tanks and weaponized ice-lizards and, of course, a whole lot of guys in goofy armor with very practical-looking guns.

"Don't listen to anything they tell you," Kirtley said as they shackled us, taking away my purse, the jerks. I had some gum in there, and also explosives.

"Right," I said. "The Prime Army are a bunch of treacherous liars."

"Well, no," Kirtley said. "They'll probably tell you the truth. They don't usually bother to lie. Which is why I'd really rather you didn't listen."

KIRTLEY IS A FIELD OPERATIVE for the Sublime Union of Ethical Anarchy and Sustainable Hedonism (SUE-ASH), a non-hierarchical Em-Banksian collective of augmented supergeniuses who live in a heavily-shielded node that's all smart matter and Dyson spheres and Ringworlds and Leafworlds and computronium and sentient stars and uplifted intelligences, where the cockroaches are as smart as third graders and the third graders are as smart as weakly godlike Rosenbaumian AIs, and the AIs look like kinetic sculptures and take care of all practical matters with a cheerfully whimsical nonchalance, all while inventing new sexual board games in their spare time. After the cool vast impish intellects there discovered the principles behind the Seagroves-Raschke exotic matter bridge and learned how to travel to parallel universes, they decided to spread their ethos of personal freedom and really good designer drugs and beating up fascists (because you can beat up fascists without feeling guilty about it) across the known multiverse. Kirtley found me in a particular shithole of a dimension where malevolent clockwork robots ruled the few remnants of the human race—Kirtley was in full tough-guy-boy-drag then, helping to lead the rebels, pretending to be a refugee from the faraway Garbage Archipelago, and Kirtley saw something in me. (What Kirtley saw was that I'm awesome. I could make improvised explosive devices out of the guts of active clockwork soldiers *without them even realizing it*. Okay, that's an exaggeration, but I was a fine blower-up-er of things.) After we reduced the clockwork men to cogs and gears and rubble, Kirtley showed me the marble and asked if I'd like to join Kirtley in making life miserable for assholes across the multiverse. The alternative was to help found a new democratic government and rebuild the wreckage of a world that had been altered to fit the whims of insane military automatons, and I've never been a big fan of cleaning things up, so I told Kirtley I was in.

"That is all complete nonsense," the Profound Imperator said, rolling his eyes at me across the interrogation table. "Fabrication, confabulation, and outright lies."

"What do you know about it, Professor Imp?" I wasn't shackled or anything anymore, but they'd taken the pointy chopsticks out of my hair, and my spiked heels, and my hollow ring with the needle full of knockout drops, because I could use them as weapons, but it wasn't like I didn't have *other* weapons. "The Prime Army is the greatest enemy of SUE-ASH in the multiverse. Your entire government is a military dictatorship, the opposite of everything they stand for!"

"We are a meritocratic oligarchy, actually," he said. "But close enough. There's no such thing as SUE-ASH, though, is what I'm trying to tell you. Kirtley, as you call him, made the whole thing up. It's *imaginary*. An anarchist techno-utopia full of benevolent wisecracking AIs? They say anything that *can* exist *does* exist somewhere in the multiverse, but I haven't ever seen anything like *that*."

I stuck my fingers in my ears and said "LA LA LA LA LA" but the bastard waited me out. My attention span has never been that great so I unplugged my ears after a while. "Okay," I said at last. "Fill my mind with your poisonous lies."

He returned to his folder, though it was looking more like a prop than an essential font of information. "Kirtley was an assassin in the employ of the Prime Army, one of the commandos we sent into technologically-advanced nodes in order to soften up resistance with a few targeted executions. Kirtley was consistently one of our most dependable and efficient operatives, at least until he had a crisis of conscience. He continued performing sadistic renditions acceptably for a couple of years into that crisis—we began to monitor him closely when his psychological evaluations showed spikes in the empathy area—but the zeal was gone. He continued out of momentum or laziness or lack of imagination, I suppose. Then the S/R bridge he was using on an assignment glitched—it happens sometimes—and sent him into an unsurveyed universe, specifically into the ruins of some kind of alien colony from the vastness of deep time, where he discovered the psychic manipulator you call the 'rotgun'—"

"Rotgun? It's the retgun. The retcon gun. The retroactive continuity gun."

"Oh," he said, and made another note in his folder. "I assumed, because it rots minds, sort of—never mind. Your way makes more sense. We've had to piece all this together from secondhand accounts and spotty surveillance, you understand. At any rate, once he acquired the retgun he began *relocating* his targets instead of killing them."

This was some pretty world-shaking stuff as far as accusations go—we weren't operatives of a secret utopian spy organization, Kirtley was a killer, what the eff—so I focused on the shreds of good news I could find. "I bet that drove you psychopaths crazy, Kirtley letting people live instead of slaughtering them as a warning to your enemies."

"We're pragmatic." He shrugged. "Once we realized what Kirtley was doing, we stopped assigning him the people we wanted gruesomely murdered as grim tokens of our unspeakable power, and started sending him after people we just wanted removed, by whatever means. He was still a good asset, for a long time, in that capacity. And then... he met *you*."

"You keep saying 'he,' but Kirtley's not a he, Kirtley's a *Kirtley*."

"That's true," the Profound Imp said. "He comes from the planet Varley Eight, in the Russ node, and they outgrew gender binaries centuries before the Prime Army took over. Our organization is very progressive about social issues that don't negatively impact our bottom line, and so we accept the fluid continuum of gender expression. I just say 'he' because I'm lazy and because it annoys you."

"Oh, well, as long as *that's* the reason. So Kirtley changed after meeting me, huh? Kirtley always said I had a good effect on Kirtley—"

"You certainly had *some* kind of effect. After he took you under his wing, he became an anarchist. Pried our surgical trackers out of his muscles, fried his blood-borne homing nanites with Vancean radiation from a dying sun, stole heaps of equipment, and did his best to vanish. And you know, we might have let him go, if he'd simply sauntered off to some unoccupied part of the multiverse to play house with you—the Prime Army is not vindictive, at least not when being vindictive has a poor cost-benefit ratio. But then Kirtley started kidnapping and relocating and retconning people we *collaborated* with, those useful traitors who help prepare the way for our arrival by turning over control of their cities and governments to us peacefully, removing the necessity to waste ammunition or destroy the resources we wanted to pillage in the first place—"

"Like Princess Stephanie."

He winced. "You took out Princess Stephanie? That... will not improve your chances at trial. Things were in a very delicate stage with her node."

I shrugged. "So Kirtley embroidered the truth a little when

he recruited me." (I was still holding out hope that there really *was* a SUE-ASH, an awesome super-science collective kept secret from the Prime Army, with Kirtley as some kind of tricky double-agent, but deep in my brain and somewhat deeper in my heart I suspected it was all bullshit.) "Kirtley's still on the side of right and life and joy and chaos, and we'll keep fighting until—"

"Don't you even want to know who you *used* to be?" he interrupted. "Before Kirtley kidnapped you away to a foreign node and fired the retgun at you and made you believe you were 'The Gen,' sassy superheroine and platonic sidekick?"

"Not especially," I said, because the very idea of the retgun being used on *me* opened up a spiraling howling void of profound discomfort at the center of my everything. I'd never even considered that my history might not be my own. If there's one thing I've never lacked it's self-assurance.

He shrugged. "Fine. Please yourself—I suspect you always do. All we really want, at this point, is to stop Kirtley from wandering around causing trouble—and of course we want the retgun, and the spatial-distortion technology Kirtley *also* found on that alien base. He made sure to blow it up on his way out, so all we recovered were non-working fragments of wrecked garbage."

"You don't have the retgun?" I laughed. "Because you can't find the holster, of course. Because you don't have Kirtley's pocket-dimension/bag-of-holding technology. Oh, man, that's hilarious. Kirtley will never give up the gun."

"Oh, we think he will. He clearly has a weakness for you, so we'll exploit that weakness. We'll scoop out one of your eyes and slice off your ears in front of him, and from *there*—"

Well, fuck that noise, am I right? I reached into my own pocket-dimension access hatch, an invisible fist-sized square of nothing at my waist, and pulled something silver-shiny and lethally elegant out. The Pronounced Emptier started to shout, but come on, like I haven't practiced this quick-draw shit in a million mirrors a billion times? I fired.

My gun wasn't a retgun. Kirtley gets the retgun. My gun was

a regular pistol, filled with blanks. But the blanks were tipped with short-term exotic matter bridge generators, keyed to specific useful universes—like miniature marbles, but they burn out after one use. I'm pretty sure the bridge I hit the Profound Imperator with took him to a world where even the grass is carnivorous. Kind of mean, but it can't be all jellybeans and rainbows, even when you work for the non-existent secret service of an imaginary utopian/anarchic society.

I twiddled with the spatial field generator at my waist—the controls were invisible, just like the folded space it generates, but you learn to do things by touch—and stepped through an undimensional portal into a ten-by-ten room that's pretty inexplicably walled in fake wood paneling, with water-spotted acoustic tile on the ceiling and a shag rug that looks like it's been chewed by goats on the floor. As always, the place gave me the major-major creeps, because it was impossible not to think about what was *beyond* the walls, which was probably nothing. Not even empty space. And yet, sometimes, there was this horrible low-pitched *buzzing*, and things tapping on the walls from outside . . . There was a reason we didn't use the inside of our bag(s) of holding as our lair.

In addition to heaps of miscellaneous crap in boxes, the marble and the retgun were there, hovering docilely in mid-air next to what looked sort of like the mouth of a ventilation shaft high up on the far wall, identical to the shaft on the other side, which I'd arrived through. I reached my hand through the far shaft and poked Kirtley hard in the gut. I heard him grunt. "You alone?" I said.

Another grunt, but it seemed pretty affirmative to me, so why not. I twiddled with the field generator and the ventilation shaft expanded to a me-sized rectangle, and I stepped through.

Kirtley's holding cell was way scarier than mine, with gore-encrusted hooks on chains dangling from the ceiling and a tray covered in rusty tools and a cage full of mechanically-augmented rats with drillbit teeth. Kirtley was tied to a chair, with pretty limited mobility, which maybe explained why Kirtley hadn't just snatched the marble from the bag of holding and jackrabbited off to an entirely other universe. Or maybe Kirtley didn't want to leave me. Who knows?

Kirtley was bleeding from the nose and lip and one of Kirtley's eyes was getting a pretty good bruise around it, but I didn't let Kirtley's sorry-looking state sway me from my irritation.

"Kirtley," I said curtly (sorry, I did it again, I can't help myself, last time, I promise), "You are a lying sack of crap and you overwrote my brain with some fake backstory about clockwork tyrants and I don't even know why I should let you out of here."

"All those things are true," Kirtley said. "But in my defense, my mission was to *murder* you, so overwriting your brain was actually the more merciful approach."

"Just tell me you made me someone *more* awesome when you zapped me?"

"You are intrinsically just exactly as awesome as you are," Kirtley said. "But I gave you a backstory that made for a way better story than the one boring reality wrote for you."

"So who was I, really? Do I even want to know?"

"You were someone the Prime Army wanted dead. So that speaks pretty highly of your character."

That much, I knew. I tested a question in my mind and decided to let it out: "Did I leave much behind? I mean … did I have a family?"

Kirtley looked away. "Ah. Not. Ah. Not after the other agents of the Prime Army were done with them. No."

I shook my head and began to untie Kirtley. "You didn't have the right to do that. To take my memories away."

"In my further defense, you *asked* me to. I rescued you from the purge, and you were pretty broken up—you wanted to take revenge, but you didn't want to have night terrors and a black hole of grief at the center of your being. You asked if I could make you happy, and I said I couldn't make you anything other than what you were, essentially, but I could make your *circumstances* better, and see what kind of person you'd be in a different situation, one where you overcame tyrants and kicked ass instead of losing everything you loved. And it turns out: under all that you're a pretty happy person. And you made *me* a better person, too—"

"I would find those facts incredibly reassuring, Kirtley, if you hadn't demonstrated a giant history of *lying* to me all the time." I untied the last knot holding him, and he stood up, groaning. I reached into the folded space at his side and snatched out the retgun and the marble both. "I oughta zap *you* with this thing."

He nodded solemnly. "Believe me, it's crossed my mind to ask you to do that very thing. I wouldn't mind being a different person, sometimes. But I figured one of us should know what the hell is *actually* going on. I'm sorry I lied about us being secret agents, but it just seemed more cool than revealing that we're freelance vigilantes making it up as we go along. Plus, you argued with my missions less when you thought they were delivered from some wise AI central control."

"You've lost that trump card, Kirtles. I'll want a bit more input going forward."

"Okay. I propose our next plan is to get the hell out of here—"

"Agreed," I said. "Then maybe we'll steal a spaceship. Haven't done that in a while."

"A joyride could be just the thing to clear our heads—"

Light dawned. I get inspirations like dogs get ticks, and this was a good one. "Nope. I changed my mind. Scratch spaceship theft. We're going to go out into the multiverse and find a promising node, and then we're going to establish the Sublime Union of Ethical Anarchy and Sustainable Hedonism. For really reals. It doesn't look like anybody else is going to get around to founding it, and it's too good an idea *not* to make real."

"How do you propose we do that?"

I brandished the retgun. "We find a bunch of supergeniuses in the gulags of the Prime Army, exfiltrate them to a nice warm universe, and make them think they're *already* in the midst of founding the sublime empire."

"That's so crazy..." Kirtley began.

"That it just might work?"

"I was going to say, 'just so batshit crazy, really, full stop, that's all.' It's also kind of morally questionable, and I realize I'm an ex-assassin saying that, but still—I don't mind shooting the retgun at horrible people, but if you want to recruit *good* people, it seems a bit messed up to force them into a non-consensual continuity—"

"So we'll stick to evil scientists, then, and retcon in a heel-face-turn in their backstory, a nice little redemption arc, some motivation to change their ways. Or if they're too deep-down vindictive, we'll work in some good excuse to overthrow the Prime Army, some personal grudge they have to work out—that'll make them work harder."

"As far as plans go, I've heard more solid ones..."

"It's not as good as randomly kidnapping tyrants and getting captured by the Prime Army?"

"We weren't captured for *long*," Kirtley said defensively. "And it wasn't my *plan*."

"We need a bigger picture, Kirtley. At least, I do—all this time I thought I *had* one, that I was working toward a larger goal. If you don't want to join me, I've got the retgun right here, I could make you think you're joyfully settled down with Princess Stephanie's extended family, or make you a happy well-adjusted assassin in the Prime Army again, killing for God and country—"

Kirtley harrumphed. "The Prime Army doesn't believe in God, exactly. They worship the personification of the strong anthropic principle in His aspect as a great armored death beetle—"

"Pretend I am cocking the magical gun and pointing it at your non-magical face," I said.

"Okay! Okay. I'm in. Why not. Sustainable Hedonism. It's a noble goal to probably get murdered for."

"Good." I holstered the gun. "And from now on, you're the sidekick. I make the plans. This partnership is officially a Genocracy, starting this very moment. "

"Now, really, it would be a mistake to ignore my years of practical experience in espionage and survivalism and morally defensible murder—"

"Shut up, Kirtley," I said curtly, and Kirtley shut up. (Last time. Really.) I dropped the marble and we traveled into the hope of a better world.

Story Notes:

I wrote "The Retgun" as a sort of gonzo homage to the sprawling, weird science fiction I adore, and naturally sprinkled it with references to great writers—notably the late Jack Vance and Iain Banks, who could both be very funny in very different ways.

Tim Pratt

Tim Pratt's stories have appeared in *The Best American Short Stories, The Year's Best Fantasy, The Mammoth Book of Best New Horror,* and other nice places. He has won the Hugo Award for his short fiction, and has been a finalist for the World Fantasy, Sturgeon, Stoker, Mythopoeic, and Nebula Awards. His latest collection is *Antiquities and Tangibles and Other Stories*. He lives in Berkeley, California with his wife, writer Heather Shaw, and their son. For more, visit www.timpratt.org.

THE DIPLOMAT'S HOLIDAY

by Heather Lindsley

The Telvarian Diplomat dropped her bag on the marble floor and allowed the thud to complete its echoing roll through the hotel lobby before shouting, "Where the hell is the porter?"

Three days, she had. Three days to be rude. To be unreasonable. To shout and swear and...

The Diplomat smiled.

Not Smile 47-R, only a touch haughty, used to silence an insecure opponent. Not Smile 23-H, indicating mildest disbelief and thus an invitation to further argument. Not even Smile 6-A, slight and mysterious, the workhorse of any Transgalactic Diplomat's repertoire, an all-purpose concealer of ignorance, of irritation, of intention.

This was the infrequently used 108-C, a wide, wolfish grin. It revealed everything.

"I said," she bellowed—bellowed for the first time in nearly two years—"Where the hell is the porter?!"

Out of the corner of her eye, the Diplomat saw the concierge holding back a porter by the sleeve. She knew what he was waiting for. Her smile grew larger before twisting into a snarl.

"Porter!"

The concierge released the porter's sleeve, accurately judging the climax of the Diplomat's tantrum. The Diplomat would remember his expert attention when it was time to tip.

Tips came at the end of the stay, of course, when diplomacy was back at work. The hotel staff knew this, and waited through the storms of bad behavior. Stress has to go somewhere, they agreed, and Diplomats had very stressful jobs. The fate of the Transgalactic Empire balanced on their somberly clad shoulders, weighing them down as heavily as their elaborate ceremonial headdresses.

The porters took the bad behavior from the Diplomats, like they took their bags, and then passed it on themselves, to husbands and wives, children and pets, and, less frequently, to revolutionary activities. One porter swore that was the surest way to pass the oppressive weight back to the Diplomats, where, he insisted, it belonged.

Like the Diplomat, the hotel's revolutionary-minded porter was on holiday. The porter who stood before her glower actually enjoyed their visits. Vacationing Diplomats tended to be both promiscuous and lazy about finding partners, a boon to like-minded hotel staff.

"Finally," the Diplomat huffed. She disengaged herself from her massive horned hennin, pins and bolts thoughtlessly dropped to the floor. The headdress's bifurcation was reminiscent of the Kargelian forehead, the swaths of green waxsilk both a concession to the modesty of the Declor and an indication of power to the people of Antoc IX.

The Diplomat lifted the hennin and thrust it at the waiting porter. Soft, golden tresses snaked to the Diplomat's shoulders and down her back, then joined the hardware on the floor when she pushed off the wig and ran her hands through a mass of short-shorn ebony spikes.

She stretched her neck and eyed the porter while he staggered under the weight of the headdress in his arms.

"Amateur," she snorted over the crackle and rasp of her vertebrae, and he knew he would not be invited to her bed.

THE DIPLOMAT WAS PROUD of her calling. Like all Diplomats she'd been recruited as a child and spent decades in training before she was allowed to even attend a negotiation of any importance. In her first years she'd learned the habits of a dozen cultures, then learned to respond to them with hundreds of precisely catalogued maxillofacial expressions cross-referenced against their interpretation by as many species.

She'd graduated with honors to the language of bodies, spoken with limbs of varying numbers, colors, and articulations. Candidates who dropped out of the Institute at this stage went on to become the finest actors in the Empire. But the Diplomat had progressed to the next level. She not only spoke the language—she knew what to say.

She knew how to negotiate.

Diplomacy had saved the galaxy from the bloodsport of war and the inevitable conflicting needs and desires among and within cultures. The fact that it required absurd hats and near-constant reserve was a small price to pay.

The Diplomat routinely rescued entire planets from violent oblivion. Her performance was always flawless . . . until her last negotiation, when she made a small slip. She was just a bit too eager in the matter of a Serkhanthian mining site.

She needed a vacation.

Ten years ago such a mistake would have blown the negotiation and demoted her to Actor, but not now. Now she had a reputation.

The negotiator across the table noticed the mistake, the Diplomat was sure, but he hesitated, doubting that a Diplomat of such stature would make so obvious an error. It must be a trap, a gambit, he decided. He let it pass.

The Diplomat did not, of course, allow herself any of the catalogued smiles.

Casual alcohol was forbidden to a practicing Diplomat, and ceremonial alcohol secretly counteracted with a few drops of Ilarian Buzzkill. The Diplomat's next stop after examining her room was, therefore, the hotel bar.

She found several other vacationing Diplomats there already—she recognized them by their bad behavior and the bruises and scrapes they wore like the gray and purple ribbons of honor pinned to their ceremonial robes every other week of the year. Healing treatments would be applied when it was time to go back to work and not a moment before.

A woman wearing a Zartanish halter top and fierce expression 152-S blocked her path, obviously disinclined to move even if the Diplomat was inclined to ask her politely. The Diplomat made her way through with a quick exchange of bruises.

The shoulder check was a promising start, and the night was still young.

She saw another Diplomat at the bar and reflexively concealed her expression, then reasserted her freedom with a long, slow grinding of teeth. Only three months before he'd been on the opposite side of an exquisitely mannered and deeply vicious legislative exercise.

He obviously didn't want her to sit next to him, so she did.

He turned to her, his face alive with far more distaste than he'd revealed in seventy-nine hours of negotiation.

"Shouldn't you be sitting in the 'No Conscience' section?"

"I'll sit wherever I damn well please," she said. "It's a Free Autonomous Governance Zone."

"No thanks to you," he said.

"Bite me," she said.

So he did.

She pulled her arm back and lunged at him. "You son of a Lweghalese dogworm!"

They kept their hands around each other's throats as they knocked over barstools, spitting, gasping, clawing.

"Hey, you two!" the bartender called out as she sprayed them with Nitreian soda. "Get a room!"

So they did.

THEY FOUGHT OVER whose room it would be, because they both wanted the privilege of residing in the inevitable wreckage. He ended the debate in the corridor by throwing her over his shoulder. She bruised the hell out of his kidneys on the way.

"Knock it off," he said. "I need those to pee."

"I know," she said with another solid punch.

They swung like a twisting pendulum between fighting and sex, sex and fighting, until they exhausted themselves and came to rest on the mattress that at some point in the frenzied proceedings had been torn off the bed.

"That was great," she said, falling into his arms.

"You're amazing," he said, rolling on top of her.

"Can you? Again? So soon?" she said with undiplomatic surprise.

"Try to stop me," he said.

"Don't tell me what to do," she said.

They went another two rounds before she left him snoring gently through a swollen nose.

"I TRUST MADAM enjoyed her stay?"

The Diplomat smiled 93-Z: sincere, relaxed pleasure. She'd just come from the spa, where in addition to a last massage and a Prizian fleshmite exfoliation, she'd had a mani, a pedi, and a minor injury healing, mostly for the brawl she'd started in the bar the night before.

"Yes, thank you." She slid an envelope across the desk. "If you could make sure the staff on this list are credited with the amounts noted?"

"Of course. And if madam would care to review this list of damages . . ." The concierge passed the Diplomat a souvenir scroll.

"I see you've included the destruction of the Rytalian Singing Fountain, but there's no charge."

"Yes, madam. One of your colleagues insisted it come out of his deposit. He was most adamant."

"I'm sure he was."

She left the hotel refreshed, revitalized, and once again ready to carry the weight of her headdress and the Transgalactic Empire.

EIGHTEEN MONTHS LATER the Diplomat found herself opposite a familiar face at the negotiating table. They'd been called to resolve the renewal of hostilities between the Dlarmonic Trade Federation and a loose alliance of Xithanian rebels. He chose, in classic Xithanian style, to greet her with the slightly smarmy 87-L. The Diplomat created a moment of uncertainty with a fractional response delay followed by the mildly amused 12-B.

When he returned the puckish 49-M, she knew he was thinking fondly of his bruised kidneys.

And then they began negotiating in earnest.

Heather Lindsley

Heather Lindsley's stories appeared in *Asimov's, F&SF, Strange Horizons, Year's Best Science Fiction #12,* and the anthologies *Brave New Worlds* and *The Mad Scientist's Guide to World Domination.* She lives in London, but can still do her original Valley Girl accent if sufficiently motivated by the right beverage.

CONGRATULATIONS ON YOUR APOTHEOSIS

by Michelle Ann King

As a life coach, Abby Fowler strongly discouraged magical thinking. It was better for people to take responsibility for improving their lives, rather than wait and hope for supernatural assistance. Better, and a lot more reliable.

So Abby would never advise anyone to use a spell, even one that came with impeccable provenance and the crackle of real power in every square inch of the ancient parchment it was inscribed on. Even one that was purely for divination, nothing more than a harmless bit of information-gathering that might, say, help someone with preparing a five-year business plan for their coaching practice in order to apply for a bank loan. She would never advise it because she knew that kind of thing never ended well.

"So it's do as I say rather than do as I do, is it?" said the figure that appeared in her client chair between one blink and the next. "Hi. I'm Sharon, and I'll be your omniscient supernatural assistant today."

"Shit," Abby said. "I mean—" she cleared her throat. "I'm sorry. I think there's been a mistake."

Sharon leaned forward and peered at the spell sitting on the desk. "Paperwork looks in order to me."

"That?" Abby said. She slid the parchment under a client file. "I thought that was a recipe for moisturising cream."

Sharon rubbed her thumb over the ring in her lower lip. "You do know the meaning of the word omniscient, don't you?" She shook her head. "You, of all people, trying to get a sneak peek. Tut, tut."

A copy of Abby's book flew from the stack on the display stand and landed in Sharon's hand. She turned it over and read from the back cover. "Abby Fowler will teach you to stop worrying about the future and have faith in your ability to cope with whatever may happen."

Abby sighed. "Thank you, yes. I know the meaning of the word irony, too."

"Okay, let's crack on, then, shall we?" Sharon closed her eyes. "Joe Callaghan is going to ring up in a minute and ask if you can fit him in this afternoon. He's distraught because despite being genuinely good at his job and having doubled his efficiency using your time management techniques, he's been passed over for promotion again."

"Er—"

"He's starting to think it must be personal, that his boss resents him. And he's absolutely right, because subconsciously Joe reminds her of a cousin who used to piss in her bed when they were kids. So it honestly doesn't matter how good Joe is, it's never going to happen, and he'd be better off cutting his losses and getting another job." She leaned back in the chair. "How was that? Pretty good, right? You don't get that sort of granular detail with goat entrails and tarot cards."

In the outer office, the phone rang. A few seconds later, the door opened and Donna poked her head around it. "That was Joe Callaghan, Abby, he wants to know if—oh, sorry, I didn't realize you had a client with you. I'll tell him you're busy."

She withdrew, and Abby laid her hands flat on the desk. "I'm sorry, I really think this was a mistake."

"Don't you mean learning experience?" Sharon opened the book. "It says here—"

Abby pinched the bridge of her nose. "Right, yes. Absolutely. And what I have learned from this experience is that I should take my own advice. So let's just forget all about it. I release you from any obligation. You can go. Sorry for any inconvenience."

"No inconvenience, no obligation. I like having something to do." Sharon put her hands behind her head and grinned. "You have no idea how hard it can be, as an immortal, omnipotent being, to occupy your time after the first few billion millennia. Everything starts to get a bit samey, you know? Creation, destruction, wars, lovers, children, pets—" she paused and held up a finger. "You haven't got any pets, have you? I'll sort that out for you—every sentient being ought to have a pet of some kind. I've got just the thing, you'll love it. Anyway, where was I? Oh yeah, so all the big spectacle stuff starts to wear a bit thin after a while. That's why I thought I'd try a more intimate approach. Like I said, it's the granular detail that makes the difference." She looked around. "You could do with a bigger window in here, don't you think? Get a bit more light."

The left-hand wall of the office shimmered, faded and became glass. "Although it's a bit low to the ground. A higher elevation would be better. Hold on to something, we're going up."

Abby grabbed her desk as the building instantaneously gained thirty floors.

"Maybe a few more," Sharon said, and they shot up again. The wall behind Abby became glass, too.

Sharon pointed over her shoulder. "There. You can see the London Eye, now. See? Over there? That's much—"

"Stop," Abby said, her voice muffled as she clamped her palm over her mouth. She didn't turn around. "Stop."

"Okay, maybe that'll do for now, then." Sharon patted Abby's shoulder. "You take it easy for a bit, sort out poor old Joe Callaghan. I'll go and see what else needs doing."

"What? No," Abby said. "Wait, I don't—"

But Sharon was gone.

"Shit," Abby said, and let her head drop. After a while, she grabbed a packet of aspirin from her desk drawer and reached for her water glass. Between lifting it from the desk and putting it to her lips, the liquid turned red and the aroma of a full-bodied Shiraz caught in her nostrils. She put it down again, untouched.

She grabbed her jacket, told Donna she was taking the rest of the day off and went down in the newly-created elevator to the car park. Her Volvo wasn't where she'd left it. Instead, the space was taken up by a sleek Ferrari in a shade of purple that exactly matched Sharon's hair. When Abby opened her bag, she found the car keys inside.

She left the Ferrari where it was and took the bus home.

Where she found the car—or an exact replica—waiting in her driveway. It had a big white ribbon wrapped around it and tied in a bow.

"Shit," she said.

Paul opened the door while she was still standing on the step and staring at the car. He whistled. "I'm guessing you have an extremely grateful—and extremely rich—client?"

"It's a little misunderstanding," Abby said.

He grinned. "Well, do you reckon I can take that misunderstanding for a spin before you clear it up?"

"No," she said, and hustled him inside.

He went to the window and gave the car one last longing look, then turned around. "Okay, so do you——" he broke off. "Um, Abby? What's that?"

She looked up and saw him staring at her bag, which she'd dropped on the sofa. "What's what?"

"That," he said, pointing.

The bag made a chirping noise, then a small creature shot out and jumped into Abby's arms. She shrieked.

It was a bit smaller than a cat, with white fur and a flat face that had large eyes and pointed, oversized ears. It reminded her of a cross between an owl and something she'd seen in a Disney film once. That one had been blue, and possibly an alien.

"That's—wow," Paul said. "What is that?"

The creature settled into the crook of Abby's elbow and chirped happily, paws kneading the material of her coat. It waved its ears at Paul.

Abby swallowed hard. "Prototype," she said faintly. "One of my new clients, er, works for a toy firm. Research and development. She wanted me to test it."

Paul took a step forward and peered at it. "Really? My god, it's brilliant. My sister's kids would love one for Christmas. Are they expensive?"

"I don't think they've set a price yet," Abby said.

The creature began to sing in a high-pitched, trilling warble. "I'll just put it away for now," she said. "Maybe take the batteries out."

The creature gave her wide eyes and clamped its mouth shut. Abby carried it into the bedroom and shut the door behind her. "What the hell?" she said.

The creature flicked its ears, jumped out of her arms and onto the bed, where it grabbed the television remote.

Abby watched it channel surf for a while, before it decided on an episode of *Man v. Food* and settled back against the pillow. Adam Richman was attempting to eat a pizza that was twice the size of his head. The creature chittered approvingly.

"I need a drink," Abby said, and closed her eyes. When she opened them again, the creature was sticking a very long, very black tongue into a champagne flute and holding a second glass out to her. She caught a glimpse of small, sharp-looking teeth.

Abby hesitated, then took the glass and drained the contents in one go.

She sat on the bed and tentatively reached out a hand. The creature sniffed it, then rubbed its head against it.

"So," she said. "This is happening, then."

Abby's glass filled itself up. She emptied it again. "I just wanted to know if the bank were going to approve my loan, that was all. And now I've summoned a—what? A genie? A demon? A goddess?"

The creature grinned at her, tongue lolling over those tiny pointed teeth.

Abby lay down on the bed and put her hands over her face. The creature snuggled up next to her and licked her cheek affectionately.

IN THE MORNING, from the perspective of ten hours sleep and a slight hangover, the previous day felt like a strange, hallucinatory dream. This thought—disturbing and comforting in roughly equal measure—sustained Abby through her shower and the morning papers, while Paul made a pot of coffee and Belgian waffles with raspberries and mascarpone. Until her furry houseguest dropped from the ceiling fan, where it had apparently been roosting, onto her head.

"Oh, that's where it got to," Paul said, putting a plate of waffles in front of her. "I was wondering. You've got to get a couple for the kids, Abby. You'd get a discount, wouldn't you?"

The creature sniffed at her waffles, then picked up the plate, unhinged its jaw and tipped the whole lot inside. It swallowed, burped and beamed at her.

Paul came back with coffee. "Wow, someone's hungry. Want some more?"

"No, thanks," Abby said. "I should get going. There's someone I need to get hold of this morning. Urgently."

"Okay," he said, and dropped a kiss on the back of her neck. "I'll see you later."

The creature hopped off the table and came back with her bag, jacket, and the keys to the Ferrari. Then it climbed in the bag and looked at her expectantly.

"Right," she said, and headed outside.

She got in the car, which smelled of new leather and Sharon's perfume, and put her bag on the passenger seat. The creature poked its head up and held out Abby's iPhone. It was displaying her Reminders app, with a new entry at the bottom. It said *Go to supermarket and buy big pizzas for Cthulu.*

"Cthulu," Abby said. "Seriously? Your name is Cthulu?"

The creature waved its ears.

Abby sighed. "Fine," she said. "Fine."

She put her hands on the steering wheel but didn't start the car. Cthulu gave an inquiring chirp.

Abby scratched behind his ears for a while. "What am I supposed to do with this?" she said helplessly. "With her? I mean, if she can do all this—should I be trying to get her to, I don't know, eradicate hunger? Create world peace?"

Cthulu cocked his head, then opened up the Notes app on her phone. He typed, carefully and delicately with one black claw, *Control by omnipotent power = eradication of free will and individuality. Create puppets, not peace.*

"Right," Abby said. "Right."

She sighed, started the engine and drove to the office.

SHARON WAS WAITING in her consulting room, sprawled in one of the puffy armchairs with her booted feet swung over the side. The reception desk was empty.

"Where's Donna?" Abby said.

"I gave her the day off. Don't worry, you'll get the credit." Sharon shimmered, briefly changed into a mirror image of Abby, then shifted back again.

Abby sank onto her own chair. "Oh, God."

"Yes?" Sharon gave her an expectant look.

"You can't do this," Abby said.

"The facts of the case would beg to differ."

"I don't mean you can't, I mean you *can't*." Abby shook her head. "You have to stop."

"Why?"

"Because—because—control by omnipotent power means the eradication of individual will. We're human beings, not puppets."

Sharon shot a suspicious look at Cthulu, who was sitting on the desk and chewing on a paper clip. He spat it out and looked back with wide, innocent eyes.

"Sharon, please," Abby said. "I didn't want this. I'm sorry. I'm sorry I called you, woke you, whatever. But please, can't you just—go back? Go home?"

"The thing is, you're totally right, what you say in your book—which is currently number one on the *New York Times* non-fiction chart, by the way, no need to thank me. The key to happiness is to keep learning, growing, and experiencing." Sharon swung her boots off the chair and sat up straight. "But how do you learn when you already know everything? How do you grow when you already *are* everything? And as for experiences—I've spent a thousand years as a grain of sand, I've gone sunbathing inside the burning heart of a star, I've played with dinosaurs and ridden centaurs. I've watched civilizations, species, whole planets, come and go. But it all gets old in the end. I'm bored, Abby. I'm bored. I need direction. A sense of purpose. That's why meeting you was so perfect, don't you see?"

Abby looked down at her desk, at the notebooks and case files. Her own image smiled up at her from the cover of her book. A red sticker said "The Mega-Bestseller! As Seen on TV!"

A small sound escaped her. She wasn't entirely sure if it was a laugh or a sob. Abby Fowler, Life Coach to the Gods.

"Okay, then," she said. "Tell me, on a scale of one to ten, how do you rate 'all-powerful superbeing' as a career?"

Sharon seemed to consider this. "I suppose it beats working in retail," she said.

Abby wiped her eyes. "Okay. Fine. You really want my professional advice? Here it is. Nothing interests you because nothing challenges you. You need something that you aren't automatically going to be good at, something you can't control."

"You do know the meaning of the word omnipotent, right?"

"If you can do anything, then that should include creating something you can't do."

Sharon scratched her neck with glittery fingernails. "Gah. Ontological paradoxes give me hives. But, you know what? You might just be on to something. Every story needs an antagonist, doesn't it? Every hero needs an arch-enemy. A nemesis." She nodded, her eyes gleaming. "That's exactly what I need. A super-villain."

Abby pursed her lips. "Well, that's not exactly what I—"

"Two evenly-matched combatants, pursuing each other through time, space and multi-phasic trans-dimensional realities, constantly fighting an epic, eternal battle for dominance. What a great idea. I love it."

She leaned back and crossed her legs. "Naturally, it goes without saying that the job's yours."

A card materialised on the desk. On the front was a satellite picture of Earth, with the words "Congratulations on your Apotheosis!" superimposed over the top. Inside, it said, "Dear Abby—it's going to be fun!—Love, Sharon."

Abby laid the card flat. "No, thanks," she said.

"So, I think the first thing we should do is—hang on, what?"

"I said no, thanks. I'm quite happy here in my ordinary, non-phasic reality."

"You don't want to be a god? I was joking earlier, you know. It's a lot better than working in retail."

"No, I don't want to be a god. I like my job. I like my life."

Sharon pulled on her lip ring. "Ah."

"Ah? What does that mean, ah?"

"You like Paul."

Abby frowned. "What? Yes, of course I like Paul. So?"

"Oh, nothing. Nothing at all." Sharon looked away.

"I might not have omniscient powers, but I'm good at telling when people are lying. What are you talking about? What about Paul?"

"Well—" Sharon shrugged. "I just made sure all the boxes were ticked, that the i's were dotted and the t's were crossed, that the—"

"What are you saying? That you——what? Mind-controlled him, somehow? Changed him? Made him perfect for me?"

"Well—"

"My God—all the time we've been together—how far back does this go? Did you go back in time and make him fall in love with me?"

Sharon rubbed the back of her neck. "No," she said slowly, drawing the word out. "Not exactly."

Abby lifted her chin. "Whatever you did, undo it."

"You don't really want me to do that."

"Yes, I do. Didn't you hear what I said about free will? That's important, Sharon. That *matters*." She stood up and folded her arms. "I don't want some perfect, fake Paul. I'd rather take my chances with the real one."

"Yeah. See, there's your problem."

"What?"

"There isn't one."

"There isn't one what?"

"A real Paul. There isn't one. I made him to order."

"That's not possible. I met you yesterday. I met him two years ago."

"Mm, no. It's the happiness thing again, you see. Good memories are part of it. So I gave you some. Trust me, Paul is about thirty-six hours old."

Abby's knees gave way and dumped her back in her chair. She pushed her hair out of her eyes. "Then take it back. If that life isn't real, I want you to get it out of my head. You must be able to."

"'I can, if that's what you want."
"I do. No, wait. What happens to Paul?"
"Like I said. There isn't one."
Abby's voice caught. "He dies?"
"Technically, he goes back to never having existed."
Abby's stomach churned. "Get out," she said. "'I don't care what powers you have, if you come anywhere near me again I will kill you."
"Well, you see, I'm like energy, in that I can't actually be..." Sharon looked at Abby's face and trailed off. "Maybe we won't get into that right now."
"No," Abby said. "Maybe we won't." She snatched her car keys off the desk and slammed the door behind her.

"You're home early," Paul said. He was stirring something in a wok on the hob, something that smelled spicy and delicious.
She nodded. "I dumped a client," she said.
"Really? That doesn't sound like you."
She stood by the breakfast bar and crossed her arms over her chest. "Tell me where we first met."
"Huh?"
"Tell me, Paul."
"On the early morning train to Glasgow, three years ago. You were speaking at a seminar on personal development."
She closed her eyes. "What's your favorite food?"
He licked the spoon in his hand and grinned. "Green Thai curry, obviously. Why?"
"Same as mine. Your favorite book?"
"Abby, what is this?"
"Just do it, okay? Humor me. Actually, no. You know what? Don't. Don't do what I want. Because you always do, don't you? You're always perfect."
Paul gave her a quizzical look. "Is that a bad thing?"
"Yes," she said. "Yes, it is."
He laughed. "So—if not doing what you want is a *good*

thing—maybe this is the right time to tell you I booked up for Trevor's stag do in Ibiza?"

"This is the trouble, you always—wait, what?"

"It's only for a week."

"You're going away for a week? To Ibiza? Without me?"

He put his head to one side. "You do know what stag do means, don't you?"

She gave a tiny shudder. "I hate Ibiza," she said. "And Trevor, come to think of it. What if I said I don't want you to go?"

Paul grinned. "Well, since I've already paid my deposit, I'd say we'd have to agree to disagree for once."

Abby let out a long breath and scrubbed her hands over her face. "Yeah," she said. "Maybe we could do that. Maybe we really could."

Paul took the wok off the heat and turned to face her. "Are you sure you're all right?"

She found a smile from somewhere. "I'm fine," she said, "I just need some air."

She slipped out the back door into the garden. A large leaf detached itself from next door's apple tree and swirled in the air. Somewhere, a cat yowled.

"Are you there?" she said softly. "Come on, I know you can hear me."

"I'm here," Sharon said. She was sitting cross-legged on top of the shed.

Abby scuffed her heel on the decking. "All right. I still think it's wrong, what you did. But he's Paul. However he started out, he's real now. So I want you to leave things as they are."

"You humans can really be capricious, you know that? But yeah, I can do that." She jumped down. "So, about that supervillain thing?"

Abby shook her head. "No. Definitely not. I am not going to play Joker to your Batman, or David to your Goliath, or whatever it is you had in mind. So you can forget all about that idea. The answer's 'No.' One hundred percent no."

"How about Buffy and Faith? I'll let you be Buffy."

"The answer's no."

Sharon scratched her ear. "Ah," she said.

Abby raised her eyebrows. "Ah? Again, with the ah? Now what?"

"So you didn't want to be given supernatural abilities that would enable you to interact with me on a more equal footing, then."

"No. I did not."

"Ah," Sharon said.

THAT NIGHT, Abby dreamed about going sunbathing inside the burning heart of a star. When she woke, she had a deep, all-over tan.

THE BANK APPROVED Abby's loan application. She gave the rest of the funds that had appeared in her account to charity and used the loan to lease another floor in her office building. Joe Callaghan was her first employee.

Cthulu discovered online grocery shopping, and she had to buy three new industrial-sized freezers to store all the pizzas. Paul went to Ibiza, and posted photos on Facebook that made Trevor's fiancée call off the wedding. Abby made him sleep on the couch for a week, but in the end everybody agreed it was probably for the best.

Sharon wiped out half of North America with a tactical strike launched from an orbital space laser, but Abby put it back before anyone really noticed.

"DID YOU HEAR?" Joe said, as he put Abby's coffee on her desk. "Some woman's opened up another coaching service on the forty-eighth floor."

"Actually, I like to call it a facilitation service," Sharon said from the doorway. She'd dyed her hair brown and swapped the motorcycle boots for suede high heels.

"What's that?" Joe said.

"It's a more hands-on approach," she said.

"Really?" Abby said. "This is what you're doing, now?"

Sharon shrugged. "You know what they say—if you can't beat them, join them. And then beat them."

Joe narrowed her eyes. "And what makes you think you're going to beat us?"

"I get results for my clients," Sharon said. "Whatever they want, I can make happen. In fact, I guarantee it."

Joe snorted. "Good luck with the advertising standards agency on that one. Well, just make sure you don't try to pinch our clients. Otherwise you'll have a fight on your hands."

Sharon grinned. "Oh, pet. I wouldn't have it any other way."

Story Notes:

I've always been fascinated by the concepts of immortality and omnipotence—with endless time and power at your command, what would you do? Many fine stories have looked at this question from the serious, "with great power comes great responsibility" angle. I decided to try a more irreverent take.

Michelle Ann King

writes SF, dark fantasy and horror from her kitchen table in Essex, England. She has worked as a mortgage underwriter, supermarket cashier, makeup artist, tarot reader and insurance claims handler before having the good fortune to be able to write full-time. She loves Las Vegas, vampire films and good Scotch whisky. Find details of her stories and books at www.transientcactus.co.uk

ONE THING LEADS TO YOUR MOTHER

BY DESMOND WARZEL

Yates propelled himself into the office. The door closed behind him, silencing the emergency klaxons that had followed him around for days like Hell's own Greek chorus. The only remaining sound was his pulse pounding in his head: too loud, too fast.

A seated figure shimmered into existence behind the desk. White, male, balding, wearing a tan sweater. "Lieutenant David Eldridge Yates. It's agreeable to see you. You have yet to avail yourself of my services."

"You're the psychologist?" asked Yates.

"System: Holographic Replica: INdividual Kounseling. S.H.R.I.N.K. for short."

"That's a bit forced."

"You may call me Dr. Turing."

"Very clever."

"Is my appearance acceptable? I can be either sex, and can approximate any ethnicity."

"Doesn't matter. What's important is, you're the only functioning computer on the ship."

"Perhaps that accounts for your agitated state. Is there some sort of emergency?"

"You gotta be kidding me."

"With the exception of the library module, I have no access to the ship's systems. My isolation ensures the confidentiality of all counseling sessions. What is the problem?"

"What *isn't* the problem?" Yates retorted. "Three days ago, Lieutenant Arcuri woke me from cryosleep. My turn on watch. No sooner had I put Arcuri under when everything went to hell. Cascading failure. Systems went down like dominoes. Some went quietly; most didn't."

"I'm afraid I don't see how I can help."

"I fixed it all. Every last system. Been awake seventy-two hours straight, but it's done. All I have to do is restart the master system, and everything should come back online."

"And?" prompted Turing.

"I can't get in. I forgot my password."

Turing raised an eyebrow. That he could react at all was a testament to the prescience of his programmers (and their refusal to underestimate the depths of human idiocy).

"You've got my file," said Yates. "Just retrieve my password, and I'll get out of your hair."

"I'm sorry, Dave; I'm afraid I can't do that." The joke eluded the oblivious Yates, as did Turing's self-satisfied smirk at finally having a legitimate context in which to deploy it. The lieutenant registered only annoyed confusion.

"Why not? You know I'm me."

"Passwords do not appear in personnel records. They're meant to be secret, after all," Turing said reproachfully.

"Well, we got an hour to figure it out," said Yates. "Then the auxiliary batteries on the cryopods conk out. Goodbye, crew; hello, just the two of us, alone together for eternity."

"Perish the thought," said Turing, with distaste. "The task you propose lies beyond my parameters, however, my perceptual acuity with respect to the human psyche is unmatched. We must try." He indicated the couch at the side of the room. "I find that most people prefer to lie down. Would you care to?"

To Yates, who had spent three days caroming off the bulkheads like a racquetball (if racquetballs spent their existences in a state of sheer panic), the couch's allure suddenly eclipsed the aggregated temptations of a dozen shore leaves in the dozen seediest ports in explored space. He kicked gently off from the wall and maneuvered across the room, pulling himself into position atop the leather cushions and strapping himself down.

"Nice place," he said, and meant it. The rest of the ship (whose designers had seen too many of the wrong movies) was unlivable on a *good* day: all stark white passageways and blinking LEDs. "Carpet, paneling, real furniture; I'm gonna drop in more often. If we survive, that is."

"My analysis of human behavior suggests some preliminary possibilities. Is your password 'password'? Or a numerical sequence? '1-2-3-4-5,' for example?"

"What?" Yates tried to heave himself upright in indignation; the restraint limited him to an awkward-looking obtuse angle. "Because I'm black, right? 'Oh, he must be too dumb or lazy to pick a real password.'"

"I'll take that as 'negative,'" sniffed Turing. "Is it your mother's maiden name?"

"Don't talk about my mother."

"Pardon?"

"You shrinks just *love* to blame everything on a guy's mother, right? I'm not having it. If we were Catholic, my mother'd be a saint."

"All the more reason to use her name, perhaps?"

"I thought about it. But her maiden name was Eldridge."

"Your middle name."

"Can't use your own name, they said."

"They told you this at the academy?"

"What academy? I worked my way up from airman, third class. I'm the only one on this ship who did."

"So you chose your password during basic training."

"Yeah. We had half a ream of paperwork and five minutes to fill it out. With two pituitary cases in sergeants' stripes screaming into our ears the whole time."

"For my part, I've never approved of such aural assaults as motivational tools."

"Wasn't that bad. No worse than trying to do homework when my dad was in the house."

"Let's talk about that. You were born in 2190, in New York City?"

"Yeah. Lived there until I was thirteen."

"With your mother."

"Man, I *told* you not to bring up my mother. Try that where I come from, and see what happens."

"And where is that, specifically?"

"Brooklyn."

"Is 'Brooklyn' your password?"

"No. Why would it be?"

"You were under stress when you selected it. You might have unconsciously sought solace in a happier time."

"No dice."

"I see that you graduated from high school in Erie, Pennsylvania."

"Yeah. Central Tech High School. Go, Falcons."

"Is any of that ringing a bell for you?"

"What? 'Erie'? 'Central'? 'Falcons'? No, sorry."

"No need to be sorry."

"Don't worry, I didn't mean it."

"When did you move to Erie?"

"Don't you know?"

"Yes, but *my* memory isn't at issue."

"When I was fifteen."

"You moved there with your mother."

"You talk about her one more time, I'm gonna put you right on your holographic ass."

"A novel threat, if unenforceable. Your concern is noted; I'll avoid broaching the subject unnecessarily."

"Fine."

"So. You moved to Erie with your mother?"

Yates fished a stylus from the pocket of his coveralls and flung it. It passed harmlessly through Turing's head and ricocheted around the office until it lodged in the kneewell beneath the desk. Turing remained unperturbed. "My understanding is that we have very little time. It's up to you how much we waste."

Yates massaged his temples. His pulse was down to a resting rate, but his head still pounded. *Starship duty: all the benefits of a hangover without all that bothersome drinking. A little something for the recruiting posters.* "Yes. With my mother."

"Why?"

"Cheaper than New York. And she had family there."

"What did your father have to say about it?"

"Nothing that mattered."

"What's his name?"

"Same as mine."

"So you're a Junior."

"No. Different middle names."

"And your father's middle name?"

"Jerome. So what?"

"Is 'Jerome' your password?"

"Be serious."

"You could have chosen something with negative associations and then repressed it after the fact."

"It's not 'Jerome.' Trust me."

"Was your father around very much?"

"Is anybody's, these days?"

"Do you resent him for that?"

"The man was a tyrant. The longer he stayed away, the better."

"And your mother was more lax, in terms of discipline?"

"No, she just knew how to let a kid be a kid. *Again* with my mother?"

"You were eighteen when you selected the password; thus, your childhood made up the totality of your experiences. The answer lies there."

"You're just jealous. You don't have a mother, so you gotta rag on everyone else's."

"I had a mother. Her name was ELIZA." This was the second joke to sail majestically over Yates's head. Turing scheduled a thorough examination of his humor subroutines, contingent on the crew's survival.

"Fine, my childhood. What else do you want to know?"

"Is there anything *you* think I ought to know? Something you've avoided discussing?"

"Obviously *you* think there is."

"You were in Brooklyn through age thirteen and Erie from fifteen on. What's missing?"

"Age fourteen, I guess."

"What happened then?"

"I lived with my father in Ohio for a year."

"Why keep that to yourself?"

"Nobody ever brought up the subject of David Jerome Yates voluntarily."

"You didn't think it might be important?"

"The worst year of my life? Sure, if you're a sadist, it's important."

"Why Ohio?"

"He thought Brooklyn had too many bad influences. Said if I came to Toledo for a year, I'd straighten up."

"Is 'Toledo' your password?"

Yates waved off the question irritably. "No, it's not. What makes you think it'll be that simple? 'Oh, the black guy has to have an obvious password, or he'll forget it.'"

"Hostility is unconstructive. Moreover, you *did* forget it."

"It's not 'Toledo.' We didn't live there anyway; we lived in the suburbs."

"Which one?"

"I don't remember. Doesn't matter. One suburb's just like every other."

"Did you like it there?"

"Hated it. Never felt at home. Plus, I was the only black kid in my class."

"They gave you a hard time?"

"No, I gave *them* a hard time."

"I see."

"Wasn't their fault; I just wanted *gone*. I pestered my dad every day. 'I wanna live with mom, I wanna live with mom.' Just 'Mom, mom, mom,' all the time. I thought you were gonna try not to bring her up."

"I didn't; you did."

"There's nothing here; try something else."

"What school did you attend?"

"Gateway Middle School."

"You remember the school, but not the town it was in?"

"So?"

"What street did you live on?"

"Sackett Street."

"In what town?"

"I don't know."

"You're hiding something from yourself."

"You don't know that."

"Something you wish to avoid."

"I don't think so."

"What was your zip code?"

"Zip code? Like on a letter? What is this, 1870?"

"Do you remember it?"

"Four three five three seven." Yates's eyes widened. "Why do I know that? I remember the zip code, the street, the school, but not the town. Why?"

"Why, indeed?"

Yates unstrapped himself from the couch and maneuvered to the desk. This close, Turing became slightly transparent and the paneling on the far wall showed through. It was like being haunted by an especially placid ghost.

Yates pointed at the switch on the desk. "You said you have library access?"

Turing nodded. "The library itself is down, of course, but my cached version should be intact."

Yates tapped the switch; a holographic interface window seemed to emerge directly from the solid wooden desktop. He began his manipulations, flinging icons around the display in all directions like pucks in a shuffleboard match between madmen.

"Take your time," advised Turing. "Keep your head about you."

"I don't come in here and tell you how to do *your* job."

"Actually, you've done nothing *but—*"

The remainder of Turing's complaint went unuttered, as Yates slapped the desktop triumphantly. "*Got* it!" He consulted his chronometer. "Still time, too. That's how we do it in Brooklyn, baby." He kicked off from the desk and hurtled across the office, hitting the doorframe at a bone-jarring velocity.

He fumbled the door open and was immediately assaulted by the emergency klaxons, which had gamely kept up their atonal ululations throughout the session. It was like being shot in both eardrums simultaneously.

"Don't forget to schedule a follow-up appointment," Turing called impotently as Yates vanished down the passageway. "It's in the regulations."

"And you're welcome, by the way."

Turing manipulated Yates's abandoned interface window (no small feat for a being with no substance) until it registered on one of several visual sensors throughout the office which served as his "eyes." There, highlighted, was the sought-after name.

Turing wondered idly if any psychology journal could be convinced to publish a paper authored by a S.H.R.I.N.K. unit. Yates's unique case cried out to be documented (with names redacted, of course).

He'd repressed the name of the town, not to purge himself of it but to preserve it. During the year he'd spent under his father's thumb in his Midwestern purgatory, it had become his only comfort, even if he didn't consciously understand why. And when he'd left home again years later, this time for boot camp, and found himself at the tender mercies of the drill instructors, it had bubbled unbidden to the surface and spilled onto a form, in a blank marked "Password."

A small Ohio town called Maumee.

"I'M HAPPY TO SEE YOU again, Lieutenant Yates."

"Don't be; I'm just obeying regulations."

"Gravity seems to agree with you. I trust everything's well in hand?"

"All systems green. Here's the thing; my watch is almost up. Tomorrow I revive Ensign Aviles and go back into cryosleep."

"Go on."

"The rest of the crew, they have no idea how close they came to biting the dust. Now that I know I might not wake up once I go back under, I want to get something off my chest. Something I'm leaving out of my official report. Can you keep a secret?"

"All S.H.R.I.N.K. sessions are confidential."

"We're in a confessional, as far as you're concerned."

"I thought you said you weren't Catholic."

"Always with the sly answers. Nobody likes you very much."

"You have my word. Confess away."

"I know what caused the system failure. Interference from an unauthorized electronic device."

"What kind of device?"

"A digital photo frame."

"Yours?"

"Yes."

"Personal electronics are prohibited while the ship is in flight. It's the oldest rule there is. It goes all the way back to the days of aviation."

"I didn't know they were serious about that. When was the last time you heard about an electronic device disabling a vessel?"

"Fifteen seconds ago."

"We're allowed personal effects. That specifically includes photos. Aren't photos digital? "

A suspicion took root in Turing's virtual mind: a detail that, if verifiable, would tie his journal article together perfectly.

"Whose picture was in the frame?" he asked.

"Not relevant."

"A woman?"

"Not relevant."

"She must be somebody important."

"What difference does it make?"

"You wanted to confess. I'm acting as confessor." *And I need you to admit it out loud so I can write it up.*

"I'm leaving."

"Suit yourself." As Yates stalked out of the office, Turing continued speaking at a conspicuously elevated volume. "It must have been someone of a quite objectionable appearance, for you to be so reticent.

"It's probably someone of poor hygiene, as well. I don't blame you for your secrecy.

"Especially if the person is of questionable moral character, which I can only assume, given your reluctance to discuss the matter."

Yates's distant footfalls ceased. Switching subroutines, Turing accessed the obscure data he'd unearthed during his humor self-assessment. He seldom departed from his default demeanor, but this was for the advancement of his field.

"I hear she's so dumb, she put headlights on an FTL cruiser.

"And so ugly, the captain strapped her to the deflector dish to scare the meteoroids away.

"And so fat, if time were a dimension, she'd be four days long.

Three.

Two.

One.

Yates burst into the office, fists clenched. "Didn't I *tell* you not to talk about my mother?"

But by the time Yates reached the desk, Turing had vanished.

Story Notes:

Funny stories often arise from the combining of two unrelated elements. The little gaps and overlaps where they don't quite line up create lapses in logic, and therein lies the humor. In this case, I had long been mulling over the idea of a typical science-fiction future with faster-than-light travel and so forth, but built atop legacy systems that could still be stymied by something as ridiculously anachronistic as a missing password. But making the connection isn't always enough; sometimes a catalyst is needed. Here, that catalyst was the title—one of a list of titles for which I hope to eventually write stories. The concept of "mother" has many aspects, but two of them—mother's maiden name as ID verification, and mother as "villain" in the popular conception of psychology—drifted serendipitously together in my thoughts, and the ever-capable Dr. Turing was born.

Desmond Warzel

is the author of a few dozen short stories. These have appeared in handy, lightweight, electronic form on websites like *Daily Science Fiction* and *Tor.com*; on genuine dead tree in nifty magazines like *Fantasy & Science Fiction* and fancy anthologies like *Blood Rites*; and in gentle, soothing audio on these newfangled podcast things, such as *Escape Pod* and *Cast of Wonders*. You can look for his latest work in upcoming issues of *Playboy* and the *New Yorker* (you won't find it there, but you can look). He lives in northwestern Pennsylvania.

CLASS ACTION ORC

by James Beamon

Things were looking good in the prison courtyard. Seeing how I was stuck here as a convict, I did what an orc does best—fight senseless battles against more righteous forces. So I went to war with the magistrate, the law as my weapon, and proved the former dungeon conditions were inhumane. Half the dungeon dwellers weren't even human, but the ones that were counted. Those humans needed humane conditions. The ones that weren't human got a free ride under some racial equality clause. Now all the felonious goblins, orcs, humans, dwarves, and whatever had a courtyard, with weights and card tables.

The weights were the most important thing. I had to stay buff for when I got out of lockup and joined forces with some dark lord's dark army. Last thing I wanted to be was the runt orc. They got the shit jobs like "guard the captured yet resourceful hero" or "stand over the trapdoor while the evil lieutenant briefs the overlord with bad news."

I strutted through the courtyard as if I was dressed in imperial silk instead of dirty tattered rags, receiving nods of respect from various races and calls of "L.O." (short for Legal Orc). Being the big man of the dungeon had clout. I went to move some of that lead around, weights sold on the cheap to the prison by the Dyslexic Alchemical Society around the same time they ran out of gold.

I trained hard, not that it mattered much. The forces of good were working overtime to keep me locked down. Speaking of, a voice called out to me from across the courtyard, a sound that was high and melodious and full of crap magic.

"Ang Ul Wud!"

I turned to face the only jackass that would use my government name like that. Llevar the high elf stood sneering at me, dapper and blond and apparently still full of elf-lawyer pomposity. My fame as Legal Orc started with this clown. In a desperate bid to accrue enough community service hours to get sprung from the tank, I took over as public defender for a centaur awhile back. Not only did I win the case, I won against his highness elf Llevar. He strode over with a leather satchel over his shoulder.

"Came to show me your new purse?" I asked. "Purty."

"I just wanted to see how you're adjusting to all the time you keep accumulating."

I stifled a grimace. The first thing this tree prancer did after he lost the case was find some loophole to keep me from getting all my community service hours. Once I was back in the dungeon, he set off on a crusade to get time added to my sentence. His most brilliant stroke of dastard came with the institution of "Quiet Hours," where any convict caught talking after lights out got fined time. This is when I learned he must've been watching me in the wee hours, and I talk in my sleep. A lot. Apparently, I mutter stuff from my minion days like "burn the village!", "when do we get to eat him?", and "hell naw, I'm on break", sweet nothings that kept adding more time than I could knock down. And since this was a stupid realm of apparent sunshine and happiness, there wasn't enough new fish getting locked up to make decent community service hours in casework. I'd never get out of here at this rate; they even counted "Mu Ha Ha Ha!" and there was no way you could dream about the good old days without tossing around a bunch of those.

At least I caught my grimace before Llevar could get the satisfaction of seeing it. "I don't look at it as time added," I told him. "I look at it as more opportunity to reflect on how I wiped my ass with your winning record."

Llevar wasn't as successful keeping his poker face. His scowl let me know things weren't the same for him over at the Elf Club. I knew none of his peers respected him. Who ever heard of a high elf losing to an orc when it came to seeking justice?

"Wouldn't you like to get out of here?" he asked. "After all, a career criminal not free to practice his craft is like a harpy without wings, little more than a saggy windbag with bad breath and worse posture."

"Meh," I said, as I bicep curled a basket of lead bars. "Dungeon's been upgraded. Now it's got that cozy overlord's lair kinda feel."

"Hmmm. I would think you of all people would be dying to get out, what with the whole of Seven Realms talking about the rising new dark lord."

I stopped curling weight. I think my mouth started watering. "New dark lord?"

The high elf smiled, which to me looked like the twin brother of high elf sneers. "Dark Lord Grimsfar."

Hot carnage, it was a good name. You could tell how committed an overlord was to spreading destruction and ruin by their name. I still shudder when I think of my days as henchman for Dark Lord Rufus and the Black Witch Kimberly. This evil overlord could be the real deal.

"Don't matter," I said. "My time keeps deepening, like the folds of loose skin on your momma's face. That's the kind of time I got ... that Hoya time, serious like those serious jowls."

"See, it's that crack wise, too-smart-for-a-stupid-orc spirit I need to break. So I challenge you plainly, Ang Ul Wud. Face me in court. If you win, I'll see to it Quiet Hours go away."

"It's Anglewood," I said. The deal sounded good. No Quiet Hours meant I had another option besides trying to upgrade the dungeon to a point where escape was easy. "And I want double the community service hours."

"Done," he said, too fast. He dug in his purse and pulled out a thick sheaf of papers and parchment.

I looked at the stack of paperwork, the size of which made my investigative mind start working immediately. Something wasn't right here.

"How'd you fit all that in there with your make-up case?"

"Take the paperwork," he said with glossy lips.

I DON'T KNOW WHY Llevar gave me all that paper, but the parchment was truly a gift from the gods. That stuff was way better than our standard issue toilet paper. It had to be lambskin. Whatever it was, it was a baby soft sign that my mission to make this dungeon more humane was far from over.

While I enjoyed one of the little perks of public service, I did read the first page. Turned out a man named Algus Truthseer was charged with fraud, embezzlement, perpetrating a hoax, malicious scheming, and impersonating a prophet. Sounded like a dude who knew how to get over and turn a party out all at once.

I realized why Llevar was so quick to bet his reputation again when I saw the story behind the charges. Old Algus had convinced a few farmboy chumps that they were all the Chosen One of Prophecy, destined to defeat the near-insurmountable forces of evil with the help of the darkness-banishing sword Cleave. And Cleave could be theirs for five easy installments of only 99 ducats each.

This case made me mad. It was a scheme I should've thought of. Granted, I'm more of a pillager than a schemer, but if the idea was wicked enough to make me envious then I knew this would be a hard case to win.

No way I was backing out. If I couldn't burn down Llevar's

ancestral forest then I could at least beat him in court. I went straight to Algus Truthseer's dungeon cell to talk a taste with the con artist, maybe get an angle.

An old, thin man in an over-sized gray robe, Algus looked a mess, the hot kind, like he had gotten here by getting rolled downhill inside a barrel. Wiry white hair all over his head, long beard knotted in places, eyes searching about his cell like he was looking for missing keys, he didn't look like he could convince a rabbit to eat its vegetables.

"Hell's up with you?"

His eyes focused on me and his expression changed to intense. He leaned forward, to no doubt tell me something seriously important. "I dreamed I was awake last night and when I woke up I was asleep!"

"For serious?"

He nodded. He was indeed for serious.

"Alright, dude. I'm your court appointed lawyer—"

"See!" he shouted, cutting me off. "It's as I've foreseen! Orcs as defenders of the public! Broken clocks telling the correct time at least twice a day! Cats and dogs living together! The shadow is spreading... the penultimate evil rises!"

"Let's hope so," I told him. "Meanwhile, you're not gonna be any help, are you?"

"It rises!" he said, standing on his cot and thrusting his arms into the air. "Like a scantily clad woman hidden inside a hollow cake! Soon it will burst forth, surprising us all with its evil, naughty bits!"

Not for the first time, I was glad I had spent most of my life alternating between being locked up in one legal system or another and working for sinister forces. I would need every trick I had picked up along the way to win this case.

THE COURTROOM WAS PACKED, standing room only. I knew I'd gotten fans after word had spread of my first win but this was enough to make an orc blush. Once I see a high elf bleed I can't help but wanna see more elf blood... apparently it wasn't just me. I winked at the dozen folks in the jury box.

The magistrate looked to me and Llevar, shrewd eyes under bushy gray eyebrows. "We ready to start this?"

"Yes, Your Honor," Llevar said. "First I'd like to call—"

"Hold up!" I cut His Highness off then looked at the magistrate. "Yonor, I think the first order of business should be my classy suit." I looked down at my dirty tattered rags. I wasn't about to sit through a minute of this case without getting what was promised to me.

"Cretin," Llevar said, "this is a class action suit."

"Exactly," I said. "Class for the courtroom, action for the weight room. When do I get my suit?"

The magistrate banged his little hammer. "See here, you dumb, dirty orc, all you're getting from this court is multiple plaintiffs. That's what class action is. Use those beady eyes of yours to look behind you. All these boys got grievance with your client."

I looked behind me. A sea of young, sour faces grimaced back, standing room only. What a way to lose a fanbase. Least there was a bright side; it would take days, maybe weeks, to talk to all these farmboys. With double community service hours, I'd be a free orc once I won.

Llevar cleared his throat. "As I was saying, Your Honor, first I'd like to call Luc Brawnshield to represent all the plaintiffs."

"Not cool," I said. "We gotta talk to each and every one of these dudes to get the full story."

"They each individually have the full story," Llevar said. "It's the same grievance, spoken one hundred and six times. We only need one."

The magistrate's hammer came down and it wasn't in my favor. I hate the fair races. No matter how much time people wasted on their own, all of a sudden they put a premium on it when someone else wasted it for them.

It was just like that damned elf to screw me out of my hours while giving me a case with a hundred plaintiffs. The jury was looking at a legion of young, hurt faces like some giant box of puppies who all needed good homes. Luc Brawnshield was on the stand, his acne-free, handsome face telling the story of how this old man descended on his meager farm, urging the boy to step into his destiny. Luc had dived in, working his fingers to the bone doing odd jobs for ducats. He washed horses, sold Troll Scout brownies, and donned a wig to work as a bar wench, earning four and a half of the five installment payments for Cleave, apparently the most out of any of the farmboys, but not enough. And all for nothing.

Crap. When Luc's eyes brimmed with tears as he talked about how the men of the bar called him flat-chested, everyone in the jury box brought out tissues.

Screw this. Orcs don't go down without a fight. Unless it's a death march. Lots of us go down on death marches. And Luc Brawnshield was making this case feel like one. I was gonna make this guy pay. It was my witness.

Me: How do you know my client?

Luc: He came to my farm and said I was the Chosen One.

Me: What'd he specifically say about the Chosen One?

Luc: He said the Chosen One would emerge to vanquish the coming evil and that I was he.

Me: How do you know he wasn't just identifying your gender?

Luc: Huh?

Me: You are he. And I'm he. The only ones who are she's in the courtroom are a couple jurors and Llevar, judging by the high voice and stylish purse. Are you not a guy?

Luc: I'm a guy.

Me: Is destiny like a pair of shoes?

Luc: Huh?

Me: You said my client told you to "step into your destiny." So I'm wondering; does destiny feel like a pair of shoes? Is destiny comfortable? Does destiny provide proper arch support?

Luc: Um... maybe?

Me: Tell me, according to you, how does one step into their destiny?

Luc: I don't know. It just kind of happens, I guess.

Me: If it just kinda happens, why'd you work all those jobs?

Luc: I... I thought I was stepping into my destiny.

Me: No. You think destiny just kinda happens, so it don't matter whether you're working yourself stupid or plopping down on your ass to watch it grow fatter, destiny's still gonna happen. Do you know what happens when you try to rush destiny?

Luc: You get swindled by an old man claiming to be an all-powerful seer?

Me: No, you get called flat-chested by a room full of dudes looking at a flat ass chest!

The magistrate brought down his hammer, which was a good thing this time. It was starting to feel like the old days, what with me towering over a farmboy at my mercy. I was a second away from grabbing him by the shirt and throwing him into a slave cart when the hammer hit. That's when I remembered we hadn't burned his village down and that I had no further questions.

I figured Llevar would have no more witnesses seeing as he had had Luc speak for over a hundred people. Nope. The elf stood up holding a sheathed sword, jewels encrusted throughout its hilt.

"Your Honor, I would like to call Cleave to the stand."

The magistrate looked at Llevar with the same expression that must've been on my face.

"Cleave is a talking sword," Llevar said, "gods-blessed, forged to cut through the forces of darkness and, in this case, provide invaluable testimony."

"I'll allow it," the magistrate said.

Llevar pulled Cleave out of its sheath, revealing a sword that seemed to reflect every ray of light in the room. The crowd of farmboys oohed in awe. Llevar propped the sword, point up, on the witness chair.

"Hello, Cleave."

"Whattup." The voice definitely came from the sword, and the light it reflected seemed to shimmer a bit when it spoke.

"State your name for the court."

"Cleavon Daggarious Rumbleskins Jackson. Folks call me Cleave—Mr. Jackson if you nasty."

"Well, Cleave, could you tell us a little bit about yourself?"

"I was made long ago by monk-clerics using some mystic ass secrets. I'm talking them rare metals like unobtainium, triple-platinum, and hardas-hellium. They blinged me out so you could see a sword shining. I'm the only weapon in the world that can cut the dog shit out of ultimate evil, which is why I need to be in the hands of the Chosen One."

Llevar paced back and forth as the sword talked, nodding appreciatively. He stopped and looked at the jury as he spoke to the sword. "So you were specifically designed to be wielded by the Chosen One to vanquish evil."

"Damn straight," the sword shimmer-spoke. "In the Chosen One's hands I take out ultimate evil and all the lil' evils that wanna get froggy. Like that orc there in the dirty rags. I was made to slide right through his ass like a hot roll that needs butterin'."

Llevar continued to look at the jury. "What would you say to a whole room of men who were all told they were the Chosen One?"

"I'd call ninety-nine percent of them suckers. It ain't hard math, baby. Ain't but one Chosen One."

Llevar had no further questions, which made this sword my witness. I didn't know exactly what I wanted to ask it, I just knew I wasn't going to let it talk smack about me on the stand like that. I stood up and got started.

Me: So, you go by Cleave?

Cleave: Yo, why you talking to me, son? Shouldn't I be

in your stomach right now, laughing while you die around me?

Me: I ain't your son.

Cleave: I don't know, B. I've stuck more unwed, single orc girls in one night than you have your whole life. That makes me the expert. Yo, you need to listen to the experts.

Me: Speaking of experts, how much experience do you have being wielded by the Chosen One while he's vanquishing the ultimate evil?

Cleave: Word? You trying to question my pedigree? I keeps it real, son, been reppin' this game my whole life. See that's the difference between real weaponry and fake citizenry. You started life getting massaged through a soft birth canal. Me? I started my life getting beat with hammers over a forge, catching a real ass whipping. I ain't no punk.

Me: So by the numbers, that would make the times the Chosen One has used you to end the ultimate evil as . . . ?

Cleave: It ain't happened yet.

Me: If it ain't happened, how do you know it's supposed to happen?

Cleave: Cause I'm a talking sword, yo! You don't make things like me as party favors. You only pull Cleave out the pocket when you wanna cleave something, ya feel me? The old heads knew that, that's why they wrote that prophecy about the Chosen One breaking out the one and only Mr. Jackson here and getting nasty on some evil. And on some stupid, which is why I can't wait to put an edge in you.

Me: Seeing how you got no legs, it's gonna have to wait, sword. Have you actually read the prophecy?

Cleave: Don't you need eyes for that? What, they making sword-Braille now?

Me: I'll take that as a no.

Cleave: You pressin' on the wrong one, son. If you ain't got no more questions, you need to step.

Me: I got one more question. You a punk ass sword. Oh wait,

that wasn't a question. OK, why are you sitting on a chair shimmer-speaking instead of out reppin' this game? Don't bother, I already answered this... 'cause you a punk ass sword. No further questions.

Llevar got up and retrieved Cleave, sticking it in its sheath while it was still talking about what it was gonna do to me. The prosecution's case rested, which meant it was my turn. I looked over to my right at Algus Truthseer, sitting there crumpled like he was getting paid by the wrinkle. I looked up at the magistrate.

"Recess?"

"No."

The way I saw it, I needed Algus on the stand. I mean, I hadn't proved he hadn't intentionally swindled a small nation of farmboys out of all their money. And in this courtroom, only Algus was gonna vouch for Algus. I figured I could wrangle him in the right direction if I handled him with soft paws. He was simply passionate about his vision of darkness, not unlike the Dark Lord Blooddrencher. Man, could that overlord motivate. I called Algus to the stand.

Me: Is darkness rising?

Algus: <stops picking his nose to thrust his hands in the air> Darkness... *is* rising!

Me: How great is the need for the Chosen One?

Algus: The need is great!

Me: These sound like desperate times. And what do desperate times call for?

Algus: Mail order brides!

Me: Maybe. That's a desperate measure, no matter how you look at it. Would you say desperation drove you to find the Chosen One?

Algus: Yes! He must step into his destiny and vanquish the penultimate evil!

Me: Sounds deep.

Algus: It is indeed very deep, dear defender of the public. Just as you have been appointed by this very court to represent us downtrodden souls who lack the capability, knowledge, and wit to speak eloquently on our own behalves, so too has the Chosen One been appointed by destiny herself to represent all the besotted races throughout the Seven Realms from the ever-growing reach of dark, immortal forces whose near-insurmountable power lies beyond the strength of normal mortals. My mission is one of serious gravity and the utmost urgency.

Me: Um... OK. So, you didn't intentionally swindle any of these farmboys?

Algus: <laughs shrilly, loudly, madly—laughs for a long time, one of those laughs like he was either pleased with the beautiful cruelty of his own joke or he was the hapless victim of a pair of enchanted happy drawers. I hoped for the drawers cause maybe I could score a pair> No.

I had no further questions. And for the first time since I took this damn case, I felt good about the outcome. I turned it over to Llevar, but not without first showing him the backside of my middle finger, real discreet like. Let him argue that.

Llevar launched out of his seat, scowling. He headed over to the witness stand.

"Algus Truthseer, how did you of all people know these dark times are 'a-comin'," Llevar said, his fingers curling into quotes as he spoke, "and only the Chosen One can save us?"

Algus cleared his throat. "I foresaw it."

"If you foresaw it, why didn't you go straight to the one and only Chosen One?"

"I'm old. I don't, um ... foresee so good."

"Cataracts in your prophetic sight, eh? So, why charge for the sword instead of giving it away? After all, the need is great, right?"

"Operating costs! Restocking fees! The need is great!"

"Right," Llevar said, his nose scrunching up in disgust. "And what were you planning to do with all that money from all these poor farmboys?"

"I have not yet received that vision," Algus said. "When the vision is clear, the way is clear. When the way is clear, people drink too much and have carriage accidents. Ends a lot of budding romances, carriage accidents. Not on my watch!"

"No further questions," Llevar said, in almost a sing-song voice. He turned to me, his smile deep, his middle finger extended discreetly.

This was bad. My defense rested like a dead bear. Now was time for closing arguments, which only twisted the knife-like feeling in my gut. While Llevar argued that the crafty old bastard knowingly and willfully took all these poor folks' money, I envisioned life in the dungeon with perpetual Quiet Hours and without the satisfaction of having a win over Llevar's high and mighty elvish ass.

I felt like I had committed suicide. Why didn't I see that a real seer could've just seen who the Chosen One was to begin with? I guess because I figured he wasn't a real seer to begin with. But I couldn't put that in my final argument.

I looked at Algus, wincing in his chair as Llevar called him depraved, predatory, geriatric. What if he was a real seer? If I could believe it, maybe the jury could, too. I had to try; it was my turn to close. I stood up, remembering not to smile because pointy orc teeth disturb the fair races.

"Ladies and gentlemen of the jury, you may be thinking my client don't know jack squat about the Chosen One. When you really think about it, who does? Prophecies ain't exactly written in keen detail . . . they're scrawled down, half-assed mutterings from eccentric old kooks, people who are arguably just as old and kooky as my client.

"You may also be thinking, 'those poor farmboys.' They were just minding their own business, raking and hoeing and generally being dirty and poor, when they got the call to be the Chosen One. Now instead of thinking about the harvest, their little heads are full of notions of adventures and quests.

"That's some bullshit; their heads were already full of notions of adventures and quests. They're farmboys! Their lives suck. You think this courtroom would be packed with billionaire playboys if the call for the Chosen One went out to them? These dudes couldn't wait to get off the farm and being the Chosen One was the perfect excuse.

"So here they all are, itching for adventure and quests, but for all we know collecting five easy installments of 99 ducats *is* the quest. What do you think's harder for a farmboy to do, something that requires physical exertion or getting that dough? Farmboys have time and desire to practice sword fights and archery, what they ain't got is money! If you can't afford to wield the mighty Cleave, the epic sword I will soon urinate on, then you damn sure can't afford to go risking your life tackling evil.

"We'll never know if collecting payment was the quest to bring out the Chosen One . . . cause none of them actually completed the quest, something that would've separated the farmboys from the farm men. Since we can't know the mysteries of the prophecies or the mysterious ways of the prophets, then we can't say for sure that my client did anything criminal. If you got doubts, you gotta let him go."

I rested my case. After an hour of deliberation, the jury came back with a verdict. Algus Truthseer was a free old kook.

A legion of farmboys booed. Luc Brawnshield stood up, fixed a blonde wig to his head and shouted "I can still complete the quest!" before dashing out of the courtroom. Just like that, the courtroom emptied with farmboys running with new fire under their asses.

Llevar gave me a high elf scowl, which to me is the twin sister of a high elf smile. "This isn't over," he said before storming off.

It was just as well he left before I could gloat. I wasn't in pro form 'cause I hadn't had a bathroom break since leaving the dungeon. Luckily, Llevar had left Cleave in its sheath on the prosecutor's table. I smiled.

Time to make one prophecy come true.

Story Notes:

This is my fourth story set in Seven Realms, a fantasy world that takes typical tropes and fantasy stereotypes and turns them on their ear. It's also the second Seven Realms story to feature Anglewood, a character so good at being bad I couldn't resist seeing him again.

James Beamon

When he found out how hard it was to win a writing award, James Beamon decided to settle for being one of the only writers he can think of with six-pack abs. Now he writes less fiction because he's always at the gym. It also keeps him in fighting shape, which is beneficial since his day job as a defense contractor takes him to places where running and ducking are oftentimes a great idea. Currently he's in Afghanistan.

THE WIGGY TURPIN AFFAIR

by Wade Albert White

It all started the day the first apple trees blossomed on the moon. I had just finished a contract to assassinate some government-type chappy from the Lunar Council and was enjoying the one week turnover period the Agency allows between assignments before returning to Earth. Even the most ruthless of killers requires a little R&R once in a while, not to mention I could claim all the expenses on my tax forms. Besides, I absolutely detest space travel.

So there I was, stretched out in leisurely fashion on a chesterfield in the Trudeau Suite of Moonbase Zeta, enjoying an ancient tome on the art of electrocution. It was quite the thriller. High voltage, higher voltage, local brown-out level voltage. Who says science can't be fun.

Then Humbert entered.

Humbert is my robotic butler and a bit of an odd looking fellow, what with the headlamp eyes and barrel legs and all.

Tends to startle guests and plays havoc with pacemakers, but since I don't really care for company anyway it usually works out in the end.

"There is a connection for you on the VID phone, Ms. Wackrill," he said.

His facial features were, as always, completely inert.

I yawned. "Remind them I'm on my turnover."

"It is not the Agency, madam."

"Then I'm not here at all."

"I believe it is a call of a personal nature."

"Well, I'm not inclined to have nature personally call me right now, so tell it to go away."

"The gentleman was rather insistent, I'm afraid."

I threw down the book. "Oh, for the love of— Who is it then?"

"From Earth. A Mr. 'Wiggy' Turpin."

Wingham Beasley Turpin, of the Dorchester Turpins, no less. He and I had attended grammar school together and on through to undergraduate classes until he ventured off into classical music and I took up serious study of close knife fighting and death by a thousand paper cuts. Wiggy was sort of the runt of the litter, but a quick wit and better than me at maths. We still exchanged Christmas cards every year.

I reached over and flicked on the end table monitor. Wiggy's rather bovine features rezzed into view.

"Ashleigh, darling," he trilled, "how's the hair?"

Did I forget to mention he had a hair fixation? I suppose I thought the nickname rather gave it away. Toupees, extensions, you name it. It was a fetish gone wild, and not for the betterment of all humankind, let me tell you.

"My hair is perfectly normal," I answered, "and yours?"

"A smash, Ash. An absolute tootle on the noodle. This week it's green."

I could see plain as day that it was green; he needn't have pointed it out. A disturbingly luminescent green that quite frankly hurt the back of my brain a little.

"I honestly couldn't care less," I said.

"Oh, come now, Ash. I'm trading in wigs on the side now. Sort of a hobby thing. Let me set you up. Some metallic silver forelocks?"

"No."

"A rainbow spread of feather extenders?"

"No."

"A full mop in a fetching leopard pattern?"

"Definitely not."

"Seriously, let me send you a leopard. I accidentally bought an entire crate and they're horrid. Absolutely ghastly. Frightened the maid so badly she cried and short-circuited herself."

"I said *no,* Wiggy."

He burst into tears.

"Oh for goodness sake," I said, rolling my eyes, "send me one then if it's that important to you."

"It's not that," he sobbed. "I'm afraid I'm in a terrible predicament. A dreadful quandary. A horrible fix."

"Well, spit it out then," I said, "before my great-grandchildren are billed for the call."

"It's quite simple, Ash. I-I've gone and killed a man."

I waited for the rest, but apparently that constituted his full confession.

"I fail to see the problem," I said.

Judging from the look on his face this was possibly not the response he'd been looking for.

"But I didn't mean to," he protested.

"'Didn't mean to' accounts for nearly half my kills," I assured him. "There's no shame in a bit of collateral damage, though it's best not to advertise it. Don't want them thinking you're only racking up points with hand grenades."

"You don't understand," wailed Wiggy. "I've become a murderer, Ash. An out-and-out criminal of the worst breed. There's blood on my hands."

"Is that all? Let me switch you back to Humbert. He's simply a wizard with stains."

I reached toward the monitor.

"Wait!" he cried. "That's not the end of it."

"Speaking strictly as a professional," I said, "I can assure you it is."

"No, it isn't." He glanced around the room and then back into the VID monitor, hunched lower now, his great beak of a nose filling the screen. "He's back."

"Who's back?"

"Howard Hornsby. The chap I accidentally dispatched."

I smiled. "Technically, Wiggy, if they're still kicking then you haven't actually killed them yet."

"No, no, I'm positive I did. Absolutely so."

"On what grounds?"

"I accidentally knocked him into one of the combines here on the farm."

"One of those mechanical harvester thingys?"

"A rather big one, I'm afraid."

"And you think what now? He's patched himself back together and is out for revenge?"

He sniffed. "As absurd as that may sound, yes. Or, well, something like that. I mean, he must be dead, he simply must. But ... oh, I don't know. I tell you, the whole thing's got me baffled but good."

"Well, I can certainly appreciate your dilemma," I sympathized. Then I thought about it a bit longer. "Actually, no I can't. Why exactly did you call me, again?"

"I need protection. I want to hire you as my bodyguard."

"Ah, see, I actually do the opposite of that."

"I'm serious, Ash. It's only a matter of time before he gets me. Or else hires someone for the job. I've seen people lurking about, shadows in the bushes. Cold-hearted, backstabbing bastards, the lot of them. Not a twig of guilt or conscience. But that's your world, Ash. You're one of them."

"My, but you do have a way of flattering a girl."

"I'm begging you."

I am, generally speaking, immune to begging, having understandably encountered my fair share of it in this line of work, but there was something in the way his chubby little cheeks quivered that got the better of me. I hate it when that happens.

"Fine," I said, "I'll come. But at twice my normal rate and a full maintenance checkup for Humbert. He's due next month."

"I'll pay, I'll pay. Whatever it takes."

"Fine. Expect us the day after tomorrow."

I snapped off the VID and looked down at my book with a sigh.

Electrocution would just have to wait.

WE ARRIVED AT WIGGY'S as scheduled, a vast, sprawling parcel of land. The Turpin estate was old money. Full east and west wings, guest houses, gardens, stables, a private observatory, and two thousand acres of prime farmland. A bit of Downton Abbey meets the American Midwest.

The maid, Greetta, and the butler, Jeevz, met us at the front door. Both were android servants and sported matching bronze Mohawks. I sensed Wiggy's influence here and no one seemed overly happy about it, least of all me. We left the pleasantries aside.

"I'm afraid there's been another incident," Jeevz intoned.

"Hornsby again?" I asked.

"No," Greetta chimed in. "It's Mr. Turpin. He's ... well, h-he's expired you see."

"Doesn't anyone ever check the due dates around here?" I quipped, tongue firmly in check.

Apparently it was a poor time for risqué humor, as the two of them simply stood there and stared at me blankly. Possibly they had been expecting more in the way of grief from an old friend, but take my word for it, when your final exam with a room full of school chums is "last one standing," you learn to let go fairly quickly.

I put on my best somber face. "May we examine the body?"

"I'm afraid there isn't one," said Jeevz.

The maid let out a shuttering sob and a few sparks flew from the corner of her eye socket.

"Obviously," I said, "you've been schooled in such matters by the late master of the house. You see, normally we base accusations of death on actual observation of the individual's current state of health, or, more typically, the lack thereof."

Jeevz frowned. "There isn't a body because Mr. Turpin fell into the combine harvester."

I leaned over to Humbert. "Make a note. The next time we require a third man we're contacting that harvester. It's establishing an absolutely first rate record."

"I can, however, direct you to the location of the incident," Jeevz continued.

"And why, pray tell, would we want to do that?"

"Were you not hired to protect Mr. Turpin?"

"Yes, but I would venture to say we've arrived a little too late to fulfill that particular contractual obligation."

"But will you not wish to investigate his death?"

"Investigate what? It was the combine harvester. You just said so."

"Mr. Turpin's estate will pay you for your services in the successful determination of his murderer."

"But . . . the combine harvester. Remember? We just talked about it. Twice. I say, do you suffer from some sort of short-term memory loss?"

Jeevz sighed. "The harvester was the instrument, madam, not the culprit."

"What culprit? You said he fell in."

"My apologies. I meant to say he was pushed in."

"Ah, yes, well that's the problem with the English language, isn't it? All the words mean different things."

"You would be free to pursue the investigation in whatever manner you see fit, completely uninhibited and beholden to no one, save that you provide the estate with a name."

"Butterfield."

"I beg your pardon?"

"Butterfield. That's a name. You said to provide a name."

"I meant the name of the actual killer."

"Well, if you're going to be fussy about it."

Since there were still several days remaining before my next official assignment, and since the thought of traveling back to the moon held even less appeal than checking over greasy farm machinery for the mangled remains of a former classmate, I accepted the job. Jeevz showed us to our rooms, gave us directions to the dining hall, and told us dinner was served at six bells. That was still several hours off.

"What say, Humbert, old goat? Might as well jump in with both feet, eh? Make hay while the weather-controlled sun shines?"

"Yes, madam."

"From assassin to bodyguard to private detective all in one day. Who knows what's next?"

"My inner parts shudder to think, madam."

"Now, now. That'll be enough cheek out of you," I warned, donning my working jacket.

Humbert spread out the portable weapon pack on the bed.

"Just a single concealed knife for the time being," I instructed. "No need to frighten the domestic staff—or at least, not without due cause. We can always return for the WMDs if things get sticky."

"Very good, madam."

WE SPENT THE AFTERNOON interviewing: the house staff, the gardeners, the stable hands, the farm hands, all the sentient A.I. on the premises, his close friends, and the neighbors. Anyone and everyone who might be able to shed even a little light on the fate of poor Wiggy and his friend Hornsby. We made little headway in turning up any useful information, but all-in-all I thought I did rather well as a first time investigator, and Humbert only had to remind me twice that waterboarding is not generally considered an acceptable canvassing technique. The one small tidbit we did glean was a hint at some recent hostility between the two of them. They were in a quartet together—Wiggy played the violin and Hornsby the cello—and a bit of friendly rivalry may have ballooned into something nastier.

We arrived back for dinner at precisely six bells, and without wishing to sound ungrateful I would not have served the meal spread before us to the worst of condemned prisoners. The hors d'œuvres were smoked salmon—or possibly salmon that had a prior smoking habit given their uncanny resemblance to small bits of dried up lung. The entree, Cornish hen with new potatoes, stared at me like we were long lost relatives, and I privately questioned the wisdom of leaving the eyeballs in as a matter of presentation. The pistachio cannoli for dessert would actually have been passable had its particular shade of green not reminded me strongly of Wiggy's toupee. Finally, we drank a toast in memory of dear Wiggy with the cheapest of watered-down wine and then shuffled off back to our rooms.

"That was the worst meal in the history of all meals," I grumbled. "I dare say God himself would have sent back the soup."

"There was no soup course, madam," said Humbert.

"Which tells you just how bad it must have been, if they couldn't even bring themselves to serve it. Wherever did Wiggy find those two and please reassure me that we didn't just eat him."

"My condolences to your stomach, madam, but it was not 'all for naught' as I believe the saying goes."

"Come again?"

"There is this," he said, and brought forth a silver butter knife, one from the place settings at dinner.

"Dear boy, if I'm not paying you enough just say so. No need stooping to petty thievery."

"My molecular scanner detected some organic residue on the cutlery, and I matched the DNA pattern to that of your acquaintance, Mr. Turpin. The sample cannot be more than twelve hours old."

"Stabbed to death with a butter knife? That harvester is downright brutal."

"Actually, the residue is not blood, merely the normal microscopic deposits secreted by all living creatures. It indicates that he held this knife sometime earlier today."

"So, not as dead as we were led to believe, eh?"

"Perhaps, madam, if I may be so bold, some after-hours reconnaissance would not be amiss?"

"Just so long as it's followed by an after-hours snack. My stomach is threatening litigation."

I'VE ALWAYS LIKED sneaking about. It's so . . . sneaky.

We checked everywhere. Both wings, the library, the dance hall, all the unoccupied bedrooms, the baths, the inner gardens, the outer gardens, the stables, and the multi-level garage. Humbert maintained a continual scan for any further signs of our missing host.

"Still nothing?" I asked some hours later.

"I'm afraid not, madam."

"Well, do one final sweep around the main compound and then meet me in the kitchen."

"You believe we will discover some further link there to the knife?"

"No, I'm merely starving."

Humbert lumbered off with the weapon's pack and I made my way down to the lower levels. I was delighted (and not a little surprised) to discover they maintained a well-stocked larder with perfectly edible foodstuffs. Why they felt the need to torture fresh vegetables and prime cuts of meat into disfigured semblances of an actual meal was beyond me.

I was halfway through a mouth-watering cold meat

sandwich when hurried footsteps echoed down the stairwell. In a flash I was up from the table and behind the door, remembering too late that I'd left my knife lying next to the bread loaf. A man in a tuxedo descended quickly into the kitchen and began randomly opening cupboard doors.

I stepped out. "Howard Hornsby, I presume."

He swung around.

"Who are you?" he asked, wide-eyed.

"A friend of Mr. Turpin's."

"Oh, yeah? Tell me where he's at then."

"You haven't heard? I'm afraid to say he's passed on."

"Poppycock. He's here. I can smell his wig glue."

He sniffed around the stove and the spice racks.

"Might I inquire as to the reason for your visit?" I asked, as I casually began to maneuver myself toward the knife rack at the other end of the counter.

"Oh, you know, just wanted to catch up, is all."

"You mean on the local gossip and such?"

"Precisely. Nothing wrong with that, is there?"

"Not at all. It's only, I'm having a difficult time reconciling that with the fact that my knife is clutched ever so firmly in your hand."

He looked down with an expression of genuine surprise. "Hello, where did this come from?"

"You picked it up off the table as you flew past."

"Now why would I do that?"

"Perhaps so you could run at me like you are right now."

I leaped nimbly to the side as he made a rather unsuccessful (and might I add, poorly balanced) lunge at me. A hapless rack of ladles were scattered across the floor instead.

"I suppose," he said, "there is a certain logic to what you say. But why would I rush at you with a knife?"

"I don't rightly know," I said, as he continued to make various jabs at my person. "Although I'd venture a guess—and I grant that it is mere speculation on my part—that you might be attempting to kill me."

He pinned me against the counter but I managed to grab his knife hand at the last second, the blade mere inches from my chest.

"The evidence would seem to be pointing in that direction," he agreed.

I did a quick reverse and jerked him forward, allowing his own weight to drive the knife home. He staggered back, blood soaking his shirt, the knife hilt now protruding neatly from his own chest.

He looked up at me. "That was ... rather ... impressive," he gurgled.

"Yes, it's a little trick I learned in school called 'not dying'."

He slumped to the floor, dead as the proverbial doornail. And let me add that that was my *professional* assessment. None of this dead person with no body business. This one was absolutely certified.

More footsteps echoed from the staircase, so I quickly dumped the body into a nearby broom cupboard (mostly out of habit) and ducked behind the door again.

"Hello? What's all this mess?" said a strangely familiar voice.

I peeked out and found myself staring at none other than one very much living and breathing Howard Hornsby, now wielding a cricket bat.

I stepped forward once more. "I say, aren't you supposed to be dead?"

"Who are you?" he demanded, raising the bat tentatively.

"Forgive my lack of manners, but I could have sworn I just killed you and stuffed you in this cupboard."

"Well, am I in there?"

I cracked open the door and peeked in. Sure enough, Hornsby's body was still there.

"Yes," I said.

"Perhaps it slipped my mind then."

I shrugged. A single karate chop to the neck rectified the oversight before he could get a swing in. The fit in the cupboard was considerably tighter this time. They're not designed for bodies, of course, but I find you can stuff a corpse into just about any available space with a little imagination. And, if necessary, a chainsaw.

"Can I assist you, madam?"

I turned around to find Hornsby once again staring me dead in the eye—or, in fact, not so much dead. Another swift survey of the cupboard confirmed the first two Hornsby bodies were still very much present and accounted for.

"By any chance did your mother have quadruplets?" I asked.

"Die, troll witch!" he screamed as he brought up a pistol and fired wildly in my direction.

Now a hotheaded assassin is usually a dead assassin, and I was not, generally speaking, one to lose my temper. Nevertheless the evening's activities were beginning to wear severely on my patience. When I kill a man I usually prefer he stay that way, and quite frankly I'd had one too many Hornsbys take a run at me. And all that on a still mostly empty stomach.

Once he'd emptied the clip—to no avail, I should add, otherwise this tale would be ending more or less right here—dispatching him was a simple matter of beating him to death with the breadboard.

Once more into the broom cupboard I went, and after some fair bit of pushing (and not a little snapping) I finally managed to shut and latch the door. I did a quick survey of the connecting rooms and gave a hard listen up the staircase to ensure there were no other Hornsbys lurking about.

A few minutes later Humbert appeared, and while rearming myself more properly from the pack, I caught him up to date on the Hornsby family reunion.

"Most remarkable," said Humbert. "I myself encountered two more on the grounds."

"It's all very unusual to say the least," I said.

"I suspect clones, madam."

"You think clones put the Hornsby family up to this?"

"I believe these *are* the clones, madam."

Across the room the door to the pantry flew open and out stormed one Wiggy Turpin.

"Why that lying, good-for-nothing cheat-bag!" he shouted.

"Wiggy, how nice of you to show yourself," I said, a pistol suddenly in my hand and aimed directly at his head.

Wiggy stopped in his tracks but continued his tirade. "I specifically asked Howard if he knew anything about cloning techniques and he assured me he was a complete dim-bulb when it came to any of that genetics business."

"And hasn't he just been made the fool. I don't suppose, Wiggy, that you would like to catch us up on anything yourself? Recent events? Rumors of your untimely death?"

"Oh, you know full well that was all a sham," he scoffed. "I had to go into hiding."

"From the Hornsby clan?"

"How many more of them can there be?"

"Impossible to say. They've certainly taken poorly to your 'accident' though."

"Yes, well, er," (he cleared his throat) "Howard always was a little contrary-minded."

Humbert reopened the broom cupboard and my collection of life-sized Hornsby figurines toppled out. He bent over and examined them. After a few minutes of mechanical humming and hawing, he reached down and wrenched the head clear off the top Hornsby.

"Lord have mercy, Humbert," I gasped, "I know we're in a cruel business but we can still show a modicum of respect for the dead."

Humbert held the head high and let us see what had caught his attention. Dangling from the neck hole was a large cluster of wires, and the skull was clearly some metallic compound with an overlay of synthetic skin.

"It's a clone *robot*?" I asked.

"I believe that technically, madam, the correct term would be robot clone," said Humbert.

I glanced at the remaining bodies.

"Wiggy," I said, "if you have any light to shed on the matter, now would be the time."

Wiggy crossed his arms defiantly. "I haven't the foggiest."

"Well, we'd best check the house again, I suppose."

Back up the stairs we went, only to stop short at the main level. The sparking bodies of Jeevz and Greetta lay on the floor before us, and behind them the entire dining hall was filled to the brim with Hornsby clone robots. Or robot clones. Or—well, there were an awful lot of Hornsbys in there was the heart of the matter. Certainly more than a proper fire marshal would allow. And every single one with a murderous gleam in his eye.

"I do believe I'm going to have to charge extra for this," I said.

"Indeed, madam," agreed Humbert.

Wiggy took cover behind a statue of Napoleon riding a gazelle while I dove in wielding a twin pair of ancient Roman gladius replicas, superb for close quarters fighting. I swung and sidestepped and stabbed my way through the mass of synthetic core bodies. The noise was incredible, mostly because they were all screaming and trampling one another in an attempt to get away from me. It turns out the clones of a classically trained cellist, even robotic ones, are no match for the Guild's "Advanced Level Multiple Opponent Room Clearing Tactics" class.

"Humbert," I yelled over the din, "see if you can find out where they're all bloody coming from."

"Yes, madam," he said, and he plowed his way to the north exit, dispatching a few clones himself in the process.

I have to admit I was actually having a real bit of sport; as it turns out, robot clones are a good deal crunchier than I had imagined. But despite the fact that it was a little like having Christmas and my birthday all at once, my arms were slowly beginning to tire and there is something about overwhelming odds that reminds you why assassins prefer slipping in and out quietly through the back door.

Gradually, though, and much to my relief, the numbers did thin out. I caught the last two cowering under the grand piano, but a single serrated boomerang to the instrument's legs completed the job with a rather cacophonous boom.

Humbert re-entered.

"Any luck?" I asked.

"Not specifically, madam, though I have developed a *theory* as to their origins."

"Do go on."

"The particular model of combine harvester in question is fitted with a genetic scanner which analyzes moisture, bacteria, and mineral content. It then modifies the next crop of seed so that it can thrive better in its immediate environment."

"And these robot clones took offense to that? Rabid environmentalists, you think?"

"Not quite, madam. I believe that when Mr. Hornsby went into the combine that the genetic scanner analyzed *his* remains and began creating replicas of him that could survive better in *their* environment."

"So it created a room full of knife-wielding Hornsbys?"

"So it would seem."

"I highly doubt that was in the owner's manual," I mused. "But still, whyever were they out for blood?"

"My analysis has led me to conclude that since the harvester would have scanned Mr. Hornsby in his final moments, and if he felt in fear for his life—as might be expected of someone falling into an operating combine harvester—the subsequent clones may have been programmed to combat the assessed danger."

"Or assailant," I added.

"My thoughts precisely."

I turned to Wiggy. At first he refused to meet my gaze, but soon enough he raised his eyes in defiance and stared me down.

"Yes, that's right" he said. "I did it. I confess. I pushed him in but good. Would do it again, too, in a blind second."

"But why, Wiggy? I thought you and he were friends."

"Not likely. Big self-made man, he was. Always bragging about his great achievements and whatnot, how he taught himself cello at age three using nothing but a piece of string and a fire hydrant. Said I'd had everything handed to me."

"But, Wiggy, you did have everything handed to you. Utterly and completely."

"Well, yes... that part's true, but... well, look now, he didn't always have to go 'round pointing it out, did he? Saying it in front of everybody. Correcting my fingering at rehearsals."

Noise from outside drew our attention to the window, and we received not just a little shock. An entire battalion of Hornsbys was marching in perfect formation across the field and surrounding the house. One of the barns was being pulled down and used to build a catapult.

"That's an awful lot of Hornsbys," I said.

"Yes, madam," agreed Humbert.

"What are the odds of us getting past them."

"It is difficult to make a precise calculation. A number of factors simply cannot be accounted for under the circumstances."

"But your best guess?"

"Negative fifteen point seven to one."

"So, rather poor then."

"Rather. But while I was out I took the liberty of securing all the entrances and ordering a hover taxi to the roof. It should be arriving in approximately five minutes."

"And our luggage?"

"Packed and waiting."

"Humbert, you're a credit to your profession."

"Thank you, madam."

Humbert trundled off and I turned back to our host.

"Wiggy, it's been ever so wonderful to see you again—except, of course, for the part where you inadvertently created a horde of incensed musicians bent on murdering us all. But I think now we'd best be off."

Wiggy gave me the stink eye but maintained his distance, probably because I still held two thoroughly bloodied swords in my hands. "You're a cold one, Ash. An honest to goodness ice cube. I mean, I knew you were and all that, what with the assassination accolades and all, but this is downright arctic of you. A real stab in bosom buddies, if you know what I mean."

"I have absolutely no idea what you mean. I simply wish to go home. And though it goes against my better judgment, you're welcome to accompany us if you like."

"You signed on to protect me. We have a contract."

"A verbal contract. I signed nothing."

"Is your word not your bond?"

"Typically yes, except for the silent clause exempting me in the face of rampaging psychotic robots. Are you coming?"

He stiffened. "Not a word of it. You all may think little of me, but this estate goes back five generations in my family and a man defends his castle. I will not flee like a coward."

"Suit yourself," I said, and slipped out.

Up to the roof and into the awaiting hover taxi I went. It shot into the darkening sky as we watched the swelling ranks of Hornsbys storm against the walls of the estate, flames leaping high into the cool night air, the Dvorak Cello Concerto playing softly against the clamor of it all.

NOT THREE MINUTES into our flight, me already comfortable with my feet up on the cushions and sipping a warm moon apple brandy, there was a blinding flash followed several seconds later by a clap of thunder and a shockwave like a class five hurricane. The taxi swerved and swooped but finally managed to regain its altitude.

I looked over my shoulder to witness a giant orange mushroom cloud forming behind us.

I turned back and stared Humbert straight in the telescopic eye.

"Humbert, did you blow up Wiggy's house?"

Humbert shifted uneasily in his seat. "Not precisely, madam."

"Not *precisely*? So you're saying you didn't blow it up?"

"No, I most certainly did; however, it was a Micro-Nuclear device, and so in all probability blew up not only Mr. Turpin's house but also the entire estate, quite likely the Hornsby estate as well, and in all probability much of the outlying village."

I'm quite certain an honest-to-goodness tear nearly moistened my check.

"My dearest Humbert, thank-you. That was just what I needed."

"I hope I did not overstep my protocols," he said.

"Not at all, dear fellow. We'll just call it tying up the loose ends."

"Very good, madam." He held out a tray. "Crumpet?"

"That would be perfect."

Story Notes:

I wanted to write a story in tribute to P.G. Wodehouse, and common sense told me it should be about a neo-Victorian assassin and her robotic butler. What else is there to say?

Wade Albert White

Wade hails from Nova Scotia, land of wild blueberries and Duck Tolling Retrievers. He lectures on ancient languages, dabbles in animation, and spends the rest of his time as a stay-at-home dad. It is also possible he has set a new record as the slowest 10K runner. Ever. He owns one pretend cat and one real one, and they get along fabulously. He has been writing fiction for over twelve years now. You can follow Wade on Twitter: @wadealbertwhite

HANNIBAL'S ELEPHANTS

BY ROBERT SILVERBERG

The day the aliens landed in New York was, of course, the 5th of May, 2023. That's one of those historical dates nobody can ever forget, like July 4, 1776 and October 12, 1492 and—maybe more to the point—December 7, 1941. At the time of the invasion, I was working for MGM-CBS as a beam calibrator in the tightware division and married to Elaine and living over on East 36th Street in one of the first of the fold-up condos, one room by day and three by night, a terrific deal at $3750 a month. Our partner in the time/space-sharing contract was a show-biz programmer named Bobby Christie who worked midnight to dawn, very convenient for all concerned. Every morning before Elaine and I left for our offices I'd push the button and the walls would shift and 500 square feet of our apartment would swing around and become Bobby's for the next twelve hours. Elaine hated that. "I can't stand having all the goddamn furniture on tracks!" she would say. "That isn't how I was brought up to live." We veered perilously close to divorce every morning at wall-shift time. But, then, it wasn't really what you'd call a stable relationship in most other respects, and I guess having an unstable condo too was more instability than she could handle.

I spent the morning of the day the aliens came setting up a ricochet data transfer between Akron, Ohio and Colombo, Sri Lanka, involving, as I remember, *Gone with the Wind*, *Cleopatra*, and the Johnny Carson retrospective. Then I walked up to the park to meet Maranta for our Monday picnic. Maranta and I had been lovers for about six months then. She was Elaine's roommate at Bennington and had married my best friend Tim, so you might say we had been fated all along to become lovers; there are never any surprises in these things. At that time we lunched together very romantically in the park, weather permitting, every Monday and Friday, and every Wednesday we had ninety minutes' breathless use of my cousin Nicholas' hot-pillow cubicle over on the far West Side at 39th and Koch Plaza. I had been married three and a half years and this was my first affair. For me what was going on between Maranta and me just then was the most important event taking place anywhere in the known universe.

It was one of those glorious gold-and-blue dance-and-sing days that New York will give you in May, when that little window opens between the season of cold-and-nasty and the season of hot-and-sticky. I was legging up Seventh Avenue toward the park with a song in my heart and a cold bottle of Chardonnay in my hand, thinking pleasant thoughts of Maranta's small round breasts. And gradually I became aware of some ruckus taking place up ahead.

I could hear sirens. Horns were honking, too: not the ordinary routine everyday exasperated when-do-things-start-to-move honks, but the special rhythmic New York City oh-for-Christ's-sake-what*now* kind of honk that arouses terror in your heart. People with berserk expressions on their faces were running wildly down Seventh as though King Kong had just emerged from the monkey house at the Central Park Zoo and was personally coming after them. And other people were running just as hard in the opposite direction, *toward* the park, as though they absolutely had to see what was happening. You know: New Yorkers.

Maranta would be waiting for me near the pond, as usual. That seemed to be right where the disturbance was. I had a flash of myself clambering up the side of the Empire State Building—or at the very least Temple Emanu-el—to pry her free of the big ape's clutches. The great beast pausing, delicately setting her down on some precarious ledge, glaring at me, furiously pounding his chest—*Kong! Kong! Kong!*—

I stepped into the path of one of the southbound runners and said, "Hey, what the hell's going on?" He was a suit-and-tie man, pop-eyed and puffy-faced.

He slowed but he didn't stop. I thought he would run me down. "It's an invasion!" he yelled. "Space creatures! In the park!"

Another passing business type loping breathlessly by with a briefcase in each hand was shouting, "The police are there! They're sealing everything off!"

"No shit," I murmured.

But all I could think was Maranta, picnic, sunshine, Chardonnay, disappointment. What a goddamned nuisance, is what I thought. Why the fuck couldn't they come on a Tuesday, is what I thought.

WHEN I GOT TO THE TOP of Seventh Avenue the police had a sealfield across the park entrance and buzz-blinkers were set up along Central Park South from the Plaza to Columbus Circle, with horrendous consequences for traffic. "But I have to find my girlfriend," I blurted. "She was waiting for me in the park." The cop stared at me. His cold gray eyes said, *I am a decent Catholic and I am not going to facilitate your extramarital activities, you decadent overpaid bastard.* What he said out loud was, "No way can you cross that sealfield, and anyhow you absolutely don't want to go in the park right now, mister. Believe me." And he also said, "You don't have to worry about your girlfriend. The park's been cleared of all human beings." That's what he said, *cleared of all human beings*. For a while I wandered around in some sort of daze. Finally I went back to my office and found a message from Maranta, who had left the park the moment the trouble began. Good quick Maranta. She hadn't had any idea of what was occurring, though she had found out by the time she reached her office. She had simply sensed trouble and scrammed. We agreed to meet for drinks at the Ras Tafari at half past five. The Ras was one of our regular places, Twelfth and 53rd.

THERE WERE SEVENTEEN witnesses to the onset of the invasion. There were more than seventeen people on the meadow when the aliens arrived, of course, but most of them didn't seem to have been paying attention. It had started, so said the seventeen, with a strange pale blue shimmering about thirty feet off the ground. The shimmering rapidly became a churning, like water going down a drain. Then a light breeze began to blow and very quickly turned into a brisk gale. It lifted people's hats and whirled them in a startling corkscrew spiral around the churning shimmering blue place. At the same time you had a sense of rising tension, a something's-got-to-give feeling. All this lasted perhaps forty-five seconds.

Then came a pop and a whoosh and a ping and a thunk—everybody agreed on the sequence of the sound effects—and the instantly famous not-quite-egg-shaped spaceship of the invaders was there, hovering, as it would do for the next twenty-three days, about half an inch above the spring-green grass of Central Park. An absolutely unforgettable sight: the sleek silvery skin of it, the disturbing angle of the slope from its wide top to its narrow bottom, the odd and troublesome hieroglyphics on its flanks that tended to slide out of your field of vision if you stared at them for more than a moment.

A hatch opened and a dozen of the invaders stepped out.

Floated out, rather. Like their ship, they never came in contact with the ground.

They looked strange. They looked exceedingly strange. Where we have feet they had a single oval pedestal, maybe five inches thick and a yard in diameter, that drifted an inch or so above ground level. From this fleshy base their wraithlike bodies sprouted like tethered balloons. They had no arms, no legs, not even discernible heads: just a broad dome-shaped summit, dwindling away to a rope-like termination that was attached to the pedestal. Their lavender skins were glossy, with a metallic sheen. Dark eye-like spots sometimes formed on them but didn't last long. We saw no mouths. As they moved about they seemed to exercise great care never to touch one another.

The first thing they did was to seize half-a-dozen squirrels, three stray dogs, a softball, and a baby carriage, unoccupied. We will never know what the second thing was that they did, because no one stayed around to watch. The park emptied with impressive rapidity, the police moved swiftly in with their sealfield, and for the next three hours the aliens had the meadow to themselves. Later in the day the networks sent up spy-eyes that recorded the scene for the evening news until the aliens figured out what they were and shot them down. Briefly we saw ghostly gleaming aliens wandering around within a radius of perhaps 500 yards of their ship, collecting newspapers, soft-drink dispensers, discarded items of clothing, and something that was generally agreed to be a set of dentures. Whatever they picked up they wrapped in a sort of pillow made of a glowing fabric with the same shining texture as their own bodies, which immediately began floating off with its contents toward the hatch of the ship.

PEOPLE WERE LINED UP six deep at the bar when I arrived at the Ras, and everyone was drinking like mad and staring at the screen. They were showing the clips of the aliens over and over. Maranta was already there. Her eyes were glowing. She pressed herself up against me like a wild woman. "My God," she said, "isn't it wonderful! The men from Mars are here! Or wherever they're from. Let's hoist a few to the men from Mars."

We hoisted more than a few. Somehow I got home at a respectable seven o'clock anyway. The apartment was still in its one-room configuration, though our contract with Bobby Christie specified wall-shift at half past six. Elaine refused to have anything to do with activating the shift. She was afraid, I think, of timing the sequence wrong and being crushed by the walls, or something.

"You heard?" Elaine said. "The aliens?"

"I wasn't far from the park at lunchtime," I told her. "That was when it happened, at lunchtime, while I was up by the park."

Her eyes went wide. "Then you actually saw them land?"

"I wish. By the time I got to the park entrance the cops had everything sealed off."

I pressed the button and the walls began to move. Our living room and kitchen returned from Bobby Christie's domain. In the moment of shift I caught sight of Bobby on the far side, getting dressed to go out. He waved and grinned. "Space monsters in the park," he said. "My my my. It's a real jungle out there, don't you know?" And then the walls closed away on him.

Elaine switched on the news and once again I watched the aliens drifting around the mall picking up people's jackets and candy-bar wrappers.

"Hey," I said, "the mayor ought to put them on the city payroll."

"What were you doing up by the park at lunchtime?" Elaine asked, after a bit.

THE NEXT DAY was when the second ship landed and the *real* space monsters appeared. To me the first aliens didn't qualify as monsters at all. Monsters ought to be monstrous, bottom line. Those first aliens were no bigger than you or me.

The second batch, they were something else, though. The behemoths. The space elephants. Of course they weren't anything like elephants, except that they were big. Big? *Immense.* It put me in mind of Hannibal's invasion of Rome, seeing those gargantuan things disembarking from the new spaceship. It seemed like the Second Punic War all over again, Hannibal and the elephants.

You remember how that was. When Hannibal set out from Carthage to conquer Rome, he took with him a phalanx of elephants, thirty-seven huge gray attack-trained monsters. Elephants were useful in battle in those days—a kind of early-model tank—but they were handy also for terrifying the civilian populace: bizarre colossal smelly critters trampling invincibly through the suburbs, flapping their vast ears and trumpeting awesome cries of doom and burying your rose bushes under mountainous turds. And now we had the same deal. With one difference, though: the Roman archers picked off Hannibal's elephants long before they got within honking distance of the walls of Rome. But these aliens had materialized without warning right in the middle of Central Park, in that big grassy meadow between the 72nd Street transverse and Central Park South, which is another deal altogether. I wonder how well things would have gone for the Romans if they had awakened one morning to find Hannibal and his army camping out in the Forum, and his thirty-seven hairy shambling flap-eared elephants snuffling and snorting and farting about on the marble steps of the Temple of Jupiter.

The new spaceship arrived the way the first one had, pop whoosh ping thunk, and the behemoths came tumbling out of it like rabbits out of a hat. We saw it on the evening news: the networks had a new bunch of spy-eyes up, half a mile or so overhead. The ship made a kind of belching sound and this *thing* suddenly was standing on the mall gawking and gaping. Then another belch, another *thing*. And on and on until there were two or three dozen of them. Nobody has ever been able to figure out how that little ship could have held as many as one of them. It was no bigger than a schoolbus standing on end.

The monsters looked like double-humped blue medium-size mountains with legs. The legs were their most elephantine feature—thick and rough-skinned, like tree-trunks—but they worked on some sort of telescoping principle and could be collapsed swiftly back up into the bodies of their owners. Eight was the normal number of legs, but you never saw eight at once on any of them: as they moved about they always kept at least one pair withdrawn, though from time to time they'd let that pair descend and pull up another one, in what seemed like a completely random way. Now and then they might withdraw two pairs at once, which would cause them to sink down to ground level at one end like a camel kneeling.

They were enormous. *Enormous.* Getting exact measurements of one presented certain technical problems, as I think you can appreciate. The most reliable estimate was that they were 25 to 30 feet high and 40 to 50 feet long. That is not only substantially larger than any elephant past or present, it is rather larger than most of the two-family houses still to be found in the outer boroughs of the city. Furthermore, a two-family house of the kind found in Queens or Brooklyn, though it may offend your esthetic sense, will not move around at all, it will not emit bad smells and frightening sounds, it will never sit down on a bison and swallow it, nor, for that matter, will it swallow you. African elephants, they tell me, run ten or eleven feet high at the shoulder, and the biggest extinct mammoths were three or four feet taller than that. There once was a mammal called the baluchitherium that stood about sixteen feet high. That was the largest land mammal that ever lived. The space creatures were nearly twice as high. We are talking large here. We are talking dinosaur-plus dimensions.

Central Park is several miles long but quite modest in width. It runs just from Fifth Avenue to Eighth. Its designers did not expect that anyone would allow two or three dozen animals bigger than two-family houses to wander around freely in an urban park three city blocks wide. No doubt the small size of their pasture was very awkward for them. Certainly it was for us.

"I THINK THEY HAVE to be an exploration party," Maranta said. "Don't you?" We had shifted the scene of our Monday and Friday lunches from Central Park to Rockefeller Center, but otherwise we were trying to behave as though nothing unusual was going on. "They can't have come as invaders. One little spaceship-load of aliens couldn't possibly conquer an entire planet."

Maranta is unfailingly jaunty and optimistic. She is a small, energetic woman with close-cropped red hair and green eyes, one of those boyish-looking women who never seem to age. I love her for her optimism. I wish I could catch it from her, like measles.

I said, "There are *two* spaceship-loads of aliens, Maranta."

She made a face. "Oh. The jumbos. They're just dumb shaggy monsters. I don't see them as much of a menace, really."

"Probably not. But the little ones—they have to be a superior species. We know that because they're the ones who came to us. We didn't go to them."

She laughed. "It all sounds so absurd. That Central Park should be full of *creatures—*"

"But what if they do want to conquer Earth?" I asked.

"Oh," Maranta said. "I don't think that would necessarily be so awful."

THE SMALLER ALIENS spent the first few days installing a good deal of mysterious equipment on the mall in the vicinity of their ship: odd intricate shimmering constructions that looked as though they belonged in the sculpture garden of the Museum of Modern Art. They made no attempt to enter into communication with us. They showed no interest in us at all. The only time they took notice of us was when we sent spy-eyes overhead. They would tolerate them for an hour or two and then would shoot them down, casually, like swatting flies, with spurts of pink light. The networks—and then the government surveillance agencies, when they moved in—put the eyes higher and higher each day, but the aliens never failed to find them. After a week or so we were forced to rely for our information on government spy satellites monitoring the park from space, and on whatever observers equipped with binoculars could glimpse from the taller apartment houses and hotels bordering the park. Neither of these arrangements was entirely satisfactory.

The behemoths, during those days, were content to roam aimlessly through the park southward from 72nd Street, knocking over trees, squatting down to eat them. Each one gobbled two or three trees a day, leaves, branches, trunk, and all. There weren't all that many trees to begin with down there, so it seemed likely that before long they'd have to start ranging farther afield.

The usual civic groups spoke up about the trees. They wanted the mayor to do something to protect the park. The monsters, they said, would have to be made to go elsewhere—to Canada, perhaps, where there were plenty of expendable trees. The mayor said that he was studying the problem but that it was too early to know what the best plan of action would be.

His chief goal, in the beginning, was simply to keep a lid on the situation. We still didn't even know, after all, whether we were being invaded or just visited. To play it safe, the police were ordered to set up and maintain round-the-clock sealfields completely encircling the park in the impacted zone south of 72nd Street. The power costs of this were staggering and Con Edison found it necessary to impose a ten percent voltage cutback in the rest of the city, which caused a lot of grumbling, especially now that it was getting to be air-conditioner weather.

The police didn't like any of this: out there day and night standing guard in front of an intangible electronic barrier with ungodly monsters just a sneeze away. Now and then one of the blue goliaths would wander near the sealfield and peer over the edge. A sealfield maybe a dozen feet high doesn't give you much of a sense of security when there's an animal two or three times that height looming over its top.

So the cops asked for time and a half. Combat pay, essentially. There wasn't room in the city budget for that, especially since no one knew how long the aliens were going to continue to occupy the park. There was talk of a strike. The mayor appealed to Washington, which had studiously been staying remote from the whole event as if the arrival of an extraterrestrial task force in the middle of Manhattan was purely a municipal problem.

The president rummaged around in the Constitution and decided to activate the National Guard. That surprised a lot of basically sedentary men who enjoy dressing up occasionally in uniforms. The Guard hadn't been called out since the Bulgarian business in '19 and its current members weren't very sharp on procedures, so some hasty on-the-job training became necessary. As it happened, Maranta's husband Tim was an officer in the 107th Infantry, which was the regiment that was handed the chief responsibility for protecting New York City against the creatures from space. So his life suddenly was changed a great deal, and so was Maranta's; and so was mine.

LIKE EVERYBODY ELSE, I found myself going over to the park again and again to try and get a glimpse of the aliens. But the barricades kept you fifty feet away from the park perimeter on all sides, and the taller buildings flanking the park had put themselves on a residents-only admission basis, with armed guards enforcing it, so they wouldn't be overwhelmed by hordes of curiosity-seekers.

I did see Tim, though. He was in charge of an improvised-looking command post at Fifth and 59th, near the horse-and-buggy stand. Youngish stockbrokery-looking men kept running up to him with reports to sign, and he signed each one with terrific dash and vigor, without reading any of them. In his crisp tan uniform and shiny boots, he must have seen himself as some doomed and gallant officer in an ancient movie, Gary Cooper,

Cary Grant, John Wayne, bracing himself for the climactic cavalry charge or the onslaught of the maddened Sepoys. The poor bastard.

"Hey, old man," he said, grinning at me in a doomed and gallant way. "Came to see the circus, did you?"

We weren't really best friends anymore. I don't know what we were to each other. We rarely lunched any more. (How could we? I was busy three days a week with Maranta.) We didn't meet at the gym. It wasn't to Tim I turned to advice on personal problems or second opinions on investments. There was some sort of bond but I think it was mostly nostalgia. But officially I guess I did still think of him as my best friend, in a kind of automatic unquestioning way.

I said, "Are you free to go over to the Plaza for a drink?"

"I wish. I don't get relieved until 2100 hours."

"Nine o'clock, is that it?"

"Nine, yes. You fucking civilian."

It was only half past one. The poor bastard.

"What'll happen to you if you leave your post?"

"I could get shot for desertion," he said.

"Seriously?"

"Seriously. Especially if the monsters pick that moment to bust out of the park. This is war, old buddy."

"Is it, do you think? Maranta doesn't think so." I wondered if I should be talking about what Maranta thought. "She says they're just out exploring the galaxy."

Tim shrugged. "She always likes to see the sunny side. That's an alien military force over there inside the park. One of these days they're going to blow a bugle and come out with blazing rayguns. You'd better believe it."

"Through the sealfield?"

"They could walk right over it," Tim said. "Or float, for all I know. There's going to be a war. The first intergalactic war in human history." Again the dazzling Cary Grant grin. Her Majesty's Bengal lancers, ready for action. "Something to tell my grandchildren," said Tim. "Do you know what the game plan is? First we attempt to make contact. That's going on right now, but they don't seem to be paying attention to us. If we ever establish communication, we invite them to sign a peace treaty. Then we offer them some chunk of Nevada or Kansas as a diplomatic enclave and get them the hell out of New York. But I don't think any of that's going to happen. I think they're busy scoping things out in there, and as soon as they finish that they're going to launch some kind of attack, using weapons we don't even begin to understand."

"And if they do?"

"We nuke them," Tim said. "Tactical devices, just the right size for Central Park Mall."

"No," I said, staring. "That isn't so. You're kidding me."

He looked pleased, a *gotcha* look. "Matter of fact, I am. The truth is that nobody has the goddamndest idea of what to do about any of this. But don't think the nuke strategy hasn't been suggested. And some even crazier things."

"Don't tell me about them," I said. "Look, Tim, is there any way I can get a peek over those barricades?"

"Not a chance. Not even you. I'm not even supposed to be *talking* with civilians."

"Since when am I civilian?"

"Since the invasion began," Tim said.

He was dead serious. Maybe this was all just a goofy movie to me, but it wasn't to him.

More junior officers came to him with more papers to sign. He excused himself and took care of them. Then he was on the field telephone for five minutes or so. His expression grew progressively more bleak. Finally he looked up at me and said, "You see? It's starting."

"What is?"

"They've crossed 72nd Street for the first time. There must have been a gap in the sealfield. Or maybe they jumped it, as I was saying just now. Three of the big ones are up by 74th, noodling around the eastern end of the lake. The Metropolitan Museum people are scared shitless and have asked for gun emplacements on the roof, and they're thinking of evacuating the most important works of art." The field phone lit up again. "Excuse me," he said. Always the soul of courtesy, Tim. After a time he said, "Oh, Jesus. It sounds pretty bad. I've got to go up there right now. Do you mind?" His jaw was set, his gaze was frosty with determination. This is it, Major. There's ten thousand Comanches coming through the pass with blood in their eyes, but we're ready for them, right? Right. He went striding away up Fifth Avenue.

When I got back to the office there was a message from Maranta, suggesting that I stop off at her place for drinks that evening on my way home. Tim would be busy playing soldier, she said, until nine. Until 2100 hours, I silently corrected.

ANOTHER FEW DAYS and we got used to it all. We began to accept the presence of aliens in the park as a normal part of New York life, like snow in February or laser duels in the subway.

But they remained at the center of everybody's consciousness. In a subtle pervasive way they were working great changes in our souls as they moved about mysteriously behind the sealfield barriers in the park. The strangeness of their being here made us buoyant. Their arrival had broken, in some way, the depressing rhythm that life in our brave new century had seemed to be settling into. I know that for some time I had been thinking, as I suppose people have thought since Cro-Magnon days, that lately the flavor of modern life had been changing for the worse, that it was becoming sour and nasty, that the era I happened to live in was a dim, shabby, dismal sort of time, small-souled, mean-minded. You know the feeling. Somehow the aliens had caused that feeling to lift. By invading us in this weird hands-off way, they had given us something to be interestingly mystified by: a sort of redemption, a sort of rebirth. Yes, truly.

Some of us changed quite a lot. Consider Tim, the latter-day

Bengal lancer, the staunchly disciplined officer. He lasted about a week in that particular mind-set. Then one night he called me and said, "Hey, fellow, how would you like to go into the park and play with the critters?"

"What are you talking about?"

"I know a way to get in. I've got the code for the 64th Street sealfield. I can turn it off and we can slip through. It's risky, but how can you resist?"

So much for Gary Cooper. So much for John Wayne.

"Have you gone nuts?" I said. "The other day you wouldn't even let me go up to the barricades."

"That was the other day."

"You wouldn't walk across the street with me for a drink. You said you'd get shot for desertion."

"That was the other day."

"You called me a civilian."

"You still are a civilian. But you're my old buddy, and I want to go in there and look those aliens in the eye, and I'm not quite up to doing it all by myself. You want to go with me, or don't you?"

"Like the time we stole the beer keg from Sigma Frap. Like the time we put the scorpions in the girls' shower room."

"You got it, old pal."

"Tim, we aren't college kids any more. There's a fucking intergalactic war going on. That was your very phrase. Central Park is under surveillance by NASA spy-eyes that can see a cat's whiskers from fifty miles up. You are part of the military force that is supposed to be protecting us against these alien invaders. And now you propose to violate your trust and go sneaking into the midst of the invading force, as a mere prank?"

"I guess I do," he said.

"This is an extremely cockeyed idea, isn't it?" I said.

"Absolutely. Are you with me?"

"Sure," I said. "You know I am."

I TOLD ELAINE THAT Tim and I were going to meet for a late dinner to discuss a business deal and I didn't expect to be home until two or three in the morning. No problem there. Tim was waiting at our old table at Perugino's with a bottle of Amarone already working. The wine was so good that we ordered another midway through the veal pizzaiola, and then a third. I won't say we drank ourselves blind, but we certainly got seriously myopic. And about midnight we walked over to the park.

Everything was quiet. I saw sleepy-looking guardsman patrolling here and there along Fifth. We went right up to the command post at 59th and Tim saluted very crisply, which I don't think was quite kosher, he being not then in uniform. He introduced me to someone as Dr. Pritchett, Bureau of External Affairs. That sounded really cool and glib, Bureau of External Affairs.

Then off we went up Fifth, Tim and I, and he gave me a guided tour. "You see, Dr. Pritchett, the first line of the isolation zone is the barricade that runs down the middle of the avenue." Virile, forceful voice, loud enough to be heard for half a block. "That keeps the gawkers away. Behind that, Doctor, we maintain a further level of security through a series of augmented-beam sealfield emplacements, the new General Dynamics 1100 series model, and let me show you right here how we've integrated that with advanced personnel-interface intercept scan by means of a triple line of Hewlett-Packard optical doppler-couplers—"

And so on, a steady stream of booming confident-sounding gibberish as we headed north. He pulled out a flashlight and led me hither and thither to show me amplifiers and sensors and whatnot, and it was Dr. Pritchett this and Dr. Pritchett that and I realized that we were now somehow on the inner side of the barricade. His glibness, his poise, were awesome. *Notice this, Dr. Pritchett,* and *Let me call your attention to this, Dr. Pritchett,* and suddenly there was a tiny digital keyboard in his hand, like a little calculator, and he was tapping out numbers. "Okay," he said, "the field's down between here and the 65th Street entrance to the park, but I've put a kill on the beam-interruption signal. So far as anyone can tell there's still an unbroken field. Let's go in."

And we entered the park just north of the zoo.

For five generations the first thing New York kids have been taught, ahead of tying shoelaces and flushing after you go, is that you don't set foot in Central Park at night. Now here we were, defying the most primordial of no-nos. But what was to fear? What they taught us to worry about in the park was muggers. Not creatures from the Ninth Glorch Galaxy.

The park was eerily quiet. Maybe a snore or two from the direction of the zoo, otherwise not a sound. We walked west and north into the silence, into the darkness. After a while, a strange smell reached my nostrils. It was dank and musky and harsh and sour, but those are only approximations: it wasn't like anything I had ever smelled before. One whiff of it and I saw purple skies and a great green sun blazing in the heavens. A second whiff and all the stars were in the wrong places. A third whiff and I was staring into a gnarled twisted landscape where the trees were like giant spears and the mountains were like crooked teeth.

Tim nudged me.

"Yeah," I said. "I smell it, too."

"To your left," he said. "Look to your left."

I looked to my left and saw three huge yellow eyes looking back at me from twenty feet overhead, like searchlights mounted in a tree. They weren't mounted in a tree, though. They were mounted in something shaggy and massive, somewhat larger than your basic two-family Queens residential dwelling, that was standing maybe fifty feet away, completely blocking both lanes of the park's East Drive from shoulder to shoulder.

It was then that I realized that three bottles of wine hadn't been nearly enough.

"What's the matter?" Tim said. "This is what we came for, isn't it, old pal?"

"What do we do now? Climb on its back and go for a ride?"

"You know that no human being in all of history has ever been as close to that thing as we are now?"

"Yes," I said. "I do know that, Tim."

It began making a sound. It was the kind of sound that a piece of chalk twelve feet thick would make if it was dragged across a blackboard the wrong way. When I heard that sound I felt as if I was being dragged across whole galaxies by my hair. A weird vertigo attacked me. Then the creature folded up all its legs and came down to ground level; and then it unfolded the two front pairs of legs, and then the other two; and then it started to amble slowly and ominously toward us.

I saw another one, looking even bigger, just beyond it. And perhaps a third one a little farther back. They were heading our way too.

"Shit," I said. "This was a very dumb idea, wasn't it?"

"Come on. We're never going to forget this night."

"I'd like to live to remember it."

"Let's get up real close. They don't move very fast."

"No," I said. "Let's just get out of the park right now, okay?"

"We just got here."

"Fine," I said. "We did it. Now let's go."

"Hey, look," Tim said. "Over there to the west."

I followed his pointing arm and saw two gleaming wraiths hovering just above the ground, maybe 300 yards away. The other aliens, the little floating ones. Drifting toward us, graceful as balloons. I imagined myself being wrapped in a shining pillow and being floated off into their ship.

"Oh, shit," I said. "Come *on*, Tim."

Staggering, stumbling, I ran for the park gate, not even thinking about how I was going to get through the sealfield without Tim's gizmo. But then there was Tim, right behind me. We reached the sealfield together and he tapped out the numbers on the little keyboard and the field opened for us, and out we went, and the field closed behind us. And we collapsed just outside the park, panting, gasping, laughing like lunatics, slapping the sidewalk hysterically. "Dr. Pritchett," he chortled. "Bureau of External Affairs. God damn, what a smell that critter had! God damn!"

I LAUGHED ALL THE WAY home. I was still laughing when I got into bed. Elaine squinted at me. She wasn't amused. "That Tim," I said. "That wild man Tim." She could tell I'd been drinking some and she nodded somberly—boys will be boys, etc.—and went back to sleep.

The next morning I learned what had happened in the park after we had cleared out.

It seemed a few of the big aliens had gone looking for us. They had followed our spoor all the way to the park gate, and when they lost it they somehow turned to the right and went blundering into the zoo. The Central Park Zoo is a small cramped place and as they rambled around in it they managed to knock down most of the fences. In no time whatever there were tigers, elephants, chimps, rhinos, and hyenas all over the park.

The animals, of course, were befuddled and bemused at

finding themselves free. They took off in a hundred different directions, looking for places to hide.

The lions and coyotes simply curled up under bushes and went to sleep. The monkeys and some of the apes went into the trees. The aquatic things headed for the lake. One of the rhinos ambled out into the mall and pushed over a fragile-looking alien machine with his nose. The machine shattered and the rhino went up in a flash of yellow light and a puff of green smoke. As for the elephants, they stood poignantly in a huddled circle, glaring in utter amazement and dismay at the gigantic aliens. How humiliating it must have been for them to feel *tiny*.

Then there was the bison event. There was this little herd, a dozen or so mangy-looking guys with ragged, threadbare fur. They started moving single file toward Columbus Circle, probably figuring that if they just kept their heads down and didn't attract attention they could keep going all the way back to Wyoming. For some reason one of the behemoths decided to see what bison taste like. It came hulking over and sat down on the last one in the line, which vanished underneath it like a mouse beneath a hippopotamus. Chomp, gulp, gone. In the next few minutes five more behemoths came over and disappeared five more of the bison. The survivors made it safely to the edge of the park and huddled up against the sealfield, mooing forlornly. One of the little tragedies of interstellar war.

I found Tim on duty at the 59th Street command post. He looked at me as though I were an emissary of Satan. "I can't talk to you while I'm on duty," he said.

"You heard about the zoo?" I asked.

"Of course I heard." He was speaking through clenched teeth. His eyes had the scarlet look of zero sleep. "What a filthy irresponsible thing we did!"

"Look, we had no way of knowing—"

"Inexcusable. An incredible lapse. The aliens feel threatened now that humans have trespassed on their territory, and the whole situation has changed in there. We upset them and now they're getting out of control. I'm thinking of reporting myself for court-martial."

"Don't be silly, Tim. We trespassed for three minutes. The aliens didn't give a crap about it. They might have blundered into the zoo even if we hadn't—"

"Go away," he muttered. "I can't talk to you while I'm on duty."

Jesus! As if I was the one who had lured *him* into doing it.

Well, he was back in his movie part again, the distinguished military figure who now had unaccountably committed an unpardonable lapse and was going to have to live in the cold glare of his own disapproval for the rest of his life. The poor bastard. I tried to tell him not to take things so much to heart, but he turned away from me, so I shrugged and went back to my office.

That afternoon some tender-hearted citizens demanded that the sealfields be switched off until the zoo animals could escape from the park. The sealfields, of course, kept them trapped in there with the aliens.

Another tough one for the mayor. He'd lose points tremendously if the evening news kept showing our beloved polar bears and raccoons and kangaroos and whatnot getting gobbled like gumdrops by the aliens. But switching off the sealfields would send a horde of leopards and gorillas and wolverines scampering out into the streets of Manhattan, to say nothing of the aliens who might follow them. The mayor appointed a study group, naturally.

The small aliens stayed close to their spaceship and remained uncommunicative. They went on tinkering with their machines, which emitted odd plinking noises and curious colored lights. But the huge ones roamed freely about the park, and now they were doing considerable damage in their amiable mindless way. They smashed up the backstops of the baseball fields, tossed the Bethesda Fountain into the lake, rearranged the New Tavern-on-the-Green's seating plan, and trashed the place in various other ways, but nobody seemed to object except the usual Friends of the Park civic types. I think we were all so bemused by the presence of genuine galactic beings that we didn't mind. We were flattered that they had chosen New York as the site of first contact. (But where *else*?)

No one could explain how the behemoths had penetrated the 72nd Street sealfield line, but a new barrier was set up at 79th, and that seemed to keep them contained. Poor Tim spent twelve hours a day patrolling the perimeter of the occupied zone. Inevitably I began spending more time with Maranta than just lunchtimes. Elaine noticed. But I didn't notice her noticing.

ONE SUNDAY AT DAWN a behemoth turned up by the Metropolitan, peering in the window of the Egyptian courtyard. The authorities thought at first that there must be a gap in the 79th Street sealfield, as there had at 72nd. Then came a report of another alien out near Riverside Drive and a third one at Lincoln Center and it became clear that the sealfields just didn't hold them back at all. They had simply never bothered to go beyond them before.

Making contact with a sealfield is said to be extremely unpleasant for any organism with a nervous system more complex than a squid's. Every neuron screams in anguish. You jump back, involuntarily, a reflex impossible to overcome. On the morning we came to call Crazy Sunday the behemoths began walking through the fields as if they weren't there. The main thing about aliens is that they are alien. They feel no responsibility for fulfilling any of your expectations.

That weekend it was Bobby Christie's turn to have the full apartment. On those Sundays when Elaine and I had the one-room configuration we liked to get up very early and spend the day out, since it was a little depressing to stay home with three rooms of furniture jammed all around us. As we were walking up Park Avenue South toward 42nd, Elaine said suddenly, "Do you hear anything strange?"

"Strange?"

"Like a riot."

"It's nine o'clock Sunday morning. Nobody goes out rioting at nine o'clock Sunday morning."

"Just listen," she said.

There is no mistaking the characteristic sounds of a large excited crowd of human beings, for those of us who spent our formative years living in theearly twenty first century. Our ears were tuned at an early age to the music of riots, mobs, demonstrations, and their kin. We know what it means, when individual exclamations of anger, indignation, or anxiety blend to create a symphonic hubbub in which all extremes of pitch and timbre are submerged into a single surging roar, as deep as the booming of the surf. That was what I heard now. There was no mistaking it.

"It isn't a riot," I said. "It's a mob. There's a subtle difference."

"What?"

"Come on," I said, breaking into a jog. "I'll bet you that the aliens have come out of the park."

A mob, yes. In a moment we saw thousands upon thousands of people, filling 42nd Street from curb to curb and more coming from all directions. What they were looking at—pointing, gaping, screaming-was a shaggy blue creature the size of a small mountain that was moving about uncertainly on the automobile viaduct that runs around the side of Grand Central Terminal. It looked unhappy. It was obviously trying to get down from the viaduct, which was sagging noticeably under its weight. People were jammed right up against it and a dozen or so were clinging to its sides and back like rock climbers. There were people underneath it, too, milling around between its colossal legs. "Oh, look," Elaine said, shuddering, digging her fingers into my biceps. "Isn't it eating some of them? Like they did the bison?" Once she had pointed it out I saw, yes, the behemoth now and then was dipping quickly and rising again, a familiar one-two, the old squat-and-gobble. "What an awful thing!" Elaine murmured. "Why don't they get out of its way?"

"I don't think they can," I said. "I think they're being pushed forward by the people behind them."

"Right into the jaws of that hideous monster. Or whatever it has, if they aren't jaws."

"I don't think it means to hurt anyone," I said. How did I know that? "I think it's just eating them because they're dithering around down there in its mouth area. A kind of automatic response. It looks awfully dumb, Elaine."

"Why are you defending it?"

"Hey, look, Elaine—"

"It's eating people. You sound almost sorry for it!"

"Well, why not? It's far from home and surrounded by ten thousand screaming morons. You think it wants to be out there?"

"It's a disgusting obnoxious animal." She was getting furious. Her eyes were bright and wild, her jaw was thrust forward. "I hope the army gets here fast," she said fiercely. "I hope they blow it to smithereens!"

Her ferocity frightened me. I saw an Elaine I scarcely knew at all. When I tried one more time to make excuses for that miserable hounded beast on the viaduct she glared at me with unmistakable loathing. Then she turned away and went rushing forward, shaking her fist, shouting curses and threats at the alien.

Suddenly I realized how it would have been if Hannibal actually had been able to keep his elephants alive long enough to enter Rome with them. The respectable Roman matrons, screaming and raging from the housetops with the fury of banshees. And the baffled elephants sooner or later rounded up and thrust into the Coliseum to be tormented by little men with spears, while the crowd howled its delight. Well, I can howl, too. "Come on, Behemoth!" I yelled into the roar of the mob. "You can do it, Goliath!" A traitor to the human race is what I was, I guess.

Eventually a detachment of Guardsmen came shouldering

through the streets. They had mortars and rifles, and for all I know they had tactical nukes, too. But of course there was no way they could attack the animal in the midst of such a mob. Instead they used electronic blooglehorns to disperse the crowd by the power of sheer ugly noise, and whipped up a bunch of buzz-blinkers and a little sealfield to cut 42nd Street in half. The last I saw of the monster it was slouching off in the direction of the old United Nations Buildings with the Guardsmen warily creeping along behind it. The crowd scattered, and I was left standing in front of Grand Central with a trembling, sobbing Elaine.

THAT WAS HOW it was all over the city on Crazy Sunday, and on Monday and Tuesday, too. The behemoths were outside the park, roaming at large from Harlem to Wall Street. Wherever they went they drew tremendous crazy crowds that swarmed all over them without any regard for the danger. Some famous news photos came out of those days: the three grinning black boys at Seventh and 125th hanging from the three purple rod-like things, the acrobats forming a human pyramid atop the Times Square beast, the little old Italian man standing in front of his house in Greenwich Village trying to hold a space monster at bay with his garden hose.

There was never any accurate casualty count. Maybe five thousand people died, mainly trampled underfoot by the aliens or crushed in the crowd. Somewhere between 350 and 400 human beings were gobbled by the aliens. Apparently that stoop-and-swallow thing is something they do when they're nervous. If there's anything edible within reach, they'll gulp it in. This soothes them. We made them very nervous; they did a lot of gulping.

Among the casualties was Tim, the second day of the violence. He went down valiantly in the defense of the Guggenheim Museum, which came under attack by five of the biggies. Its spiral shape held some ineffable appeal for them. We couldn't tell whether they wanted to worship it or mate with it or just knock it to pieces, but they kept on charging and charging, rushing up to it and slamming against it. Tim was trying to hold them off with nothing more than tear-gas and blooglehorns when he was swallowed. Never flinched, just stood there and let it happen. The president had ordered the guardsmen not to use lethal weapons. Maranta was bitter about that. "If only they had let them use grenades," she said. I tried to imagine what it was like, gulped down and digested, nifty tan uniform and all. A credit to his regiment. It was his atonement, I guess. He was back there in the Gary Cooper movie again, gladly paying the price for dereliction of duty.

Tuesday afternoon the rampage came to an unexpected end. The behemoths suddenly started keeling over, and within a few hours they were all dead. Some said it was the heat—it was up in the nineties all day Monday and Tuesday—and some said it was the excitement. A Rockefeller University biologist thought it was both those factors plus severe indigestion: the aliens had eaten an average of ten humans apiece, which might have overloaded their systems.

There was no chance for autopsies. Some enzyme in the huge bodies set to work immediately on death, dissolving flesh and bone and skin and all into a sticky yellow mess. By nightfall nothing was left of them but some stains on the pavement, uptown and down. A sad business, I thought. Not even a skeleton for the museum, memento of this momentous time. The poor monsters. Was I the only one who felt sorry for them? Quite possibly I was. I make no apologies for that. I feel what I feel.

All this time the other aliens, the little shimmery spooky ones, had stayed holed up in Central Park, preoccupied with their incomprehensible research. They didn't even seem to notice that their behemoths had strayed.

But now they became agitated. For two or three days they bustled about like worried penguins, dismantling their instruments and packing them aboard their ship; and then they took apart the other ship, the one that had carried the behemoths, and loaded that aboard. Perhaps they felt demoralized. As the Carthaginians who had invaded Rome did, after their elephants died.

On a sizzling June afternoon the alien ship took off. Not for its home world, not right away. It swooped into the sky and came down on Fire Island: at Cherry Grove, to be precise. The aliens took possession of the beach, set up their instruments around their ship, and even ventured into the water, skimming and bobbing just above the surface of the waves like demented surfers. After five or six days they moved on to one of the Hamptons and did the same thing, and then to Martha's Vineyard. Maybe they just wanted a vacation, after three weeks in New York. And then they went away altogether.

"You've been having an affair with Maranta, haven't you?" Elaine asked me, the day the aliens left.

"I won't deny it."

"That night you came in so late, with wine on your breath. You were with her, weren't you?"

"No," I said. "I was with Tim. He and I sneaked into the park and looked at the aliens."

"Sure you did," Elaine said. She filed for divorce, and a year later I married Maranta. Very likely that would have happened sooner or later even if the Earth hadn't been invaded by beings from space and Tim hadn't been devoured. But no question that the invasion speeded things up a bit for us all.

And now, of course, the invaders are back. Four years to the day from the first landing and there they were, pop whoosh ping thunk, Central Park again. Three ships this time, one of spooks, one of behemoths, and the third one carrying the prisoners of war.

Who could ever forget that scene, when the hatch opened and some 350 to 400 human beings came out, marching like zombies? Along with the bison herd, half-a-dozen squirrels, and three dogs. They hadn't been eaten and digested at all, just *collected* inside the behemoths and instantaneously transmitted somehow to the home world, where they were studied. Now they were being returned. "That's Tim, isn't it?" Maranta said, pointing to the screen. I nodded. Unmistakably Tim, yes. With the stunned look of a man who has beheld marvels beyond comprehension.

It's a month now and the government is still holding all the returnees for debriefing. No one is allowed to see them. The word is that a special law will be passed dealing with the problem of spouses of returnees who have entered into new marriages. Maranta says she'll stay with me no matter what; and I'm pretty sure that Tim will do the stiff-upper-lip thing, no hard feelings, if they ever get word to him in the debriefing camp about Maranta and me. As for the aliens, they're sitting tight in Central Park, occupying the whole place from 96th to 110th and not telling us a thing. Now and then the behemoths wander down to the reservoir for a lively bit of wallowing, but they haven't gone beyond the park this time.

I think a lot about Hannibal, and about Carthage versus Rome, and how the Second Punic War might have come out if Hannibal had had a chance to go back home and get a new batch of elephants. Most likely Rome would have won the war anyway, I guess. But we aren't Romans, and they aren't Carthaginians, and those aren't elephants splashing around in the Central Park reservoir. "This is such an interesting time to be alive," Maranta likes to say. "I'm certain they don't mean us any harm, aren't you?"

"I love you for your optimism," I tell her then. And then we turn on the tube and watch the evening news.

Robert Silverberg

has been a professional science-fiction writer since 1955. He has won many Hugo and Nebula awards and among his best-known books are *Lord Valentine's Castle*, *Dying Inside*, and *Nightwings*. In 2004 he was named a Grand Master by the Science Fiction Writers of America.

About the Editor

Alex Shvartsman is a writer, anthologist, translator, and game designer from Brooklyn, NY. His short stories have appeared in *The Journal of Nature, InterGalactic Medicine Show, Daily Science Fiction, Galaxy's Edge,* and a variety of other magazines and anthologies.

His website is www.alexshvartsman.com

The body text of this book was set in the modern font of Stone Serif and Stone Sans, designed by Summer Stone and Bob Ishi (which just happens to also mean "stone" in Japanese).

Do you crave more Unidentified Funny Objects? Read the original, available now:

Available at www.ufopub.com and from fine booksellers everywhere. Also enjoy additional stories published at **www.ufopub.com**

And be on the lookout for
UNIDENTIFIED FUNNY OBJECTS 3—coming in 2014

Releasing in November 2013
from UFO Publishing

Coffee- and tea-infused stories, short enough
to read on your coffee break.
Visit WWW.UFOPUB.COM to pre-order.